***Standing on tiptoe, Becky planted a
kiss on his cheek.***

Carter felt a surge of heat rush though him.
Her face had *my hero* written all over it, and what
flesh-and-blood male could resist such unmasked
admiration? To top it off, she looked precious in her
Santa Claus hat. "What's a nice Jewish girl like you
doing in a hat like that?" he asked gruffly, mixed
emotions raging through him. At that moment,
Carter wished *he* were Santa, so he could pull her
onto his lap.

He took her arm and led her down the hallway, into
the study. "Mistletoe," he whispered, motioning to
the rafter in the ceiling. He kicked the door closed.
With an urgency he couldn't suppress, he pulled
her to him and wrapped her in his arms, his lips
finding hers, his hands in her hair, then down her
back. The way she smelled, the way she tasted, the
way her body fit so well with his, released feelings
he'd kept restrained for months.

"Marry me," he said for what seemed like the
hundredth time.

D0018187

Dear Reader,

Well, it's that time of year again—and if those beautiful buds of April are any indication, you're in the mood for love! And what better way to sustain that mood than with our latest six Special Edition novels? We open the month with the latest installment of Sherryl Woods's MILLION DOLLAR DESTINIES series, *Priceless*. When a pediatric oncologist who deals with life and death on a daily basis meets a sick child's football hero, she thinks said hero can make the little boy's dreams come true. But little does she know that he can make hers a reality, as well! Don't miss this compelling story....

MERLYN COUNTY MIDWIVES continues with Maureen Child's *Forever...Again*, in which a man who doesn't believe in second chances has a change of mind—not to mention heart—when he meets the beautiful new public relations guru at the midwifery clinic. In *Cattleman's Heart* by Lois Faye Dyer, a businesswoman assigned to help a struggling rancher finds that business is the last thing on her mind when she sees the shirtless cowboy meandering toward her! And Susan Mallery's popular DESERT ROGUES are back! In *The Sheik & the Princess in Waiting*, a woman learns that the man she loved in college has two secrets: 1) he's a prince; and 2) they're married! Next, can a pregnant earthy vegetarian chef find happiness with town's resident playboy, an admitted carnivore... and father of her child? Find out in *The Best of Both Worlds* by Elissa Ambrose. And in Vivienne Wallington's *In Her Husband's Image*, a widow confronted with her late husband's twin brother is forced to decide, as she looks in the eyes of her little boy, if some secrets are worth keeping.

So enjoy the beginnings of spring, and all six of these wonderful books! And don't forget to come back next month for six new compelling reads from Silhouette Special Edition.

Happy reading!

Gail Chasan
Senior Editor

Please address questions and book requests to:
Silhouette Reader Service
U.S.: 3010 Walden Ave., P.O. Box 1325, Buffalo, NY 14269
Canadian: P.O. Box 609, Fort Erie, Ont. L2A 5X3

The Best of Both Worlds

ELISSA AMBROSE

Silhouette

SPECIAL EDITION

Published by Silhouette Books

America's Publisher of Contemporary Romance

For my mother.

Acknowledgments

Special thanks to Anne Lind, Sharon Skinner and
Sarah Mlynowski, critique partners par excellence;
and to Mireya Merritt, gourmet chef extraordinaire.

 SILHOUETTE BOOKS

ISBN 0-373-24607-2

THE BEST OF BOTH WORLDS

This edition published by arrangement with Harlequin Books S.A.

® and TM are trademarks of Harlequin Books S.A., used under license.
Trademarks indicated with ® are registered in the United States Patent
and Trademark Office, the Canadian Trade Marks Office and in other
countries.

Visit Silhouette at www.eHarlequin.com

Printed in U.S.A.

Books by Elissa Ambrose

Silhouette Special Edition

Journey of the Heart #1506
A Mother's Reflection #1578
The Best of Both Worlds #1607

ELISSA AMBROSE

Originally from Montreal, Canada, Elissa Ambrose now resides in Arizona with her husband, her smart but surly cat and her sweet but silly cockatoo. She's the proud mother of two daughters, who, though they have flown the coop, still manage to keep her on her toes. She started out as a computer programmer and now serves as the fiction editor at *Anthology* magazine, a literary journal published in Mesa, Arizona. When she's not writing or editing or just hanging out with her husband, she can be found at the indoor ice arena, trying out a new spin or jump.

Chicken Soup without the Chicken

From Rebecca Roth's *The Lover's Guide
To Vegetarian Cooking*

*Just as comforting as chicken soup with the chicken,
this recipe will soothe any man—body and soul.*

3 tbsp olive oil
1 1/2 onions finely chopped
3 carrots, sliced horizontally
2 stalks celery, sliced horizontally
1 small turnip, cubed in to 3/4-inch pieces (optional)
1/2 tsp Hungarian or Spanish paprika
2 quarts cold vegetable stock
1 1/2 tsp salt
1/4 tsp black pepper
2 tsp fresh dill, minced; or 1/2 tsp dried leaf
2 tsp fresh parsley, minced; or 1/2 tsp dried leaf
1 cup dried bow tie noodles

Procedure:

Heat oil in large pot over medium heat. Add onion and
sauté until transparent.

Add carrots, celery and turnip, then let sweat for
10 minutes. (Sweating means allowing the vegetables
to cook with the onions until they start releasing their
juices and begin to mingle with the onions and oil.)

Add paprika and stir for one minute.

Pour the cold stock over the vegetables and bring to
a boil. Turn down the heat, cover and simmer for about
20 minutes, until the vegetables are somewhat tender.

Stir in salt, pepper, dill and parsley, then add noodles.
Simmer for another 10 to 12 minutes, or until the
vegetables and pasta are tender. Check for seasoning.

Serving Suggestions:

Get your man into bed and cover him with a comforter.
Place a bowl of hot soup on a serving tray with plenty of
saltine crackers, then spoon-feed him the soup and hand-
feed him crackers. It won't take him long to feel a new
surge of strength!

Chapter One

"Now you've done it," Becky said. "You didn't have to yell at her. Christina is sobbing in the storeroom, and all because of you. Sometimes you're as sensitive as a steamroller."

The round-faced, fuzzy-eyebrowed owner of Merlin's Fine Diner glared at her from behind the counter. "Christina got the order wrong again," he snarled. "The customer's always right."

"In this case the customer was wrong. He ordered a BLT without the bacon, tomato on the side, and that's exactly what he got!"

"Yeah, right. Who orders a BLT without the bacon?"

"Me, for one," Becky answered. "Not that I've ever been inclined to eat in this dive." These days, however, just seeing all that grease sizzling in the kitchen, never mind the smell, was enough to send her stomach reeling.

"I'd better check on Christina," she mumbled, fighting back a fresh wave of nausea.

"You people are all alike," Merlin said. "Trouble-makers, everyone of you."

Becky whirled around. "You people? What is that supposed to mean?"

"You vegetarians. It's as if you all belong to the same secret club. It's un-American, I tell you. Downright subversive. Now get back to work."

"Work, shmirk. You heartless clod! Christina is in the back room, crying her eyes out, and all you can think about is work? What kind of person are you?"

He waved a finger in her face. "I'll tell you what kind of person. Someone who plans on staying in business. Someone who doesn't need back talk from the help. I've had it, Rebecca. If I'd wanted a cook with a mouth, I would have hired my wife. You're fired. From now on I'm doing all the cooking myself, just like when I first opened."

Another fine mess, Becky thought after saying goodbye to Christina. Another job down the drain. Fired again, and for what?

Little silver bells jingled as she pulled open the door to the diner, a blast of cold air assaulting her face. She pulled her scarf up over her chin and stepped onto the sidewalk.

It wasn't her fault she couldn't hold down a job. She just hadn't found her niche in the world. But she wasn't thinking about her sudden unemployed state, and she wasn't thinking about the weather as she bundled her jacket close to her body and made her way down the street. She was thinking about *it*. The problem. The predicament she planned to dump on her family at dinner.

No use putting it off. They'd find out sooner or later. Might as well let the cat out of the bag when the whole family—the whole *mishpokhe* as Bubbe liked to say—was gathered around the table.

For as long as Becky could remember, no one in the family had ever been excused from Friday-night dinner at Ma's. To be excused, you had to have been run over by a truck or be in the process of having a baby. When Becky was married and living in New York, she'd taken the train back to Middlewood every Friday evening. But she'd always traveled alone. Her husband, Jordan, had been excused. He was almost a doctor, and doctors, according to her mother, made their own rules.

Becky could just imagine the scene that evening when she broke the news. In the center of the polished oak table would be her mother's favorite crystal vase, filled with an arrangement from the florist. Her father would complain that nothing could equal the prize roses he grew every summer in his garden, and her mother would roll her eyes.

"Pass the knishes, please," Becky might say to her brother, David. "Guess what, Ma? I lost my job today. Oh, by the way, I'm three months pregnant."

"Again you got fired?" Becky's mother might answer. As usual, Gertie Roth would hear only what she expected to hear, and the last thing she'd expect to hear was that her divorced daughter was pregnant. Refusing to do the math, the last thing she'd *want* to hear was that Jordan Steinberg, her ex-son-in-law the doctor, wasn't the father.

On second thought maybe I shouldn't tell them right away, Becky debated, imagining the mayhem that would follow. Her mother, once understanding set in, would hold her hand over her heart and feign an attack. Gertie Roth—who, barring mild hypertension, was as healthy as a horse—was convinced she was going to die young. "It's too late for that," Becky's father liked to tease her, only now he'd be in no mood for jokes. He'd insist that Becky get a second opinion, all the while lamenting, ''Where did we go wrong?'' And Bubbe would nod her head sadly, in the way that grandmothers did, while thanking God that Chaim, Becky's grandfather, had already passed on, because if he hadn't, the news would probably kill him.

No, Becky decided, she wouldn't tell them tonight. She couldn't drop a bomb like this between the chicken soup and gefilte fish—which, being a vegetarian, she'd never get to eat—and not expect a fallout. She considered not telling any of them, ever. She could blame her weight gain on her depression, and when the time came she could...she could what? Give her baby up for adoption? No way, she told herself, just as terminating the pregnancy hadn't been an option when, just hours ago, she had hidden in the ladies' room at the back of the diner, waiting for the results of the home pregnancy test.

Positive.

Bracing herself against the wind, she rounded the corner at the end of the block, and, like Dorothy after she had landed over the rainbow, found herself in another world. Here, in the older part of town, the houses were different from the contemporary split-level bungalows in Becky's neighborhood. In striking contrast, they were large and stately in the Colonial style of days long ago. Here was where Carter had grown up.

She turned another corner and stopped outside a bed and breakfast. Set against a woodsy landscape, the old home was a picture of old-fashioned charm. The posts on the corners of the house were ornamentally molded, the chamfered beams under the overhang embellished with large teardrop shapes. On a sign in the window, Vacancy was written next to Starr's Bed & Breakfast, underneath that, Assistant Cook Wanted. On sudden impulse she walked up the stone pathway. She reached for the large brass knocker, then hesitated.

In the yard stood a large Douglas fir, silver streamers and multicolored lights woven through its branches. Since Thanksgiving, Christmas decorations had sprouted everywhere, candles in windows, wreaths on front doors, Santa with reindeer on snow-covered lawns.

She pulled her hand away. Not my world, she thought, and headed back to the street.

The job in Phoenix had taken ten months to complete, but it was nothing compared to what lay ahead, the project that would ensure him a full partnership with Sullivan and Walters, Middlewood's prestigious architectural firm. Joe Sullivan had called him on his cell phone only moments ago, informing him that the New Zealand job had been approved.

At the moment, though, New Zealand was the farthest thing from Carter's mind.

He sat in the booth, examining the stained checkerboard oilcloth that covered the table. Bored with that, he turned his gaze to the torn red vinyl of the seat. He'd never been here before and now he knew why. A Meal You'll Never Forget, the sign outside boasted. If the coffee was any indication of what the food was like, *never forget* was right. Your stomach wouldn't let you.

The day had been long, starting with a five-hour flight from Phoenix to LaGuardia, followed by another hour's trek by car service to Middlewood, Connecticut. All he'd wanted was to stay home and unwind, but he knew his mother was expecting him. After dropping off his bags at his apartment, he headed straight for the garage to get his car and was on the road again.

And then he'd seen the sign. He'd made a U-turn and headed for the diner.

No time like the present.

Becky hadn't returned any of his calls, and he was tired of her ice-queen attitude. The sooner they got it out in the open, the sooner they could get on with their lives. They were adults, weren't they? This kind of thing happened all the time, didn't it?

So why did he feel like a heel?

Three months ago, after seven uninterrupted months on-site, he'd flown back from Phoenix to be the best man at David's wedding, intending to return to the job the following morning. After the reception Mrs. Roth had invited the guests to take home anything they wanted. Although she'd been referring to the sweet-table and flowers, Carter had taken home the groom's younger sister.

"The decor doesn't do much to whet the appetite, does it?" Armed with a pot of coffee, a fresh-faced young woman no older than eighteen, her long blond hair in a ponytail, stood by the table. "The diner's only saving grace is that it's across the street from the bookstore. More coffee?"

"Sure, why not?" If the first cup hadn't killed him, nothing would. He read her nametag and asked, "Christina, can you tell me when Becky will be back from her break?"

She frowned. "Sorry, mister, Rebecca left just before you got here. She was let go. I guess she went home." A worried expression crossed her face. "I hope she's okay. That storm out there is pretty nasty. She was on foot."

"Christina!" a large, beefy man called from behind the counter. "How many times do I have to tell you not to fraternize with the customers! Get back to work!"

"I'm not fraternizing, I'm working!" She took out her

order pad and pretended to write. "I feel pretty bad about the whole thing," she said quietly. "She was fired because of me."

"I doubt that," Carter replied. "Becky's made a career of getting fired. She's perfected the technique all on her own, without any help from anyone." He had to give her credit, though, for sticking it out this long. Who would have thought someone as pampered as Becky would work in a rattrap like this in the first place? He dropped a five-dollar bill onto the table and stood up. "Thanks for the refill, but I think I'll skip it. Maybe I can catch up with her."

"Coffee's only a buck-fifty. What about your change?"

"Keep it. Working for someone like him—" he motioned to the man behind the counter, who was scowling in their direction "—I'd say you've more than earned it."

By the time he reached the car, it was already buried in snow. Grumbling, he proceeded to clear the windshield with his bare hands. Dammit, it was only the first week in December, too early for a major storm. He should have remembered his gloves. In seconds his hands were stinging with the cold.

This is what happens when you don't plan ahead, he thought.

Like Becky, for instance. He should never have let it happen.

As kids they had flirted innocently. She'd been cute and funny and charming—and spoiled worse than an overripe peach. A princess-in-training, her brother used to call her. She was also five years younger. But as she grew into womanhood, the age difference began to fall away, and cute gave way to radiant, funny to endearing, charming to devastating. Ringlets of long sable-brown hair tumbled freely down her back, as though daring someone to tame it. Her large brown eyes were unfathomable, and her mouth, which seemed to curl in a perpetual half smile, half pout, was sinfully tantalizing. She was, however, from a different world. Without ever having to say a word, his family had made sure he knew the boundaries.

Not pursuing a relationship was a mistake he'd regretted for years. And three months ago, on the night of David's wedding, he'd made another one.

Since then sleep had evaded him. He'd lain awake in his hotel room, trying—without success—to drive the memory of that night from his mind. As much as he hated to admit it, she'd gotten under his skin.

But he wasn't going to do anything about it. Except apologize.

What had he been thinking, letting her come back with him to his apartment? He no longer felt that the difference in their backgrounds was a barrier, but these days, thanks to a failed marriage and a fast-paced lifestyle, any kind of involvement was at the bottom of his wish list. Becky was the kind of woman who needed a husband. She wasn't the type who would settle for an affair.

That devil-may-care, free-spirit act didn't fool him for a minute. She might look like a temptress, might act like a temptress, but he knew the truth. Becky Roth was as homegrown as apple pie, or in her case, apple kugel.

Of course, if the truth were told, she had seduced *him*.

And that's why he felt like a heel. He should have turned her down.

Three teenagers, bundled in coats and scarves and gloves, ran out of a large saltbox-style house. A boy around sixteen stopped to roll a snowball, then shot it at the girl, who appeared to be a few years younger. The girl squealed and the two boys laughed.

"Oh, you think you're so macho!" the girl shouted, retaliating with a bull's-eye shot to the taller boy's shoulder.

"I think I'm going to defect to the other side," the taller boy called to his friend. "With a windup like that, your sister could pitch for the pros."

For a brief moment Becky was that young girl, and the taller boy was Carter, her teenage crush, her brother's best friend. She closed her eyes, trying to conjure up memories of her youth, a carefree time when life wasn't encumbered with complications. Back then there weren't as many choices, she thought. You did what was expected of you.

Without warning a snowball smashed against her forehead, causing her to lose her balance. Her legs slipped out from beneath her, and a moment later she was down on the sidewalk. "Oh, no," she said, noticing the rip in her panty hose. Along her shin was a nasty red patch. At first she felt nothing but the cold, but then the pain took over. She wasn't bleeding, but her skin felt as if she'd been whipped with steel wool.

"Are you all right?" the taller boy asked, concern written across his brow. "Gee, I'm sorry, ma'am. With all this snow, I didn't see you. I didn't mean to clobber you."

Ma'am? Did he just call her ma'am? Just when she thought the day couldn't get any worse, some kid has to come by, practically knock her unconscious and then call her ma'am.

"He meant to clobber *me*," the girl by his side said. "Randy, you moron, don't just stand there. Help her up."

Becky squeezed her eyes shut in an attempt to squeeze out the pain. It was a trick she'd learned when Jordan left, and it had worked. She hadn't cried, and afterward she had gone about her life as though nothing had changed. And nothing had, really. All that had happened was that she'd moved out of her husband's domain back to her parents, where she'd been living in limbo these past nine months.

Nisht ahir un nish aher, Bubbe would say. Neither here nor there.

A tear rolled down Becky's cheek. The trick wasn't working. "My leg," she moaned. "It hurts."

"I'll take care of her," she heard someone say. It was a man's voice, deep and resonant. She opened her eyes and winced, but not because of the pain. Carter. Above her stood Carter Prescott, III, her brother's best friend, her teenage crush. Carter Prescott, III, father of her unborn child.

She felt her head spinning, and it wasn't because of the fall. His massive shoulders, his lean, trim waist and his muscular, perfectly proportioned frame were only part of the reason. With smoky-gray eyes a dramatic contrast against his fair hair and skin, his ruggedly handsome face had always sent her head reeling, but it was more than his appearance that made her pulse fly off the charts. It had something to do with the way he carried himself, tall and proud, as though the world had been created for him to command.

She'd always been a sucker for a take-charge kind of guy, and Carter Prescott, III, was no exception. As a teenager she'd flirted with him innocently, but she'd been David's kid sister, five years younger. Too young for Carter.

So what did the jerk go and do? He married someone older than he was. All right, so the bride was only two years his senior, not exactly a Mrs. Robinson. But she was the hoity-toity Wendy St. Claire. Wendy Wasp, Becky had called her behind his back. If her blood were any bluer, it would be ink.

"Take my hand," he was saying now. "Let me help you, Becky."

Maybe she'd always been a sucker for a take-charge kind of guy, but all that was about to change. Over her dead body would she let him touch her. Never again. She pushed away his hand and stumbled to her feet. "Ouch!" Another wave of pain surged though her leg and she fell against him, cursing.

"Such language from a nice Jewish girl," he said, catching her in the circle of his arms. "Your mother would be shocked."

If all it took were a few choice words to throw her mother into a tailspin, Gertie Roth would probably lapse into a coma after what Becky had to tell her. "Let go of me," she demanded. "I'm better now." She took a step forward, trying not to let the pain register on her face. "There, you see? It's just a scratch. Nothing broken. Not even sprained."

The teenagers looked at each other with relief. "You lucked out," the girl said to the boy named Randy. "She could have sued you. If she's smart she'll still sue you, for assault and battery."

"I'll show you assault and battery!" Randy said, laughing. He picked up a handful of snow and threw it at the girl, who ran off squealing with mock indignation.

"Have a nice day, ma'am!" the other boy called as the three of them disappeared around the corner, their laughter ringing in the air like sleigh bells.

Have a nice day? Too late for that. She turned to Carter and sighed. "Was I ever that young?"

"Tell you what, old lady," he said, wrapping his arm around her waist. "Pretend I'm a Boy Scout and I'll help you cross the street. My car is parked on the other side."

Suddenly very tired with the whole situation and too

drained to argue, she answered, "All right, I'll let you drive me home. But I can walk to your car on my own." She moved out of his reach. "I thought you were off somewhere in the *ruchas,* playing with your building blocks. What are you doing here, anyway?"

"A little cranky, are we? For your information, Phoenix isn't the sticks, and building a resort hotel isn't what I'd call playing with blocks."

Becky knew darn well where Carter had been and what he had been building. Her brother, who had remained in contact with him the whole time he'd been away, had felt the need to give her a detailed account of his friend's activities. Nevertheless, there was no way she'd admit to Carter she'd been paying attention.

"I meant, what are you doing here out on the streets?" she asked, limping by his side. "Were you following me?"

"Following you! Now that's what I call nerve. Just because you walked out on me that night, then refused to take my calls, you think you've driven me to the brink of despair? Sorry to deflate your ego, princess, but I'm no stalker. I was on my way to my mother's when I decided to swing by the diner, but Chrissy told me you'd been fired. So I left. I saw you fall, and like any Good Samaritan I came to your rescue."

Chrissy? Did he mean Christina? Becky assumed that Carter had just met her, but here he was, calling her by a nickname. She should have known he'd get friendly right away. Christina—*Chrissy*—was female, wasn't she? And she was blond. Carter always did have a penchant for tall, full-bosomed blondes.

"I wasn't fired," she said tersely. "I quit."

He raised an eyebrow.

"Okay, so I didn't quit. Let's just say the owner and I had a parting of the ways."

"Right. He wouldn't do something your way, so you parted." He opened the car door and eased her inside. "You must be freezing in those stockings. I don't know why you chose to walk in the first place."

"Maybe it has something to do with my not being able to afford a car," she snapped. "That and the fact that Middlewood isn't famous for its public transportation. Besides, the diner is only a mile from home, and it wasn't snowing this morning when I left for work."

He removed his jacket and draped it over her legs, his hand brushing against the red patch of skin where she'd torn her panty hose. "I'm sorry," he said when she flinched. "I didn't mean to hurt you."

She felt the color rise in her cheeks. It wasn't pain that had caused her to draw back. It was the heat she'd felt when his chilly fingers had made contact with her leg. Heat that could melt the snow off the North Pole, if she let it. But she had no intention of allowing another meltdown, ever again. The consequences of that mistake would last a lifetime.

"You didn't hurt me. I told you, it feels much better."

"In that case it must be revulsion that made you recoil. Let me put your mind at rest. I can honestly say that no woman has ever died from my touch. But don't worry, I won't touch you again." Then, as if echoing her thoughts, he added, "That's one mistake I won't repeat."

She waited until he was in the driver's seat before she responded. "I believe your exact words were 'I hope you don't think this means anything.' As far as lines are concerned, that one's a gem. Not mean anything! Who do you think you are?"

"Look, I admit it was a pretty callous thing to say, and

I apologize. I would have apologized sooner, but you never gave me the chance. You're the one who ran out in the middle of the night. You're the one who refused to talk about it.''

And you're the one who left me alone and pregnant, she thought. She leaned back in her seat and sulked. She knew she wasn't being fair. He'd told her he'd be returning to Phoenix. He also had no idea she was pregnant. But the way he was sitting there, so smug, so collected, trying to exonerate himself by making her feel guilty, infuriated her. "First you lure me to your apartment, then you seduce me, then you dismiss me as though I'm some little harem girl, and now you accuse me of abandoning you?''

"What are you talking about? You practically tore off my clothes right there in the elevator! We didn't even make it to the bedroom.'' He sighed. "I didn't come after you today to pick a fight. I was hoping we could talk this out like adults, calmly and rationally. I already told you I was sorry for my crude remark. I know how it must have made you feel, but I do have an explanation.''

"Why is it men always start singing the old commitment blues *after* they have their way with us? Well, I have news for you. I've heard that song before. If it's understanding you want, I'm the wrong audience.''

He grumbled something unintelligible and slammed the car into gear. An uncomfortable silence fell over them as they drove down the snow-bordered road. "Tell me something,'' he said finally, as he flicked on the signal and turned onto her street. "Why do women think they're the only ones allowed a moment of weakness? I know you were vulnerable that night, and I know I shouldn't have taken you up on your offer, but—''

"My offer! Why you egotistical, self-centered, conceited—"

"You're being redundant."

"I beg your pardon?"

"Redundant. As in superfluous. Repetitive. Pleonastic."

Enough already! What was he, a thesaurus? "You bet I was vulnerable. You knew how I was feeling that night, and you took advantage of it. I thought you were offering consolation, not an invitation to do the horizontal bop! Before we left for your apartment, I made it clear I wasn't going to sleep with you."

Amusement shone in his eyes. "Your memory is faulty. As I recall, princess, you said that the only way you'd ever sleep with me was if we were driving in the middle of a blizzard, and we were forced to stop. The only shelter around for miles would be an old barn. It would be cold and desolate inside, and we'd have to huddle for warmth. Outside the storm would continue to rage, turning the landscape into a frozen wasteland. It wouldn't just be a blizzard, it would be a disaster. Certain we'd never live to see another sunrise, we'd give in to our basic need and allow our passion to take over."

It was obvious he was enjoying this. "Don't mock me, Carter. I was in a highly sensitive state that night."

"Sensitive? Tipsy would be a more apt description. I have just two questions," he pressed on mirthlessly. "Number one, where exactly is this hypothetical barn?"

"I don't know. Somewhere. What difference does it make?"

"It makes a lot of difference. For instance, if there's a barn, there's a farmhouse nearby, and a farmer who feels sorry for us and offers us lodging. Number two, why are we out in a blizzard?"

"Maybe we're coming back from a business trip. I don't see what—"

"What business could we have together? You're too busy getting fired, and the last time I checked, I was still an architect."

"You said you had two questions. That's three. Why do you always do that? Why do you always go on and on? All I meant by the story was—"

"Oh, I know what you meant. All that talk about huddling and need and passion—the truth is, you seduced *me*. But I'll admit to my part of the blame. I should never have let it happen. Now all I want is for us to get past it. I wouldn't want anything to jeopardize my friendship with David."

David. So this was what it was all about. She should have known. What was it about men? They made fun of women for going to the powder room in twos, yet they lived by the Eleventh Commandment, "Thou shalt not let a woman divide a man from his buddies."

Jerk. Carter Prescott, III, still had the power to knock her socks off—and a lot more than her socks—but he was still the same jerk.

He was right about one thing, though. He shouldn't have let it happen. But it *had* happened. The child she was carrying was proof.

"I wouldn't lose any sleep over it," she said as they pulled into her driveway. "It's not as if my brother would come after you with a shotgun."

Carter grimaced. "No, but your father might."

She almost laughed out loud. She could just imagine her meek, mild-mannered father, prodding Carter down the aisle with the business end of a rifle. Well, here's a news flash, she thought. It would take more than a rifle to make her marry Carter. Or anyone else, for that matter. Marriage was an experience she had no desire to repeat.

She regarded his profile and sighed. No matter which path she chose, nothing could change the fact that Carter was the father of her child, and as much as she was determined to raise the baby alone, he had a right to know.

A shock like this would serve him right for being such a jerk.

She drew in a breath. "I have something to tell you."

"Apology accepted."

"No, you don't understand—"

The front door to her house opened, and David appeared on the porch. Carter rolled down the window. "Hey, Roth!" he called. "How's it going?"

David sprinted through the snow to the driver's side of the car. "Pres, you old son of a gun, when did you get back? Come in for a glass of wine—and stay for dinner. It's been a while since you've had one of my grandmother's feasts. Either you're traipsing across the country or you're out on a date. Bubbe's cooked up a storm, chicken soup, roast brisket and potato knishes—and you can't say no to her gefilte fish."

Becky's stomach turned over.

"Thanks, but I'll have to take a rain check," Carter said. "I'm off to my mother's. If I don't show up tonight for dinner, she'll probably stay awake all night, figuring out new, inventive ways to make me crazy."

Mothers will do that, Becky thought, opening the car door.

Gertie stepped onto the porch, wearing her lamb's wool coat. "David!" she called, waving frantically. "Put on a jacket! It's cold out here!"

Becky turned to Carter. "Thanks for the lift. I can manage from here."

"Stay put. I'll help you to the door."

"I told you, I can manage." She glanced over at her brother, who hadn't even acknowledged her presence. What, was she invisible? "God forbid I should come between you and your buddy." Before Carter could protest, she was out of the car, hobbling up the front pathway.

"Where are your boots?" Gertie scolded. "In this terrible storm you don't wear boots? And why aren't you wearing a hat? Get in here before you catch pneumonia. What's the matter with you, can't you see it's snowing? It's not a blizzard, it's a disaster!"

Becky followed her mother into the house. You don't know the half of it, she thought. If she hadn't felt so miserable, she might have laughed.

Chapter Two

"Finally, a grandchild." Gertie's hands flew into the air as though she hoped to embrace the world. "But the word *pregnant* is so harsh-sounding. I prefer *expecting*. Even better, *in the family way*."

"No matter what you call it," Bubbe said, "a baby is a blessing. Have some more soup, Hannah. Now you eat for two."

Aaron stood and raised his glass in a toast. "A finer daughter-in-law there never was. May your son be strong and healthy. May you have many more sons, and daughters, too. May all your children bring you joy. May all—"

"Sit down, Aaron," Gertie said. "Your soup is getting cold. So, Hannah, when is the baby due?"

"According to the obstetrician, the last week in May. I wanted to tell you all sooner, but David wanted to keep it our special secret a little while longer."

"You're supposed to add seven days to the date of your

last menstrual cycle, then subtract three months," Becky said. She knew. She'd looked it up after missing her period. But hoping the problem would somehow go away, she'd put off taking a pregnancy test for another two months. It was only this morning, after studying her disappearing waistline in the diner's bathroom mirror, that she'd drummed up the courage to confirm her suspicions.

"Watch how you talk," Gertie reprimanded, handing a plate of sliced *challa* to Hannah. "There are men here."

"I wasn't hatched from an egg," David said, laughing. "Anyway, Becky is right. That's the calculation the doctor used. But the ultrasound scheduled for next week will give us a more accurate picture." Looking at Hannah adoringly, he took her hand as though she was as fragile as a china doll.

Becky could tell that her mother was performing a few of her own calculations. "This is the first week in December," Gertie said slowly. "That would make Hannah three months preg—in the family way." She looked at David accusingly. "Right?"

He rolled his eyes. "Don't worry, Ma. The baby won't dare show his face until the appropriate amount of time has passed."

"I wasn't saying anything, so wipe that look off your face." Gertie pretended to be offended, but her joy was obvious. "Not that I'm complaining, but I have to say, you didn't waste much time."

"They didn't go on a honeymoon to play golf," Aaron said.

"Shame on you, Aaron. Such a way to talk in front of your children." She turned to Becky. "Finally I'm going to have grandchildren, and here I thought the first one would come from you."

It just might, Becky thought. She wasn't sure of the

date of her last period, but she knew exactly when she had conceived: Labor Day weekend, the night of David's wedding. Which meant that she and Hannah would be delivering around the same time.

"Don't start on her, Ma," David said. "She'll get re-married one day. Besides, she's a lot younger than I am. She has time. She'll have a family when she's good and ready."

As a matter of fact, before I'm good and ready, Becky thought.

"From your mouth to God's ears," Gertie said.

Becky let out a nervous breath. This was as good an opening as any to tell them about the baby. But she had to do it gradually, to soften the blow. Step one, marriage is out. Step two, adoption is in. Step three, forget step two and tell them I'm pregnant. "Actually, I don't think I'll ever get married again."

Gertie dismissed the comment with a wave of her hand. "Of course you will. Jordan will come back. Just be patient."

When was her mother going to accept the divorce? "I wouldn't take him back if he crawled on his hands and knees, not after what he did," Becky said. "He used me, and he used you, too. Without the money he borrowed from you, he never would have been able to go to medical school. And don't forget, I was the only one bringing home the bacon, you should pardon the expression. Don't get me wrong. I'm not angry that he went to school while I worked—yes, Ma, I do have some skills—but it's funny how he dumped me as soon as he got what he wanted."

Gertie frowned. "Do we have to talk about this at the Friday-night table? *Shabbes* is supposed to be a time of rest, and that means a rest from all this bickering."

"You're the one who brought it up," Becky answered

indignantly. "If you like Jordan so much, why don't *you* marry him?"

"Is that how you talk? Listen to how she talks! Aaron, say something!"

Aaron cleared his throat. "First of all—"

"First of all she needs a husband," Gertie interrupted. "Which she had, I might add, but she sent him away. What kind of daughter sends a man like that away?"

"I didn't send him away, Ma. He left."

"Yes, I know. He used you and then he left. Well, I have news for you. A husband and wife are supposed to use each other. They're supposed to turn to each other in times of need. Did you want him to use someone else?"

Becky sighed with frustration. "Jordan did turn to someone else, or have you forgotten that already?"

"You mean that *shiksa?* He'll get tired of her, mark my words. He'll come back when he comes to his senses. What was her name again, Bambi?"

"Barbie, Ma, and I wish you wouldn't use that word."

"What, *shiksa?* You're worried you might insult her? Next you'll be saying she's a wonderful woman and if circumstances were different, the two of you could be friends. What kind of wife makes friends with the husband's mistress? What's wrong with you?"

Becky gritted her teeth. "I'm not the one at fault here. Nothing's wrong with *me*." Nothing except that she was unmarried, pregnant and unemployed. "Why can't you ever take my side? After Jordan and I separated, I'm surprised you asked me, not him, to move in with you."

"Calm down. You don't have to make a scene. All I'm saying is that men don't leave. Women let them go."

"And daughters don't leave, either," Becky retorted. "Mothers drive them away." She pushed away from the table. "I'm going for a walk." She stood up and gave her sister-in-law a warm squeeze on her shoulder. "*Mazel tov,* Hannah. I'm so happy for you and David. But I have to warn you, you're going to need all the luck you can get to survive in this family."

"Where are you going?" Gertie demanded. "In this weather you want to go for a walk? Aaron, do something!"

"Listen to your mother," Aaron said.

Bubbe looked up at Becky. "Eat something, *bubeleh.* At least have some soup. I made it just for you. Chicken soup with no chicken, the way you like it."

"I'm sorry, Bubbe. I'm sure it's delicious, but I'm just not hungry." She gave her grandmother a peck on the cheek, then whirled around to face her mother. To heck with softening the blow. Bombs away! "Oh, I forgot to mention that I was fired. And there's one other thing. I'm in the family way."

"I realize it's only the first week in December," Eleanor said, "but this is Connecticut, for pity's sake. It's supposed to snow. Why does the town always go into a tizzy at the first sign of a flake? Schools close, roads back up and people crowd into grocery stores to wait at the checkout for hours, convinced that if they don't stock up they'll perish."

Carter sat at one end of the long mahogany table, facing his mother. At the center of the table was a spray of orchids in a Baccarat crystal vase. At each end, arranged in a formal place setting were Eleanor's sterling silver, her Royal Worcester dinnerware and a crystal wineglass. It's just the two of us, he thought, yet she sets the table as though she was expecting the queen of England. But even when his father was alive, it had been this way. Carter suspected she dined like this even when she was alone.

"It's the mentality of the masses," she continued. "They always cause such havoc whenever the slightest thing goes wrong. Is that why you're so late?"

"Excuse me?"

"The traffic, Carter. I'm talking about the traffic."

"There was no traffic, Mother. I'm late because I gave Becky Roth a lift home."

She drew her lips into a tight curl. "Oh, Rebecca. Yes, I heard she was back in Middlewood, living with her parents. It's been a while since I've seen her or her people. I understand that her brother Daniel bought his own pharmacy. I'm sure he'll do well—but those people always do, don't they?"

"His name is David. And he and his *people* are fine."

"You needn't take that tone. You know what I mean." She took a sip of her wine. "You haven't touched your coq au vin. Should I ask Martine to prepare something else? You haven't met my new housekeeper, have you? I think I'll keep this one. She's a real gem."

You mean you hope she doesn't quit like all the others before her, Carter thought. He put down his fork and stared at his plate. "The chicken is fine. I'm just not hungry."

His mother continued speaking, but Carter barely heard her words. Yet it wasn't his mother who was the cause of his distraction. At the moment the only person on his mind was Becky. She was acting as if he'd been responsible for what had happened that night three months ago. Hell, she'd known what she was doing—she was twenty-seven, not some blushing schoolgirl. Okay, so maybe afterward he'd been a jerk, but he'd apologized for his crude remark, hadn't he?

"She wants you to call her."

Carter looked back at his mother. "Excuse me?" he asked again.

"You haven't been listening to a word I've been saying. I said that Wendy called. She wanted to know when you'd be back." Eleanor took another sip of her wine. "This is a 1976 Chateau d'Yquem, in case you're interested. I've been saving it for a special occasion."

Carter regarded her with suspicion. "What special occasion?"

"I'm celebrating your homecoming. That and the New Zealand job. Can't a mother show pride in her son? As much as I hate to see you gone for two years, I know what this project means to you. You'll finally be made a full partner, something you've wanted for a long time. Anyway, I can come down at Christmas to visit, if you'd like. It's summer then, isn't it? I'll even stay the whole season."

Good Lord, was there nowhere he could go to escape her? "The partnership is not the primary reason why I'm going," he said curtly. He immediately regretted his tone. Eleanor was just being Eleanor. After thirty-two years he should be used to the way she tried to run his life—and the lives of everyone around her.

But either the insult had evaded her or she had chosen to ignore it. "Of course it's not the main reason," she said. "I know how much you enjoy your work. But you have to admit, the prestige that goes along with being a full partner is a definite plus."

"Tell me something, how many country clubs are there in Middlewood? And what's the sense of joining if I'm never here?" He was sorry he'd told her about the trip in the first place. He should have known she'd zero in on the partnership. Even though the promotion wasn't contingent on his going to New Zealand, it was true that the trip would cement it. He removed his napkin from his lap and tossed it onto the table. "I should go home. It's getting late and I still haven't finished unpacking."

Eleanor looked up at the grandfather clock behind him. "But it's still early! What about dessert? We're having your favorite, crème caramel, in honor of your return."

"I'm sorry, Mother, but I'm tired and I have a lot to do tonight. But thank Martine for me, will you?" After unpacking, he wanted to review his notes on the Denver project. The school for the performing arts was small potatoes compared to the New Zealand job, but it was coming up fast. Even though tomorrow was Saturday, he and Mike Walters, one of the firm's two senior partners, were meeting in the morning to go over the plans.

"I insist that you stay, Carter." Once again she glanced at the clock.

And once again Carter eyed her with mistrust. "What is it, Mother? Are you expecting someone?"

"Promise me you won't get angry. I invited Wendy for coffee. She happened to be in town visiting her parents, and I thought that inviting her would be the decent thing to do."

"Right. She happened to be in town." He stood up and headed toward the hallway, then abruptly turned around. "The decent thing to do? Now that's almost funny. I don't think Wendy would recognize decency if it slapped her in the face. I'm going home. Make my apologies for me, will you?"

"Come back here!" Eleanor called after him, a note of panic in her voice. "What am I supposed to say to her?"

"I'm sure you'll think of something. You always do."

She shouldn't have delivered the news that way. Becky had been sure that Bubbe would drop her teeth, right there at the table, into her soup. The last person she ever wanted to hurt was her grandmother, dear Bubbe, whose entire world revolved around her family, but Becky had had enough. Her mother was driving her crazy. Becky knew she'd have to move out soon, or she'd end up in a strait-jacket.

She trudged through the blowing snow, hugging her chest as if at any moment she would be lifted up and blown away. She could feel the wind right through her jacket. Her leg still felt tender underneath the warm camel slacks she'd changed into before dinner, but at least the sting was gone. A person needs snowshoes in this weather, she thought, not two-inch-heeled boots from Macy's sale catalogue.

No one else was out walking tonight—in this weather who in their right minds would be?—and for a moment she imagined herself alone and lost, trying to find her way out of a forest. Worried about the future, her fears assailed her as she walked without aim, her boots crunching rhyth-mically on the frozen snow.

Lions and tigers and bears, oh my! Lions and tigers and bears, oh my!

Pregnant, unmarried, unemployed, oh my!

Not that she didn't want to be a mother. On the con-trary, she wanted to be a mother more than anything in the world—someday. But right now there was this one small detail. She wasn't married. It wasn't the stigma that bothered her; she was terrified at the prospect of raising a child alone. She couldn't even support herself, never mind a baby.

I do have some skills, she'd told her mother. Unfortu-nately, she just hadn't discovered what they were. She'd studied Greek mythology in college, but these days there wasn't much of a need for Greek mythologists, especially in a small town like Middlewood. After graduation she'd flitted from job to job, trying to make ends meet. I'm just not cut out for office work, she'd told herself. Was it her fault she didn't have the filing gene? Or the answer-the-phone-without-alienating-the-customer gene?

Anger filled her as she pushed on, fighting the wind. Nothing had gone according to plan. She was supposed to help put Jordan through medical school, and once he was on his feet, it would be her turn. Maybe she'd go to graduate school. Maybe she'd start her own business. Or maybe she'd be a stay-at-home mom. But all those dreams had ended. During his first year of internship—after four years, eight months and three weeks of marriage, not that she was counting—Jordan had up and left.

How did one fall out of love, precisely? The salon-bought redhead with the surgical bosom had nothing to do with it, her husband had insisted while packing his new Louis Vuitton suitcase. Becky had even helped him pack, making sure everything was folded just right. Was that new underwear? she'd wondered absurdly. Not only had the redhead bought him new luggage, she'd bought him new shorts. Designer underwear with the labels sewn on the outside so they wouldn't chafe.

"Fold your own underwear," Becky had said defiantly. There. *That* would teach him.

At this time, however, concerns other than her ex-husband's preference for designer shorts and big-breasted redheads demanded her attention, and she forced her anger aside.

How would she raise this baby alone?

She didn't want Carter in her life as the father of her child. What kind of parent would he make, spending most of his time gallivanting away from home? She didn't want him in her life under *any* circumstance. He'd already walked out on one wife, and Becky had already been there, thank you very much. Not that she expected him to propose once he learned the truth. He was a man who relished his freedom. He went through women the way she went through jobs.

She plodded along aimlessly, snow swirling in front of her eyes as thoughts of Carter swirled in her head. What had she been thinking that night? She knew exactly what she'd been thinking, all right, as they'd faced each other under the wedding canopy. She'd been thinking of his smoky-gray eyes, his lean, sexy body, the way her insides would turn to matzo meal whenever his gaze met hers. But the whole insanity—the whole *mishegoss,* as Bubbe would say—had started before the family had even left for the synagogue:

Becky had been getting ready for her brother's wedding, thinking that for the first time in a long while she wasn't miserable. Here it was already September and she'd been working at the same job for more than a month. She'd even started thinking about getting her own apartment. She couldn't sponge off her parents forever, not that her mother believed the situation was permanent. "Jordan has lost his senses," Gertie had kept insisting, "but he'll come around." But it had been six months since Jordan had misplaced his senses and he still hadn't found them. At first Becky thought she'd disintegrate, but a half year later, to her surprise, she discovered she was still in one piece, getting on with her life.

And then her bubble had burst, the day of David's wedding. She'd stepped outside the house to pick up the mail, expecting letters and cards from the out-of-town relatives who wouldn't be attending the wedding. Recognizing the court insignia, she'd ripped open the envelope, and the pain she'd felt upon Jordan's departure immediately re-surfaced.

After nearly five years of marriage Mr. and Mrs. Jordan Steinberg had become a statistic. Their marriage was over. Finally, officially and irrevocably over.

Tucking the letter in the pocket of her bathrobe, she'd returned to the house. "You look as wrung out as a *shmatte*," Gertie said. "It's that horrible diner that's turned you into a rag. I don't know why you insist on working there—it's not even kosher. Jordan will soon be a bona fide doctor. How does it look, a doctor's wife working in a place like that?"

"You know I don't keep kosher," Becky reminded her, "and Jordan's not coming back."

"If it's a hobby you need, what's wrong with canasta? All those germs in that dirty place, no wonder you look the way you do. Stay away from Hannah. A bride doesn't need to catch something just before her wedding. Is there any mail?"

"Just bills," Becky replied.

How could she play the role of matron of honor? she'd thought miserably, the idea of matrimony leaving a bitter taste on her tongue. After receiving her final divorce papers, no woman should have to march down the aisle.

Yet in spite of her mood, four hours later she'd found herself smiling as she waited for her cue to walk to the altar. She was filled with happiness for her brother and Hannah. They were a perfect match, even though it had almost taken a bulldozer to get him to the altar. Hannah, his longtime girlfriend, normally quiet and shy, had decided that her biological clock was ticking away and had given him an ultimatum, and David, self-proclaimed bachelor at the ripe old age of thirty-two, after being nagged ad nauseam by Gertie, had finally given in. Mrs. Gertie

Roth wanted a grandchild, and since Becky didn't seem to be in a hurry to provide one, the spotlight had fallen on Hannah.

But everyone knew that David and Hannah belonged together; he'd just needed a little push. David loved her, everyone could see that. Becky could see it in his eyes every time he looked at her. She had no doubt they would have a long, strong marriage, once he got used to the idea.

Why was it that the men who balked most made the best husbands?

Becky walked down the aisle, following her parents and David, and took her place under the *chuppah*. Carter, David's best man, was waiting at the other side of the canopy. Becky had almost forgotten how good-looking he was, and now, seeing him standing there, tall and striking in a tuxedo, a red boutonniere on his lapel, she felt a familiar pang.

And then her mood sobered. He was a statistic, just like her. Another marriage gone under. Another example of love gone sour. Maybe it had been better in Bubbe's day, she thought. A friend or matchmaker introduced you to a suitable partner, and the marriage was based on respect. "We learned to love each other," Bubbe always said. "Chaim was a good man, may he rest in peace. What was not to love?"

"Hey, stranger," Carter said quietly. "It's been a while. I can't remember the last time I saw you. You're looking good, princess."

Aware of his eyes sweeping over her in appreciation, she felt herself blushing. "You're looking snazzy yourself," she answered back, and for an instant she was a teenager again, flirting with him, yearning for his attention.

Then came Hannah's parents, and after that the organist

began to play the wedding march. All heads turned toward the double doors. Hannah appeared, exquisite in a gown of satin and tulle, her skirt made up of several layers of the flowing material. As she walked down the aisle, the crystal beads of her bodice glistened in the soft lighting. Bubbe had wanted the bride to walk with her parents, as in a more orthodox ceremony, but David had insisted that his bride share her moment of glory with no one. "We're Reformed now, Bubbe," he tried to explain. "We choose the laws and traditions we want to follow."

Tears welled in Becky's eyes as she watched Hannah walk down the aisle, tears of happiness for Hannah, tears of sadness for herself. She thought about her own wedding, remembering the promises that were made and then later broken.

At the *chuppah* David met his bride and put his arm through hers. Becky barely heard the ceremony. Afraid she would break down entirely, she held her head low, looking up only when it was time for her to perform her duty as matron of honor and lift Hannah's veil.

After the bride and groom each took a sip from the cup of wine, the rabbi wrapped the glass in a cloth and placed it on the floor. "*Mazel tov!*" the guests cheered after David had stomped on the glass, smashing it to pieces. The tradition of the breaking glass was supposed to be a solemn reminder of the fragility of life, but now that the ceremony was over, all somberness was to be banished.

"On with the festivities!" Aaron called jovially, then led the way to the reception hall.

After the meal, the hall was cleared for dancing. The guests formed a circle around the bride and groom, who were seated on chairs, holding opposite ends of a handkerchief as the custom dictated. "To the king and queen of the night!" someone called out, and when Hannah and

David were lifted in their chairs into the air, Becky quietly sneaked away.

She was in no mood for a party, but she could hardly leave her brother's wedding. She hid out in the bride's lounge, drinking glass after glass of champagne, emerging every now and then to make a brief appearance, resolving, for Hannah's sake, not to reveal her misery. All she wanted was to be left alone, and when the reception was finally over, she told her parents she planned on walking home.

"You want to walk in those heels?" Gertie chided.

"We live just down the block," Becky reminded her mother. "Besides, there won't be any room for me in the car after you've packed it up with leftovers."

Outside, the September air was cool and crisp, a preview to the coming fall. Her head ached from too much champagne, and she wanted to be alone. A walk will do me good, she thought, even though it'll be a short one.

"Bailing out?"

Becky jumped. "Carter! You shouldn't sneak up on a person that way."

"Is there any other way to sneak up on a person?" He tilted her chin with his fingers. "Hey...what's the matter, princess? Those aren't tears of happiness."

His soft caress was enough to break the last of her resolve, and before she could stop herself, she began to sob against his shoulder.

He wrapped his arms around her. "It can't be that bad. Just think of that old saying, 'You're not losing a brother, you're gaining a sister.'"

"You have that all wrong," she managed through her sobs. "The saying is, 'You're not losing a daughter, you're gaining a son.' But that's not why I'm crying." Suddenly embarrassed, she pulled away from his embrace.

Not meeting his eyes, she wiped at the moisture on his jacket. "I'm sorry. I don't know what got into me."

"Don't apologize. The tux can be cleaned." A fresh stream of tears rolled down her cheeks, and he said, "Aw, I'm sorry, princess. I shouldn't have been so flippant. David told me what happened between you and Jordan. If it means anything, I understand what you're going through."

She stopped sniffling and looked at him warily. Of all the people in the world who could offer consolation, she had to get stuck with Carter Prescott, III, deadbeat husband and playboy of the Western Waspy World. "I don't think so! You left your wife—it wasn't the other way around. Why am I even talking to you? You're the last person who could understand what I'm going through."

"You seem to forget there are at least two sides to any story," he said softly. "Did you ever consider that there might be two sides to mine? Maybe I'm not the big bad wolf you make me out to be. Personally I think Jordan is a complete idiot, leaving you. Someone with such poor judgment isn't even fit to shine your shoes."

Then again, maybe a dose of Carter's sugarcoated words was just the medicine she needed. She managed a small smile. "Go on. I'm listening. I'll take all the flattery I can get. My divorce papers came in the mail today, and I'm feeling pretty low."

"Hell, if it's a husband you want, I'll marry you. According to some ancient law, isn't it my duty? Something about the best man and the matron of honor?"

"You're thinking about the story of Ruth. Except you'd have to be Jordan's brother, and he'd have to die. But even if Jordan's parents adopted you and then you went out and hired a hit man, you should know that I'm never getting married again. And you can't fool me with your talk about marriage. You feel the same way I do.''

''In that case,'' he said, winding a lock of her hair around his finger, ''since marriage is out, how about we go back to my place and check out my etchings?''

She laughed. ''Carter Prescott, I wouldn't go to bed with you if you were the last man on earth, not with your track record.''

''Hey, I never said anything about sleeping arrangements.'' His face sobered. ''Kidding aside, come over for a while. I make a mean cup of coffee, and you sure could use one. Truth is, I'm feeling pretty low myself. I was out of town for seven months and no one even knew I was gone.''

''You don't give up,'' she said, shaking her head. ''And I don't buy what you're selling for a minute. What about your mother? She must have missed you. And David. And your co-workers.'' And your long string of women.

''It's my duty as best man to take care of the matron of honor. Just one cup of coffee, I promise. I'll take you home whenever you're ready. I have to hit the sack early, anyway. I'm going back to Phoenix in the morning.''

She hesitated, then smiled. ''Misery loves company, right? All right, just one cup. But I should tell my parents I'm going to be late.''

''As always, the dutiful daughter. You can always depend on Becky to do the right thing.''

She was back at his side momentarily, after informing her parents—and offering no other information, to Gertie's obvious curiosity—that she was going out with a friend.

Arm in arm she and Carter walked to the parking lot. He opened the passenger door of his car, and then, with a straight face, turned to her and asked, "So what about those etchings?"

She swatted him playfully on the shoulder. When they were kids, Carter had made a career of ignoring her or teasing her, but whenever she was hurt, he'd always made her laugh. After she'd fallen, or come home crying because of something someone had said, he'd say something outrageous to take her mind off her troubles.

Now he had her laughing again, and it felt good—even if the joking was risqué. But that was okay. They weren't kids anymore. And she could handle it.

"Here's the scoop," she said, as she climbed into the car. "The only way I'll ever sleep with you is if we're out on the highway and there's this terrible storm..."

Something about her drove him to the brink. It had always been there, and it had been there earlier today when he'd seen her fall. Slim and delicate in a petite frame, she made him feel larger than life. Important. Made him want to be her hero. When he was near her, he felt like protecting her, coddling her. But it wasn't just her compact size that made him want to pull a Tarzan; she had a way of looking at him that turned his resolve to mush.

But coddling wasn't what he'd felt like doing as he'd watched her standing across from him, under the wedding canopy.

The memory of that night burned in his mind as he drove back to his apartment from his mother's. At the ceremony Becky had worn a long-sleeved jacket that matched her rose-colored gown. Her quiet elegance and regal beauty had taken his breath away. He couldn't pull his gaze from her, even when Hannah had walked down the aisle.

After the ceremony Becky had discarded the jacket, and he felt as though he'd been hit with a freight train. This was David's kid sister? The jacket, outlined in sparkly beads, must have been buttoned up right to her chin, because he sure as hell would never have missed the plunging neckline on that dress. Narrow rhinestone straps barely held up the satiny folds that caressed her full breasts, and more sparkles curved at her waist, the fabric falling into soft pleats across her hips. When she turned away to shake some other lucky guy's hand, Carter almost moaned. Her dark hair cascaded in ringlets down toward her tiny waist, curling against the rhinestone strands that crisscrossed her naked back.

He'd been entranced, no use denying it.

Not that he'd planned to do anything about it. Becky might be single again, but she was still David's sister. And she wasn't someone whose name belonged in a little black book. He knew he'd have to keep his distance.

As it turned out, he saw her only for brief moments during the reception. He wasn't disappointed, he told himself. Nope, not in the least. He was feeling sorry for himself because he felt so out of place. The guest list had been enormous, but the only people he knew were Becky's immediate family and a few of David's friends. He wanted to leave, but as best man he knew he was expected to stay. So he chatted, danced and shook hands with strangers—with an eye out for Becky. When the musicians finally stopped playing and packed up their instruments, he sighed with relief. Now he could go.

He saw her at the doors in the foyer. He hadn't meant to startle her, but she'd been so preoccupied, she obviously hadn't seen him coming. "You shouldn't sneak up on someone that way," she reproached him.

"Is there any other way to sneak up on a person?" he

returned, trying to disguise his discomfort with humor. She wasn't the only one who'd been caught by surprise. Feelings he'd suppressed for years had suddenly resurfaced—and he didn't like it. Didn't like it one bit. He pushed his unease aside. "So why the glum face?"

"I'm not glum. I'm gaining a sister, aren't I? Add one sister, subtract one husband. It's an even trade. Me, glum? I'm having a wonderful time, can't you tell?" She twirled around, layers of skirt swirling at her feet. Losing her balance, she fell against him.

"Whoa, I think the lady needs a shot of caffeine. What do you say? There must be someplace open at this hour."

"This is Middlewood, remember? Not even Merlin's Diner stays open, not that I'd suggest we go there. I'm not that cruel." She leaned her head against his shoulder and closed her eyes. "But I'm not ready to go home," she said, her voice suddenly quiet. "I can't...I just can't..."

"Rumor has it that I make a mean cup of coffee," he offered. "How about my place?"

She drew back and smoothed the wrinkles on the shoulder of his jacket. "I'm sorry, Carter. I'm making a mess of your tux—and I'm making a spectacle of myself." She looked up at him with large, dark eyes. "Maybe I will take you up on that coffee."

Snuggling close to him on the drive to his apartment, she murmured, "Have I mentioned that I think you're sweet?"

Sweet? He'd been called a lot of things by a lot of women, but he couldn't remember *sweet* being one of them. And at that moment sweet wasn't how he was feeling. With Becky nestled beside him, the alluring aroma of her perfume was scrambling all his senses. He had to struggle to keep from slamming on the brakes and taking her in his arms.

In the elevator going up from the parking garage to his fourth-floor apartment, she wrapped her arms around his neck and said, "Maybe there'll be a power failure. Maybe the doors won't open and we'll be stuck in here for hours. This way you won't be able to leave—I hate when people leave. This way I'll have you under my control."

Gently he disengaged her arms. With all the willpower he could muster, he said, "This isn't what you want, Becky. You're feeling low and you've had too much to drink."

"Why, Carter Prescott," she said, looking up at him with innocent eyes. "What could you be thinking? I should tell you that the only way I'll ever consider going to bed with you is if there's this terrible snowstorm—"

"I guess I'm out of luck," he said as the doors to the elevator opened. "It doesn't look like it's going to snow anytime soon."

She turned to him, her eyes shining with sudden lucidity. "I'm not drunk," she said softly. "I admit I've had a little too much champagne, but I know exactly what I'm doing. My whole life has just gone down the drain, and at the moment I don't want to think about tomorrow. Right now is all I have. And right now," she said, running her fingers along his arm, "I'm pretending that it's the middle of winter...."

Now, three months later, he was the one pretending. Pretending that what had happened between them had meant nothing at all. It was ironic, he thought as he plowed his way back to his apartment. He was the one who usually gave that speech about not wanting to think about tomorrow.

I hope you don't think this means anything.

He turned onto Elm and his heart stopped beating. Becky. There she was, on the corner. He tried to follow her, but visibility was poor. By the time he reached the place where he had seen her, she had vanished.

He must have been mistaken. What would Becky be doing out on a night like this? But then again, where she was concerned, he'd learned to expect the unexpected.

A car turned onto the street, and for a moment she thought it was Carter's. But in the blowing snow she couldn't be sure. She rounded the corner and found herself outside the bed and breakfast where she'd stopped earlier that day. The ad for an assistant cook was still in the window.

She walked up the pathway, past the Douglas fir with the twinkling lights and silver streamers. Once again she hesitated, but this time she didn't turn back. Not my world, she thought, but a job is a job. She picked up the brass knocker and banged on the door, then waited for her life to change.

Chapter Three

"I knew you were coming," Starr said, clapping her hands together like an excited child. "I dreamed you came with the wind and appeared on my doorstep. You told me that you had brought the winter and that you were seeking shelter. And here you are, just like in my dream."

"I'm afraid I'm not much of a believer in dreams." This could be a mistake, Becky thought warily. She noted the disappointment on Starr's face and quickly added, "But I have an open mind."

"Of course you do." Starr scooted from the kitchen's floor-to-ceiling cabinets to the industrial-size refrigerator and then back to the cabinets, pulling out cups and saucers, honey and milk, spoons and napkins. Her long flowered skirt *whooshed* with each abrupt movement, her flowing sleeves flapping like wings. She sat down next to Becky at the table. "You might be logical and analytical, but you're also adaptable and versatile. An interesting combination, I must say. Gemini is the sign of the Twins for good reason.''

Becky's mouth dropped open. "How did you know I was a Gemini?''

Starr's eyes shone with amusement. "Relax. I can read cards and tea leaves, and I can see auras, but I can't read minds. I saw your birth date on your driver's license. I'm sorry I had to ask you for identification, but a person can't be too careful, even a seer like me. When someone materializes like Mary Poppins at your front door, you have to wonder. Not that I was worried, just cautious.'' She smiled warmly. "Did you know that Gemini is an air sign? It's as if I conjured you up, right out of the air. I wanted a cook, and here you are.''

Though not a follower of astrology, Becky was familiar with the traits of her sign, and one of those traits was flightiness. Her family called her scatterbrained, and she had to admit, at times it aptly described her. When she used to help out at home and her mind would be somewhere else, Gertie would say, "Don't go off *fartootst*.'' When Becky left home to get married, it was the same thing. She'd darted from interest to interest, from one job to another, like a butterfly fluttering from flower to flower.

Was it her fault she had a curious nature and couldn't stay focused on any one thing? Starr must know this, Becky surmised, glancing at a framed chart of the zodiac on the kitchen wall. Apparently, though, her new employer wasn't concerned. In fact, she'd hardly asked any questions about Becky's previous experience. "I base all my decisions on intuition,'' she'd explained. When Becky told her that she was a vegetarian, Starr had hired her on the spot, convinced that destiny was at work.

"Who will I be reporting to?'' Becky asked, remembering the sign in the window. It had advertised for an assistant.

"'Reporting to'? This isn't an office, Becky. It's just you and me. Technically you'll be my assistant, but I'd like to think of us as kindred spirits. We'll be working together, planning and making the meals. For the time being all we do is breakfast, but I'm expecting a group of vegetarians over the holidays and we'll be serving dinner. Where else can people go in this town for fine vegetarian dining? I'm also thinking about opening the dining room to the public on Saturdays." A frown crossed her brow. "Maybe I shouldn't have used the word *assistant*. Maybe I should have used the word *slave*. I'm afraid I can't pay you much, but as I already mentioned, room and board are provided."

"The money is no problem," Becky said, crossing her fingers behind her back. "Without my having to worry about food or rent, I can save almost every cent I earn." Until the baby comes, she thought. Diapers and food and clothing would add up pretty fast, never mind the doctor bills. Which was another thing. What about prenatal care? What about the hospital? And, of course, there was the loan from her parents. She made a quick calculation. With what she'd be earning, she could probably pay off the loan in two hundred years.

Maybe working here wasn't such a good idea. The pay *was* meager. Her options, however, were limited. No one else seemed to be clamoring for her services, and she was tired of running home to Mommy and Daddy whenever the going got rough.

Starr picked up the teapot and began to pour. "Oh dear, where are my manners? I didn't even ask if you liked herbal."

"Herbal is fine," Becky answered, noticing the cracks

in the china. Starr was turning out to be more of an enigma than Becky had imagined. Despite a clutter of statuettes and dolls, the living room was charming, furnished in French provincial with embroidered sofas and cherrywood tables. Charming and expensive, Becky thought. Yet here in the kitchen was a chipped tea service. "I don't use caffeine," she said, picking up her cup.

Starr nodded approvingly. "We have so much in common, we could be soul sisters. I still can't believe my luck—I wanted a vegetarian cook, and here you are." She lowered her voice as though she were sharing a secret. "I should warn you. There are still vegetarians out there who aren't as enlightened as we are. Unfortunately, we'll have to provide coffee. But what can I do? I tell myself I shouldn't be so narrow-minded, but I can't help it. Not only do we have a commitment to the earth not to consume its life force, I believe we have a commitment to ourselves not to poison our bodies. After all, we're part of the earth. That's how I see it, anyway. What about you? Why did you give up meat and caffeine?"

Gertie had once accused Becky of becoming a vegetarian just so she wouldn't have to keep two sets of dishes, one for dairy and the other for meat, according to kosher law. As for Jordan, he hadn't cared one way or the other. He'd rarely eaten at home—when not at school or the hospital, he'd been out cavorting with the redhead.

"Uh, it was because of the earth," Becky answered. Truth was, until now she'd never even considered the environment. Compared to the global dilemma, her reasons now seemed frivolous. She'd given up meat simply because she didn't like the taste and because the thought of the slaughter made her squeamish. Why kill an animal when she could eat a stick of broccoli? As for giving up caffeine, she'd made this choice only that morning, after learning she was pregnant.

Over the rim of her cup she studied Starr surreptitiously. The woman was as complex as she was strange. She was also one of those women who looked ageless. She could have been forty or sixty, but Becky's guess was somewhere in the middle. Although Starr's skin was smooth and youthful, her long dark hair was streaked with gray. Worn straight and parted down the center, it made her appear otherworldly. But it was her eyes that Becky found so unnerving. Large and green, they shone with an unnatural luminescence.

Above the kitchen doorway were strings of red-and-blue beads, and on the ceiling bright silver stars. But it wasn't the beads or stars that gave Becky an uneasy feeling. Everywhere she looked were dolls—on the counter, on the floor, on the shelves, even on the walls: miniature dolls, baby dolls, porcelain dolls and fashion dolls, some handcrafted, others store-bought. One in particular, suspended on a gold hook on the wall next to the refrigerator, held her attention. Made of straw and about a foot long, it was clothed in a long white gown, the hem of the skirt hoisted up and draped across one shoulder. Becky shivered, trying to eradicate thoughts of voodoo from her mind.

"Don't worry, it's not black magic," Starr said as though she was, indeed, psychic. "That's Hestia, my favorite doll, Greek goddess of the hearth. I found her in Barbados, of all places. She reminds me of the Statue of Liberty, except that instead of a torch, she's carrying a ladle. It's the straw that throws people. Not exactly typical of a Greek goddess." Her eyes suddenly twinkled, making them appear even more unearthly. "Speaking of Greek goddesses, I have the perfect thing for you to sleep in.

It's a nightshirt I bought last year at a craft fair. You'll see what I mean by *perfect* when I show it to you.''

Becky hesitated. ''I don't know, Starr. I should go home. I walked out angry, and I know my parents will be worried. I'll call my father. He'll pick me up.''

''Nonsense. The storm is worse, and the roads won't be cleared until morning. No one in his right mind would attempt to plow through this mess. Tomorrow I'll drive you to your parents' house, and you can collect your things. Why don't you call your mother? There's a phone in your room, if you want privacy. Each room has its own extension. Come, and bring your tea with you. I'll show you where you'll be staying.''

Becky followed Starr down a long hallway and up a narrow staircase. ''The house was built back in the late nineteenth century,'' Starr said as they climbed to the third floor. ''It's been in the family for generations. My great-great-grandfather built it after he came over from Holland…there I go again, jabbering about my ancestry. I hope I'm not boring you. I have to keep reminding myself that family history is interesting only to the family involved.''

It must be nice to be able to trace your ancestry that far back, Becky thought with a touch of bitterness. Must be nice to feel so connected. Most of Becky's ancestors had perished in World War II, leaving no records behind. Bubbe was her only living grandparent, and she hardly ever talked about the past. The memories, Becky knew, were too painful.

''I'm not bored,'' Becky told Starr. In truth, she'd always been fascinated with family history, as though someone else's lineage could make up for the lack she felt inside. ''Please go on.''

''How about if I bore you with details of the neighbors

instead?'' Without waiting for Becky to reply, Starr continued, ''The house on the left belongs to the Davidsons. You won't be seeing much of them. They're both lawyers, and they commute to New York. The Logans live in the house on the right. Such a sweet girl, that Laura. Has the cutest two-year-old named Caroline, and a baby on the way.'' She handed the key to Becky. ''Here we are. Go on, you open it. The room's yours now.''

Becky opened the door and switched on the light. What she saw filled her with delight. She'd been expecting more of what she'd seen in the kitchen, but to her relief the motif here matched the casual yet elegant style of the living room—without the dolls. The wallpaper was of a textured jacquard with a subtle floral pattern. The dresser against the far wall was French country with a rich cherry finish, and above the chest of drawers hung an antique mirror. A queen-size canopy bed, its four posts intricately carved, was draped with exquisite white lace.

''This room is fit for royalty,'' Becky said in awe. ''Are all the rooms like this?''

''Glad you like it. And yes, all the rooms are done in this style. Believe it or not, I don't subject everyone who stays here to my hocus-pocus.'' She smiled wryly. ''And this is the reason I can't pay you more. I went overboard with the renovations, and now money is tight. I confess I'm not much of a businesswoman. Next time I plan to consult a crystal ball before making changes—oh, I know what you're thinking, but let me tell you, a crystal ball is far more reliable than the economy. But enough of this financial mumbo-jumbo. On with the tour! Bathroom to the right. In fact, all the rooms have private baths.'' She motioned across the room. ''Look over there. That alcove will make a wonderful nursery.''

Once again Becky's mouth dropped open. ''You

couldn't have gotten that from my driver's license. How did you know? Did you see it in my aura?''

Starr laughed. ''No special magic. It was the way you were sitting. There's something about the way a pregnant woman sits, as if her whole center is off balance.''

Now that's an understatement, Becky thought. In these past few months her whole universe had shifted. ''My pregnancy won't be a problem, will it?'' she asked uneasily. ''I can work until the last moment, and I'll only take off a day or two after the delivery.''

''Work until the last minute? Start cooking right after the baby pops out? I don't think so! I was only kidding about that slavery business—this isn't ancient Greece, for heaven's sake. But to answer your question, no, the pregnancy isn't a problem. On the contrary, it'll be good karma having a baby in the house. New life means rejuvenation. Now, why don't you make that phone call while I get the nightshirt?''

Becky waited for Starr to leave, then kicked off her shoes and lay back on the bed. She knew she had to call her mother, but her courage had melted faster than an ice cube in a bowl of hot chicken soup. Why did her mother always make her feel this way? After Jordan walked out, Becky had waited until she was nearly flat broke before breaking the news and returning to Middlewood. When she'd received the final divorce papers, she'd kept that a secret, as well. She hadn't wanted to be a cloud over David's wedding, she'd rationalized. Then, when she first suspected she was pregnant, she'd gone about her life as if in a trance, hoping that she would wake up.

And now she was afraid to tell her mother that she was planning to live at Starr's bed and breakfast. Compared to what Becky had previously kept hidden, this bit of news seemed trivial, but nevertheless she remained rooted to the bed, unwilling to pick up the phone. She could almost hear Gertie's high-pitched, nasal retort. Imagined her saying, ''Not only is that woman not Jewish, she's *meshugeh*. You want to live with that crazy?''

Starr returned in a few moments and handed the night-shirt to Becky. On the front was an illustration of a woman in a long, loose gown, and underneath that, Demeter Saves the Earth. ''I told you it was perfect. Demeter was the goddess of the harvest, and just like you did in my dream, she brought the winter.''

''Demeter agreed to let her daughter spend half the year with Hades,'' Becky said. ''When Persephone was away in the underworld, Demeter allowed nothing on the earth to flourish, and that's how winter and summer came to be.''

Starr let out a gleeful laugh. ''I can't believe you know this! We're definitely soul sisters. I prayed for someone like you and here you are. We're going to have a lot of fun, Becky. Just like *real* sisters.''

At least someone finds me amusing, Becky thought. After Starr left, Becky reached for the phone on the night-stand. Demeter was also known as the goddess of fertility. Gertie just might get a kick out of that.

Right. And the forecast in the underworld was calling for snow.

Carter raised his racquet and delivered a fast, hard serve. David immediately reacted with a low forehand, blasting the ball into the ceiling. Cocking back his racquet like a baseball bat, Carter stepped into the ball after it had bounced, then swung with full force, his well-practiced forehand slamming the ball against the front wall.

''That's game,'' he said when David failed to return

the shot. "Looks like married life has sapped the life right out of you, bud."

"Or maybe I had too much of my grandmother's cooking last night," David said, wiping the sweat from his forehead. "As for married life, maybe you should think about trying again. Might make you more human."

Carter picked up the ball and followed David into the locker room. "And maybe you should forget about racquetball and take up croquet. Looks like you've lost your edge."

"Here's an edge you won't forget," David said, pulling a towel from the bin and snapping it against the back of Carter's knees. "Did you say 'croquet'? Is that what you do on your dates? Play lawn games? Lost *your* edge, buddy?"

"You wish. No, I take that back. You'd better hope I don't lose the old edge—how would you live vicariously?"

Joking amiably, they headed for the showers. Carter turned on the water in his stall and allowed himself to give in to the pain. Every muscle in his body ached as he stood under the biting, hot spray. But it wasn't the game that had him feeling so sore. He always felt like this the day after flying, and today was no exception. Even though he'd flown first class, his six-foot frame had felt crowded in the seat, his long legs cramped in the tight space.

To top it off, he was exhausted, but like his aching body, his fatigue wasn't because of the game. Last night he'd lain awake for hours, Becky on his mind. Even though three months had passed since they'd made love, he could still picture her lying in his bed, her long, dark hair spilling down her neck, fanning across her breasts. He forced the memory aside.

After changing back into street clothes, Carter waited

in the lobby for David. He thought back to the conversation they'd had earlier that afternoon when he'd called his friend, asking him to meet him on the courts. It had been tough convincing him to come out for a game. Saturday was the Jewish day of rest, but Carter knew that David's reluctance had nothing to do with religion. He knew it was because of Hannah. Marriage did that, he recalled. It changed a man.

Five minutes later David emerged from the locker room. "Still here, Pres? No date?"

Carter laughed. "It's still early. I've still got time."

"Translated, that means no date. What was it you said about losing the edge? As for me, I don't even remember having one. It's been a while since I played the dating game."

Carter flung his sports bag over his shoulder and followed his friend out the front door. "You don't remember it because it never existed. You and Hannah have been together forever." He looked at David questioningly. "Kidding aside, Roth, do you ever regret not playing the field?"

David hesitated. "There was this one time, after Hannah and I had an argument. I went to a bar. The woman was a stranger, no more to me than a face in a crowd. She was a nurse, I think. Worked at Danbury Hospital."

Carter looked at his friend with surprise, not just because of what David had said, but because he'd never mentioned it. Then again, Carter wasn't exactly an open book himself. Some things he preferred not to talk about; others were best left unsaid. Like the events surrounding his divorce. Or what happened between him and Becky.

Although he was reluctant to probe, curiosity got the better of him. He didn't want to believe that David could cheat on Hannah. "What happened?" he asked, hoping the answer would be what he wanted to hear.

"Nothing. We had a few drinks, and that was all. But sometimes I find myself wondering about that night, about how things might have changed if something *had* happened. But nothing did, and I never saw her again. Do I regret not playing around? No, I can honestly say I don't."

Carter felt a moment of envy. One guy in a thousand had what David had. In this day and age, David and Hannah went against all the odds. Not that Carter was looking for something permanent. He wasn't a man who bet against the odds.

Suddenly he didn't feel like going home. "You feel like a beer? We can talk about the old days—I'll fill you in on everything you're missing."

"Sorry, Pres, I have to get back. I promised Hannah I'd paint the back room."

Carter shook his head. "You really *are* married." Without warning, the emptiness he felt whenever he returned from a business trip hit him like a punch in the stomach. As much as he hated to admit it, these days he and emptiness were becoming old pals.

"Like I told you," David said, "you should try it sometime. Again, that is."

"No thanks. I'm not looking to become a half couple. Two's a crowd."

"You've got that wrong. Three's a crowd. Not that I'm complaining." David broke into a wide grin. "I'm talking about a family, Pres. Hannah's pregnant."

Carter stopped walking and grabbed David's arm. "That's great," he said, giving his hand a hearty shake. "Congratulations. So when do I get my cigar?"

"Not for another six months. A half year away, and

already she's preparing for the arrival. This week it's the nursery, next week she wants to shop for baby clothes— soon she'll have me going with her to one of those breathing schools. Did you ever hear of anything so bizarre? There are classes that teach you how to breathe.''

''Admit it, you love this whole baby thing. You were made for it.''

David began walking again, and Carter followed, waiting for David to make a snappy comeback. When he didn't, Carter asked, ''What is it? Hannah's okay, isn't she?''

''She's fine.''

But Carter could tell that something was wrong. When they reached David's car, David turned around and said, ''I know I shouldn't be telling you this, but I'd rather you hear it from me than from any of this town's wagging tongues, and trust me, they'll be wagging like signal flags. It seems that Hannah's not the only one about to increase Middlewood's measly population. Looks like I'm going to become an uncle.''

Carter's whole body stiffened. ''Run that by me again.''

''You heard me the first time. Becky's pregnant.''

Carter knew he looked ridiculous standing there in the middle of the parking lot, his mouth wide open. Pregnant. As in baby. A baby that couldn't be his—she would have told him if he were the father. Looks like little Goody Two-Shoes Becky wasn't so Goody Two-Shoes, after all. Here he'd been feeling sorry for the way he'd treated her, when all the while she'd been running around. Apparently, she'd used the old ''I'm so depressed, why don't you console me'' on someone else, as well. He had to hand it to her, it was usually the man who played the role of fisherman, casting out lines with smoothness and skill.

Immediately Carter chided himself. With his past, who was he to judge her? And then anger set in, surprising him. Why should he care that after being with him she had run straight into the arms of someone else?

Maybe it was pride. Or maybe he was just a little bit hurt.

He dismissed both possibilities from his mind. "I'll bet your mother is beside herself," he said, redirecting his focus. He could just imagine Gertie's reaction. In many ways Becky's mother was just like his. Both women were more concerned about what other people thought than about the happiness of their children. Yet they both gave the old "What will the neighbors say?" a new slant, since neither one of them even spoke to their neighbors.

"That's putting it mildly," David answered. "She called me this morning, demanding that I come right over. The way she sounded on the phone, I was sure something had happened to my grandmother. When I got there, she sent me upstairs to talk to Becky, but then Becky came down the stairs with Starr DeVries—she's that space cookie who owns the B and B on the corner of Elm and Old Mill. Becky, so it seems, is going to live there, of all places. My mother got hysterical and tried to stop them from leaving. She kept repeating, 'A girl needs her mother in times like these.' She stood in the doorway, blocking the exit, but Becky pushed past her."

On second thought, Carter realized, their mothers were nothing alike. If he had a sister who was unmarried and pregnant, Eleanor wouldn't insist she remain at home. No, not Eleanor. She'd probably deny she even knew her.

"Want to know what I think?" David asked. "What's bugging my mother has nothing to do with Becky's moving out. She's upset because the baby isn't Jordan's."

"That's crazy. Why would she think it could be? Becky

hasn't even seen him since they separated.'' Or had she? He dismissed the idea from his mind. Becky despised Jordan. Or so she'd kept repeating on the night of the wedding. An unsettling feeling began to stir in Carter's gut. ''Whose baby is it?''

''She won't say. All I know is that I'm going to become an uncle around the same time I become a father. So that would make her about three months along. Which brings us to the night of the wedding. I know she went out after the reception. My mother said she heard Becky sneaking back into the house about four in the morning. You talked to her that night, didn't you? Do you have any idea who she left with? You don't think it was Nick Patterson, do you? I remember the way he was ogling her. I swear, if it was—''

''It wasn't Nick,'' Carter said quietly.

''Now that I think of it, I hardly saw her during the reception. Every time the photographer wanted to take a family picture, we couldn't find her. Nick wasn't around much, either. They were probably on the balcony, or in the bride's room, getting friendly. That scumbag. I swear, when I get him face-to-face—''

''It wasn't Nick,'' Carter repeated. ''Give your sister some credit. Do you honestly believe she'd go off with that sleaze?''

David opened the door to his car, then turned to face Carter. ''What makes you so sure? Do you know something I don't?'' When Carter didn't answer, David said, ''Spill it, Pres. Now.''

''David, I…'' He let his voice trail off. This wasn't going to be easy.

David let out a curse and exhaled loudly. Then, with one quick, fluid motion, he landed his fist in Carter's face.

Carter fell and hit the pavement, breaking his fall with

the palms of his hands. He looked up, and for a moment all he saw was a swirl of colors. "Let me explain—"

"Save it," David spat, and climbed into the car.

For one frightening moment Carter almost believed that David would run him over, but then realized his thinking was crazy. David was angry—angry as hell—but he wasn't homicidal. With a squeal of the tires, the car sped away.

Carter scrambled to his feet. His head was still reeling from the blow, and he stumbled to the nearest car. Bracing himself with his arms, he leaned forward against the white sedan, trying to keep himself from blacking out.

Croquet, Carter had suggested. With a right hook like that, David should think about taking up boxing. Even though the earth had stopped spinning, Carter still felt shaken.

He knew he deserved the hit he'd taken. Not only for taking Becky back to his apartment that night, but also for thinking, even for a minute, that she'd been with someone else. Even though they had allowed their passions to take over, Becky wasn't someone who took sex lightly. She wasn't someone who flitted from man to man. He'd known how vulnerable she'd been that night. Maybe he'd been deluding himself. Maybe he'd been the one to cast the line.

Maybe the truth about what had happened that night wasn't as cut-and-dried as he'd originally believed, but the one thing he was certain of was that he was the father.

A baby.

As in family.

As in…marriage.

He walked to his car in a daze, his head aching from the blow, his mind in turmoil. One mistake didn't mean you had to make another, did it? Single women had babies all the time, didn't they? No to the first question, yes to the second. Morality had changed in the past few decades, and people no longer felt compelled to get married just because a baby was coming. Nevertheless, Carter was the father and he intended to do the right thing. He'd see to it that Becky and the baby wanted for nothing.

He'd missed his chance at fatherhood once before. He didn't intend to let it happen again.

After Becky and Starr returned from Gertie's, they spent the rest of the morning and the early afternoon planning menus. Although only a handful of guests were registered at the inn, Starr was expecting a crowd next weekend and throughout the holiday season. Equally important, she wanted to open her Saturday bistro before the end of January. They were poring through recipe books when a cacophony of birdsong filled the kitchen. Startled, Becky looked up. "What is *that?*"

"Doorbell. Just like the ones in the rain forests. I'll get it." Starr returned momentarily, her mouth pulled into a sardonic smile. "And thus the saga continues. The father has come to stake his claim. Carter Prescott is here, straight out of the society pages, demanding to see you."

"How...how did you know he's the father?"

"He has that sheepish look. You can't disguise guilt. I parked him in the living room, but I'll send him away, if you want."

"No, I'll see him."

Carter was seated on the sofa near the window, his jacket open, revealing a crewneck sweater. She felt her throat constrict. She'd always been a sucker for a man in a crewneck. No, she'd always been a sucker for Carter, period. Even now, after her life had been turned upside down, he still had the power to send her pulse racing. The memory of that night came back in a rush, and she tried to push it away. It was because of her foolish attraction she was in this predicament in the first place.

She gathered her courage and approached him—and stopped in her tracks. "That must have been some fight," she said, noticing the black and blue that circled his eye. "What happened?"

"Let's just say I had a mishap at the racquetball club." He looked around the room and frowned. "Why are you here, Becky? What are you doing in this hippie haven?"

"What I'm doing here is none of your business, and for your information the decor is French provincial."

"I was referring to the smell. Is that incense?"

"It's not incense, it's strawberry and kiwi." She pointed to the candles on the bookcase. "Scented," she explained. "Starr lights candles all over the house. My house," she added. "I live here now."

"So your brother said." He stood up and walked over to the fireplace. "Since when is Buddha French?" he asked, picking up the green jade statue on the mantel. He put it back down and motioned to a basket on the floor. "And what are those? Voodoo dolls? Have you lost your mind? Is this any place to bring up a child?"

Her heart dropped to her stomach. He knew. Carter knew and now he was here to…to do what? To reprimand her for getting into this predicament? He'd already proven how well he could delegate blame, she thought, remembering their conversation yesterday. Did he honestly believe she'd been alone in the room at the time of the conception? Or was he here to drag her off to the altar, wanting, as Starr had put it, to stake his claim?

Becky rested her gaze on his injured eye, and realization took hold. "Looks like you and my brother talked about more than my new living arrangements. You didn't have a mishap playing racquetball. He hit you, right? How did he know you're the father?''

"What difference does it make? Why didn't you tell me you were pregnant, Becky? Why did I have to find out from him?''

"I was going to tell you. Soon. I only found out yesterday.''

"Yesterday! David's wedding was three months ago. You've been pregnant all this time and you only confirmed it yesterday?''

"Three and a half,'' she corrected.

"Excuse me?''

"I'm three and a half months pregnant. You're supposed to count back from the start of your last period. Not that I remember when it was, but if I conceived in the middle of the month, all I need to do is go back two weeks. Isn't that silly? That means that theoretically a woman can be pregnant before she's pregnant. When she's one week pregnant, she hasn't even—''

"Becky, stop. You're being ridiculous. The bottom line is that I'm the father and I won't have my child living in this sorcery saucepan. Pack your bags. I'm taking you home.''

She was ridiculous? Standing there with his arms folded rigidly across his chest, his chin jutting stubbornly into the air, he looked liked a pouting child. "Sit down,'' she ordered. "You obviously don't understand. I need to make some things clear.''

Scowling, he sat back down on the sofa, and she took the armchair next to him. "Why not just lend me your crystal ball?'' he asked sarcastically.

Thinking about Starr, she smiled inwardly, silently blessing her new friend and employer. The woman might be a little strange, but she was a godsend. She had opened up her home and her heart, and for this Becky would always be grateful.

"This *is* home. I'm not going anywhere. I'm the new cook here—assistant cook, that is—and the pay is, uh, great. On top of that I get free room and board. Starr is wonderful, and this place is filled with positive vibrations—can't you feel them?"

Carter looked at her as if she'd just arrived from another planet. "Vibrations," he repeated, muttering the word as if it was spelled with four letters. "What are you saying? That you don't want my help?"

"Bingo."

"This child is mine as much as it is yours. I should have worn protection that night. I'm responsible, and I intend to do the right thing."

"The right thing," she echoed. "That's all you care about, isn't it? Look, I appreciate your coming here and offering to help, but this is my problem."

"It's my problem, too, remember? You make it sound as if wanting to help is some sort of crime. What's wrong with doing the right thing?"

"I'll tell you what's wrong. Right now my father is probably conjuring up ways to get you to the altar, and my brother is probably shopping for a gun. As for my mother, she's probably concocting ways to convince Jordan that the baby is his. I don't even want to think about what his perception of *right* might be, but one thing I'm sure of, it has something to do with a redhead in a hot tub." She could see she wasn't getting her message across, and raised her voice. "The right thing? By whose standard? I'm sick and tired of everyone telling me how to run my life. From now on the only standard I intend to live by is mine."

His tone was calm yet patronizing. "You don't live in

a vacuum. There are others involved. The baby, for instance. You can't possibly be thinking of raising it on your own.''

''I'm sick to death of people telling me what I'm thinking! And I'm sick to death of people telling me what to do. This is *my* life, Carter, and I'll do what I want.''

A look of panic crossed his face. ''You're not thinking of doing something stupid, are you? Because if you are, I won't let you—''

''Won't let me what?'' Understanding set in, and her fury almost choked her. ''What kind of person do you think I am? I'm already in the second trimester—the baby has a heartbeat! But even if it wasn't too late, I would never think of ending the pregnancy.''

''I didn't mean to imply—''

''All I'm saying is that from now on I intend to live my life my way. I'm a responsible adult, even though the rest of the world seems to disagree. While we're on the subject of responsibility, I want you to know that I take full blame for what happened that night. You had no reason to believe that I wasn't protected. Furthermore, I should have insisted you wear a condom. I had no idea who else was in bed with us, given your past and Jordan's, too.''

''I'm not here to talk about blame,'' he said curtly. ''It's a little late for that. Besides, I already admitted it was my fault. Why are you being so difficult? I want to provide for you and the baby. Why won't you let me help you?''

She leaned back in the chair. ''How can I make you understand?'' she asked in a tired voice. ''I lived at home when I went to college. After I graduated, I moved from my parents' house to live with my husband, and after Jordan left, I moved back home. This is the first time I've ever been on my own, and you know what? It feels good. It feels good not having anyone telling me what to do. Telling me how to live my life. Good karma, Starr would say. That's why I don't want your help. It's my body, Carter, and this is my baby. I intend to raise it—her—by myself.''

"I hate to interrupt," Starr said, appearing in the entranceway, "but your mother's on the phone."

"I suppose that means I'm dismissed," Carter said icily. "All right, I'm leaving. But I'm not giving up. This is my baby, too, and I demand a say in how it's going to be raised."

"You can take the call in the kitchen," Starr said to Becky. "I'll see Carter to the door."

"I know where the door is," he retorted. He stood up and walked toward the hallway, then suddenly turned to face Becky. "We're not done yet. No matter what you've decided, you can't change the fact that this baby is mine."

Becky rose from her chair and walked past him, feeling his stare on her back. On to the next round, she thought, not looking forward to what awaited her in the kitchen.

What was it Starr had said?

And thus the saga continues...

Chapter Four

Carter sat at his desk, staring at the open folder. He tried to blame his lack of focus on post-weekend blues, but he knew he was fooling himself. He loved his job any day of the week, Mondays included. He often worked evenings, as well, which did wonders for his social life.

He almost laughed. What social life? People seemed to think he was a party animal, but the truth was, after his divorce he'd buried himself in his work, and it had become a way of life. Now, when he wasn't working, he felt restless. Yesterday, for instance, he'd been bored, sitting alone in his apartment. He couldn't even call David. Even if his best friend had been inclined to talk to him, Carter knew he'd be busy with Hannah, preparing the nursery and doing whatever else expectant fathers did.

He closed the folder and leaned back in his chair. He had just come from a meeting on the New Zealand project. He and Phil Thompson, one of the other junior partners, would be going over there in July.

New Zealand's seasons were opposite from those in North America, January being the warmest month, July the coldest. But the temperatures were moderate even in winter, and construction would be in progress year-round. Carter was looking forward to skiing in the South Island. The Southern Alps was home to some of the most spectacular resorts in the world.

The timing was perfect. The baby was due in late May. He wouldn't be leaving until well after the birth.

A nagging feeling settled inside him. Should he be going at all?

When he'd joined the firm more than seven years ago, it had been a small operation with only Joe Sullivan at the helm. Although several companies had approached Carter in his last year at Harvard Design School, he'd wanted to settle in Middlewood, where he'd grown up. The lifestyle was slower and more relaxed, and he'd had no desire to climb the corporate ladder. Wendy, however, hadn't shared his sentiments regarding small-town life. She hadn't gone through Harvard Law to practice her profession in a hole-in-the-wall like Middlewood, she'd argued. In the end, though, she'd agreed to settle here. After they were married, they'd bought a house, and they'd been happy. Or so he'd believed. They were young, they were healthy and they each had a rewarding career. His was based in Middlewood, and she commuted to New York.

After four years it all unraveled. Without giving him a definition of what the word entailed, Wendy told him she wanted more. Carter said he would be willing to sell the house and move to New York—he'd be the one to commute—but she dismissed his suggestion with disdain. That was when he realized she'd been referring to *him* when she'd used the word *more*. Technically he'd been the one to walk out, that night of the argument, but in reality it was she who had ended the marriage.

By then Joe had formed a partnership with Mike Walters, and they'd hired more architects. The firm had expanded, and it was still growing. Instead of building bungalows, they were erecting hotels. At his own request, Carter found himself spending most of his time away onsite. He sold the house and rented an apartment. Middlewood had become no more than an address; it made no difference where he hung his coat.

But now circumstances were different. He had a reason for staying put. Even though Becky insisted on raising the baby by herself, he was the father. He had obligations.

He cursed her silently. As far back as he could remember, she'd always been so undemanding, so compliant. Why now of all times did she have to go and get independent on him? He didn't look forward to the months ahead. He had a feeling she'd fight him every step of the way. Well, he didn't intend to give up. The baby was his, and Carter wasn't someone who shirked responsibility. He almost felt sorry for her. Not only did she have him to contend with, she had her mother. Not to mention her bodyguard brother.

Carter's hand automatically rose to his eye. Here it was Monday, and the bruise still smarted. But it sure got attention from the women in the office, he thought, smiling to himself. Not to mention the ribbing from the guys. He tried to imagine what they'd say if they knew the story behind it. And that stumped him. He had no idea what they would say. Truth was, he didn't know his co-workers very well. He never saw any of them socially, Joe and

Mike included. Until now he'd never even considered that they might have lives outside the workplace.

And this stumped him, as well. Why was he considering it now?

Maybe becoming a father-to-be changed you without your knowing it, he thought. Made you more human, he imagined David saying. He gazed out the window, wondering what it was like to have a kid. Might be nice to have a miniature Prescott tagging along. Maybe when the kid was older, Carter would take him on-site.

Him. He was sure it was a boy. He'd read somewhere that if the mother had been aggressive at the time of conception, the baby would be male. He thought back to that night, and his pulse started hammering. Maybe he'd been the one to initiate what had happened, but once they got started, she'd had no qualms about moving into the driver's seat. Not that he had complained. He remembered the way she had maneuvered him to the wall and pressed her body against his, right there in the elevator. For a moment he'd been tempted to push the emergency stop.

Aggressive? If that old wives' tale were true, she was carrying Rambo.

He laughed out loud. Old wives' tale? Why didn't he just go over to the B and B and hang his shingle next to Starr's?

He glanced at his watch, amazed to see that it was almost one. He'd been sitting at his desk for hours, unable to work. His thoughts returned to Becky. She'd made it clear she didn't want his help. If anything, she had guts. She'd been given a raw deal by that rat of a husband, and now she was determined to make a life for herself. But soon there would be another person involved. The baby. His baby. Dammit, even though she was determined to change her life, she was just as irresponsible as he remembered. How could she live in that nuthouse? How soon would it be before she left that job, too? And speaking about irresponsibility, he couldn't believe she'd waited this long to confirm the pregnancy.

A disturbing thought occurred to him. What if she wasn't planning on prenatal care? He knew she was in a dire financial state. Maybe Starr had a friend who was a midwife, or maybe she knew a witch doctor. Good Lord, what else was that strange woman putting into Becky's head? What if Becky was considering having her baby underwater? He'd read about this practice. It was supposed to be relaxing for both mother and baby, but this was his child they were talking about, not some Olympic swimming star. Carter would be damned if he would allow her to take any unnecessary chances.

His son was going to get the best health care that money could buy, and that meant no witch doctors or swimming pools. He grabbed his jacket and headed for the door. It was time to take action.

"What is that wonderful smell?" Starr asked, poking her head into the kitchen.

"Come here, I want you to taste something." Becky stirred the pot simmering on the stove, then scooped out a spoonful of stew. "What do you think?"

"Mmm. If we were in ancient Greece, this would be food for the gods. What is it?"

"Lunch. Zucchini herb soup and tofu stew, both my own recipes." Becky took two plates from the cabinet and set them on the counter. "Actually, we're just having stew. The soup's not quite ready. But I don't think you'll be disappointed. The stew is one of my favorites. I call it Napoleon's Delight."

Starr pulled out the flatware and napkins, then sat down

at the table. "Why? Do you have a thing for short megalomaniacs who hide their hands in their jackets?"

Becky dished out two generous servings and took the chair next to Starr. "Supposedly this dish was served to Napoleon after his victory in Marengo. His chef used findings from the nearby countryside. But I've changed a lot of the ingredients. For one thing, I took out the meat and added tofu."

"I knew it was destiny when I hired you," Starr said, after devouring her portion. "That was wonderful. But you don't have to make lunch for me. It's not part of your job."

Becky dismissed the comment with a wave of her hand. "Nonsense. I enjoy it. You know, it's funny how fast my morning sickness disappeared once I left the diner."

"And I'm grateful that you did. Food this good is going to put the B and B on the map. I'd like to add this dish to the dinner menu when we open to the public." Excitement gleamed in Starr's large green eyes. "I just had the most brilliant idea! Why don't you write a cookbook? You could mention this place in your acknowledgments. I've always wanted to be famous." She rose from the table, carrying her plate. "Do you want more stew? Seriously, I think you should consider it."

"No more for me. I'm full. It's a myth that pregnant women have to eat for two."

"I mean you should consider writing a cookbook."

"Me, write a book? I can't even spell."

Starr refilled her plate and sat back down. "You need to develop a positive attitude. Unborn babies feel what their mothers feel." She shook her head slowly. "It's a sad thing when a woman loses her confidence."

Lose her confidence? Becky never had any to begin with. How was she supposed to gain confidence when she couldn't do anything? Except that wasn't true—she could cook. "Maybe you're right. I don't want to hand down a negative attitude to my baby. It's time I stopped agonizing over what I can't do and start focusing on what I can."

"Exactly," Starr said between mouthfuls. "So when did you learn to cook like this?"

"When I was married. My husband left me alone a lot, and I needed something to do. The more he left me to myself, the more depressed I got. The more depressed I got, the more I cooked. To this day, whenever I'm upset or whenever I have a difficult decision to make I run to the kitchen. Cooking calms me. Thank goodness I've always been health conscious, otherwise I'd have a weight problem. What you're sampling is the latest fruit of my misery."

"It's delicious. I'll have to make sure you stay upset."

"The odds are on your side." Becky's eyes suddenly filled with tears. These days the tears came with no forewarning, at the least convenient times. "The morning sickness was bad enough, but no one ever warned me about the mood swings."

Starr jumped to her feet and was at Becky's side in an instant. "Aw, honey, I'm sorry. I was only joking. What happened to make you start cooking today?"

Becky cast her a woeful glance. "With a mother like mine, I'm surprised I don't develop a vice worse than cooking. She's been calling me every hour on the hour. Do you know what she did? I can't believe the nerve of that woman! She made an appointment for me with Hannah's obstetrician."

Starr looked confused. "And the problem is…"

"I'm perfectly capable of making my own appointments. Not only that, I'd like to pick out my own obstetrician. Hannah is very sweet, but she has this crazy idea that the older the doctor is, the more competent he must be. This Dr. Boyd is probably a dinosaur.''

"So have you?"

"Have I what?" Becky asked, reaching behind her for a tissue on the counter.

"Picked out a doctor?"

Becky blew her nose. "Uh, not yet." She looked back up at Starr. "Oh, all right," she grumbled. "I'll keep the appointment. But if this doctor starts talking about trepanning, I'm going to turn him in to the AMA."

"Trepanning, as in drilling holes in your head? I think you need a vacation. You're sounding as crazy as me." Starr stood up and took the dishes to the sink. "You know, you should think about writing that cookbook. Don't worry about the spelling, that's what spellcheck is for. I've been thinking about biting the bullet and buying a computer. It would make the accounting much easier— you know I don't have a head for figures."

"You're going to enter the modern era?" Becky asked, chuckling.

"Haven't you heard? I've traded in my broomstick for an electric scooter. That reminds me," she added, wiping her hands on a dish towel. "It's time I got started on the vacuuming."

After Starr left the kitchen, Becky sat at the table, mulling over the idea about writing a cookbook. She knew that Starr wouldn't buy a computer; the woman couldn't even program her VCR. I'm one to talk about being modern, Becky thought. I don't even own a cell phone. Those things cost money, and right now money wasn't an available resource.

Having a baby would be expensive, let alone raising a child, but she was determined to do it by herself. She hadn't realized just how determined she was until she'd had that argument with Carter. She'd surprised herself with her outburst, and by the look on his face she could tell she'd surprised him, too. She'd never been one to stick up for herself. She'd never even admitted to herself that she had needs of her own.

Like the need to stand on her own two feet.

Life is funny, she thought. If I weren't pregnant, I wouldn't be feeling this streak of independence. I guess a baby will do that. Makes you reevaluate your priorities. This baby is dependent on me, and I won't let her down.

She smiled to herself. Won't let *her* down. Starr had dangled a gold chain over Becky's palm, explaining that if the medallion on the end moved in a circle, the baby was a girl. If it moved back and forth in a line, the baby was a boy. Not that Becky believed in old wives' tales, but secretly she'd been glad when the medallion had moved in circles.

She'd always wanted a little girl, to love and to nurture, to provide with all the understanding Becky felt she had missed as a child. She would teach her daughter to think for herself, to be proud of her accomplishments. Her daughter would learn to respect all living things, her own life included.

Of course, the baby could be a boy. She considered what it would be like to have a son. It might not be so bad, she decided, especially if he looked liked Carter, with those smoky-gray eyes, that lopsided smile whenever he was amused, the way the left side of his mouth turned down whenever he was worried. No, having a son would be perfectly fine. Kids were kids, right? You loved them unconditionally, boys and girls alike. What she'd planned to teach her daughter she could teach her son: compassion, self-esteem, respect.

Especially respect.

Respect was something Carter lacked. It was obvious he hadn't taken seriously anything she had said. Did he think he could just come waltzing in demanding parental rights? It took more than a drop of the pants to be a father.

He wanted to do the right thing. Just what did that mean? A nagging feeling settled in the pit of her stomach. As much as she hated to accept his help, could she refuse? Babies were expensive. Could she deny her child what Carter could offer? She knew that doing the right thing meant doing what was right for the baby, but at what price? "I demand a say in how it's going to be raised," he'd said. Would he insist on raising the baby on his own terms? And what about his traveling? Did he intend to pull the strings from clear across the country? From clear across the world?

She rose from the table. She'd do what she always did whenever faced with a tough decision. The refrigerator was already filled with an assortment of soups and stews, but the freezer had plenty of space.

You'd think the woman would have cats, he mused as he waited on the doorstep, ringing the doorbell, listening to birdsong. And what kind of name was Starr? Her real name was probably something like Harriet or Bertha. Here comes Bertha now, he thought, listening to the footsteps echoing in the hallway.

But it was Becky who answered, her face flushed as though she'd spent the past hour doing aerobics. "Sorry I took so long," she said, slightly breathless. "I didn't hear you over the vacuum cleaner."

"You've been vacuuming? Are you crazy?"

"I'm pregnant, not an invalid. Why shouldn't I vacuum?" She narrowed her eyes. "What are you doing here, Carter? I have nothing more to say to you."

"What do you think I'm doing here? I'm here to make you listen to reason, and I'm not leaving until you consent to do what's best for the baby. For starters, there'll be no more housework."

"And who's going to do the cleaning? You?" A glint of amusement flickered in her eyes. "Although, I have to admit, there's something enticing about a man in an apron."

Yesterday she'd just about split her gut arguing with him, and today she was flirting? Mood swings, he thought. Pregnant women were supposed to be temperamental, right? His eyes roamed over her clingy sweater and snug-fitting jeans. Maybe there was a little more to her than he'd remembered—especially her chest—but she didn't *look* pregnant. Weren't pregnant women supposed to glow? He studied her face carefully. Nope, no glow. Another old wives' tale. Her eyes met his, and, embarrassed to have been caught scrutinizing her, he averted his gaze. "I thought you were hired as a cook, not a maid," he muttered.

"Don't get your apron all ruffled. Starr was vacuuming, not me. We have a cleaning service, but they only come by twice a week. I was in the kitchen doing what a cook normally does in the kitchen—cook. I admit I overdid it and now I'm feeling a little tired, but…omigosh, the soup!"

Carter followed her as she darted into the kitchen. "What smells so good?"

"Zucchini herb soup. Want some?"

He made a face. "I think I'll pass."

She rolled her eyes. "What is it about men? If it's not meat and potatoes, it's not real food." Napoleon's Delight, still too hot to freeze, was cooling down in a large bowl on the counter. She spooned a healthy portion onto a plate. "Here, try this," she said, handing him the food and a fork.

He sat down at the table. "Now this is more like it." He shoveled a forkful into his mouth, then looked up with surprise. "Say, you really *can* cook. What's in this?"

"Just the regular stuff. Eye of newt, toe of frog, leg of lizard."

He laughed. "I thought you didn't eat meat."

"I don't. No animal whatsoever has contributed to this dish. It's made up of mushrooms, olives, tomatoes, a few secret seasonings…and tofu."

At the mention of tofu, he groaned. "Haven't you heard the expression, 'Real men don't eat tofu'?"

"Quiche. Real men don't eat quiche." After sprinkling some black pepper into the pot, she stirred the soup, then glanced down at his empty plate. "Finished already? Must have been the eye of newt you found so tasty. Do you want some more?"

"Actually, I was thinking I'd try the soup."

"Spoons are in the top drawer. While you're up, get two glasses from the cabinet behind you." She ladled the soup into a bowl, then took a pitcher from the refrigerator. "How about some carrot juice?"

"Don't push it."

"You'll never know if you like something until you try it," she said, turning off the stove. "But I'm proud of you, Carter. You charged into the tofu and you didn't let it kill you. What next? The possibilities are endless."

"Are you calling me inflexible? That's like the pot calling the kettle black. You're the one with the stubborn streak."

She sat down next to him. "Yeah, how so?"

"You know what I'm talking about. All I want to do

is help out with the baby, and you make it sound as if I want to control your life.''

''Okay.''

He put down his spoon. ''Okay?''

''Okay, I'll let you help. And, Carter?''

''What?''

''Thank you.'' She poured herself a glass of juice. ''You sure you don't want any?''

Just like that she changes her mind? What happened to ''I want to live my life my way''? He looked at his empty plate with suspicion. Maybe she was trying to poison him. He raised his hand to his black eye. Maybe maniacal tendencies ran in her family.

He glanced back at the plate. That stuff she'd made him eat sure hadn't tasted like tofu, but then again, he'd never tasted tofu before. ''Carrot juice. Sure, why not? This is a day for miracles. You've relented and I've discovered I don't hate tofu.''

He caught himself staring at her as once again she reached across to pick up the pitcher. Staring at her neck. Slender and pale, long and regal. His gaze dropped. There should be a law against pregnant women wearing tight sweaters. He gulped down the juice.

''Well?'' she asked. ''Do you like it?''

''I survived.''

''I'll alert the media,'' she answered back. ''By the way, that juice is my own secret recipe. You won't find anything like it anywhere.''

He raised a brow. ''I didn't realize there were so many ways to juice a carrot.''

''You'd be surprised. I can be very inventive. In fact, Starr thinks I should compile all my recipes into a book. I have so many, I could fill a library. Do you know where

I can pick up a secondhand typewriter? I can't exactly submit a handwritten book to a publisher.''

"First get your recipes into some sort of order. That should take some time. In the meantime, I'll look around for a typewriter." He shook his head. "You never cease to amaze me, princess. Just when I think I have you all figured out, you throw me a curveball. For one thing, I had no idea you could cook like this, and now, just when I thought I'd have to tie you up to make you listen, you tell me you're willing to let me into the baby's life.''

Her lips pulled into a tight line. What now? he thought.

"I never said anything about you being part of the baby's life," she said, answering his silent question. "If you want to help with the medical bills, that's fine with me. But that's it.''

Curveball? Spitballs seemed more her style. "Gee, thanks, Becky. That's very generous of you, allowing me to dig into my wallet. But that's not enough for me. I plan to provide for this baby even after he's born, and I want to be a part of his life.''

Her eyes flashed with anger. "Yes, I know. You want a say in raising the baby. But what does that mean? Does it mean you intend to monitor my every move? Does it mean you get to breeze in and out of my child's life whenever it suits you? This isn't a business we're discussing, this is a child. Fatherhood isn't a part-time job, Carter. It's all or nothing.''

"Just what do you have in mind?" he said, alarm bells going off in his head. "Are you saying you want to get married?''

To his surprise—and irritation—she laughed. "Us, married? Don't be ridiculous. We come from different backgrounds, different faiths. Talk about confusing a child! It's hard enough as it is, trying to find a place in this world. Why make it more difficult? All that aside, I never intend to get married again, and I suspect you feel the same way. Admit it, Carter. You like your freedom. You like gallivanting all over the country.''

He felt his skin prickling. Her interfaith reasoning made sense, but they could work it out. After all, didn't they worship the same supreme being? What irked him was that she presumed to know what he was feeling. She was wrong. Maybe he was getting a little tired of his lifestyle. Maybe he wanted to stay in one place. Maybe staying rooted was all he'd thought about since learning about the baby.

Well, no. He'd thought about a lot more than geography. He'd thought about Becky. A hell of a lot about Becky.

Before he could stop himself, he found himself saying, ''My life won't always be like this. In fact, this morning Joe and I were discussing my future with the firm. When I become a full partner, I won't have to travel as much. Sure, I've always liked watching my buildings go up, but the real pleasure is in the design. I'm more than willing to let someone else supervise at the site. I could easily settle down here in Middlewood, make a life, raise a family.''

She stared at him, wide-eyed. ''Are you asking me to marry you?''

''I think we should at least consider it an option.''

''Don't you think you're carrying your I've Got To Do the Right Thing motto a little too far? This isn't the old country. People—women—have choices. A marriage based on obligation is no marriage at all. What kind of message would I be giving my daughter? Besides, what about New Zealand? David told me the job has been approved. You can't fool me with all this talk about staying put, and you can't fool yourself. You love working on-site. You love watching the seeds of your imagination grow into something real."

He hadn't realized he'd been holding his breath. He hoped his relief wasn't too obvious. Yet part of him was offended. She had turned down his marriage proposal, such as it was. And part of him felt let down. He couldn't help wondering what it would be like to crawl into bed with her, night after night, year after year....

She reached for his hand, and a surge of heat flowed through him. "I appreciate the gesture," she continued softly, "but it's not necessary for you to marry me. And don't worry, no one's going to come after you with a shotgun." She let out a chortle. "I never knew my brother had it in him." She pulled her hand away to caress the wound around his eye. "That's some shiner he gave you. Looks like a rainbow."

She would have to stop touching him. As it was, that sweater of hers had him close to melting a circuit. He cleared his throat. "What does it feel like?"

"Tender. It's still a little swollen."

He gently cupped her hand with his, then brought it down to her abdomen. "No, I mean the baby. What does it feel like?" He looked up at her face. And there it was. The glow. "Do you feel anything yet?" he asked, his voice catching.

"All the books say it's too early, but I swear I can feel her moving."

He felt a ripple under his fingers. Startled, he quickly pulled his hand away.

"See what I mean?" she said. "It's as if she can't wait to get out into the world and give us a piece of her mind."

"You keep saying *she*. How can you be so certain it's a girl?"

"I can't. But I hate calling the baby *it*. Anyway, I'm having an ultrasound on Thursday. I intend to ask the sex. I'm not one of those mothers who want to be surprised."

So, she'd made an appointment with a doctor. Relief swept through him—relief and a dose of shame for doubting her. "I'm going with you," he said with rising anticipation. When he'd felt that little ripple, no more than a burp, he'd thought the world had stopped on its axis. If all it took was one little burp to stop his world from spinning, what would the actual birth do?

Suddenly he found himself looking forward to the whole drill—visits to the doctor, shopping for the baby, Lamaze class…breathing classes, David had called them. Carter felt he could use a breathing class himself, just to calm him.

"I'd rather you didn't come with me," Becky said, her words chilling him out of his reverie. "It would be better in the long run if you didn't get too involved. I'm thinking of both you and the baby. Soon you'll be off in New Zealand. After that, who knows where? It'll be easier on you if you don't become attached, right from the start."

"We both live in the same small town. We're bound to run into each other. What do you plan to do every time I come home? Hide the baby until I leave?"

"I've thought about this a lot, Carter. One thing I know for sure is that I can't stay here in Middlewood. By the time you get back from New Zealand, I should be on my feet financially. I've been thinking about moving back to New York. It's a great city, and I still have friends there."

A single mother with no skills, living in New York? Where did she get her ideas?

His gaze darted from the stars on the ceiling to the red-and-blue beads strung over the doorway, and then to the spooky straw doll next to the refrigerator. Thoughts of sorcery and voodoo—and, for some reason, swimming pools—swirled in his head.

"No way," he said.

"Excuse me?"

"There's no way I'll let you give birth to my son underwater."

She looked at him sideways. "Are you all right, Carter?"

"If I'm footing the bills, I have a right to know you won't do something stupid."

"Something stupid," she repeated dryly. "Don't worry, stupid is something I have no intention of repeating." She sighed heavily. "Fine. You can come with me to the doctor. You have a right to know that the baby is being well cared for. But just this once, Carter. That's it, I swear. Like I said, fatherhood isn't a part-time job."

He hated to admit it, but her words made sense. No child should have a here-today, gone-tomorrow dad. It wouldn't be fair. Nevertheless, whether or not Becky agreed, after the birth he would continue to provide for her and the baby. But it would have to be from the sidelines.

He knew she was right. So why did it feel so wrong?

Chapter Five

On Thursday morning, when Carter showed up on her doorstep, he was equipped with a large cardboard box. On top of it lay a thick, heavy book. "Don't just stand there," he said cheerfully. "Grab the manual, will you?" Becky cast him an inquisitive glance, then picked it up. He brushed by her and headed toward the stairs.

"Where do you think you're going?" she asked, following closely behind. "We have a doctor's appointment in less than an hour."

He suppressed a smile. Her exasperation was just what he'd expected, but he was sure she'd soften when she found out what he'd brought. Some men come bearing flowers, others bring chocolate, he thought. Not him. His present was, well, different.

"This won't take long to set up," he said once he'd reached the top of the stairs. "Which room is yours?"

"Third one on the left, but—"

"Are you going to open the door, or do I set up right here in the corridor?"

"I don't know what you think you're doing, but if you think you can just barge in—"

"I'm not barging in. You're letting me in." When she didn't open the door, he put down the box and tried the knob. It turned in his hand. "What's the matter with you?" he reprimanded. "You shouldn't leave your room unlocked. You never know who could be lurking in the corridor. Next time use your key."

"Not that it's any of your business," she replied huffily, "but the last of the guests from the weekend left on Tuesday, and we're not expecting anyone until tomorrow night. Furthermore, I would appreciate if you didn't use that tone with me. I'm not a child, Carter. Don't patronize me. I've had it with people who feel it's their moral duty to protect me."

She had a point about people who wanted to protect her. He raised his hand to his eye. The bruise was healing nicely, but he could still feel the sting of the punch he'd taken from David.

Nevertheless, he felt he had to watch out for her. She had that effect on him. She had that look, a damsel in distress begging to be rescued.

"But you're absolutely right," she said, her dark eyes meeting his. "Apparently, there are all sorts of intruders milling about. Tell me something, if this isn't what you'd call barging in, then what is?"

A damsel in distress with an attitude, he grumbled to himself.

He picked up the box and entered the room. She might not need rescuing, but she could use a computer. He glanced around, then rested his gaze on the small desk in the alcove. "Perfect place for a computer," he said, and set the box on the floor.

"A computer?" she asked, wide-eyed. "You brought me a computer?"

"To help you write your cookbook. The monitor is still in the car—I only have two hands. So what do you think? It sure beats banging away on a secondhand typewriter."

"And I'd say you're out of your mind. I can't accept this, Carter."

He was no fool. He'd anticipated her refusal and had come prepared. "I upgraded my home office," he said matter-of-factly. "If you don't take my old computer, it'll just sit at the back of my closet, taking up space."

"You can always sell it," she countered. "Or donate it."

"With all the new technology on the market, no one would pay a nickel for this old heap. It's slower than a turtle on tranquilizers. Still, for the time being it's good enough for what you need. All you want is word processing, right?"

"Yes, but this is too much! Providing for the baby is one thing—she's your daughter—but I can't start accepting gifts like this."

One thing about Becky, she was consistent. Stubborn as usual. "It's not as if I went out and bought it. It didn't cost me anything, but if it makes you feel better, consider it a loan. When you're ready for something with a little more horsepower," he added, purposely downplaying its value, "you can donate this relic to the charity of your choice. This way it won't be relegated to the back of my closet, along with all my other obsolete castoffs."

She frowned and said, "If it's obsolete, it's not much of a gift, is it? Or even a loan."

Someone was a little testy this morning. He was about

to make a snappy comeback, when she raised her hands as though in resignation. "All right, Carter. I'll take the computer. I wouldn't want you to lose any of your precious space. Speaking of space, the alcove is going to be a nursery, not an office. Will you please move the desk over to the window?"

"No problem." Damn, he was good. He'd known she would accept his offer if he handled it right. He picked up the desk and positioned it under the window. He was about to move the box, when it occurred to him that although he was skilled in manipulation, she had written the book. Somehow she had managed to make him feel as though she was doing him a favor.

"On second thought," she said, her brow deeply furrowed, "maybe you should set up the computer in the study downstairs. That way Starr can use it, too. She has such a hard time with the bookkeeping."

He picked up the box and headed toward the door. "You're sure you want it downstairs?"

"Of course I'm sure," she snapped. "Didn't you hear me?"

Hormones, he thought. The coming months were going to be long ones.

He followed her down the stairs. "I'll have to pick up an accounting package," he said as they entered the study. "The only program installed, besides the operating system, is word processing."

"If this is your old computer, why isn't it fully loaded? Where are all the other programs? Like games, for instance. I have to have chess."

Why hadn't he known that Becky played chess? Well, if chess was what she wanted, chess was what she'd get. "My old software was outdated, so I bought you a new package. But I'll pick up whatever else you need."

Immediately he realized his mistake. Becky was a proud, stubborn woman. Now that she knew he'd spent his own money to get her digitized, she'd probably toss the whole thing straight to cyber-heaven. Uh-oh, he thought, noting her expression. Here it comes.

She waved a finger in his face. "You said it didn't cost you anything."

"I was referring to the computer itself. I didn't spend a cent on the hard drive."

"Hard drive, shmard drive," she intoned. "What difference does it make? You lied to me, Carter."

Lied? Bent the truth was a more apt description. Now she was questioning his ethics? "Wait just one minute—"

"And I don't see why I need new programs in the first place," she continued with her assault. "It's not as if the stuff breaks down." She looked at him suspiciously. "You said you upgraded your home office. If you wanted me to have the latest software, why didn't you just make a copy of your new programs?"

Aha! He had her now. "Because it's a crime to pirate software," he said smugly. "Or videos. Or CDs. Or DVDs. People do it all the time, but it's illegal. You wouldn't want me to break the law, would you?" There. She couldn't argue with that. And the next time she got it in her head to question his integrity, maybe she'd think again.

"In that case, I want you to take back what you bought. I'll buy my own software."

"No returns. Store policy." When she didn't reply, he took her silence to mean acquiescence. He supposed that was her way of thanking him. At least it was an improvement over the flak she'd been shoveling.

He pulled the computer, keyboard and mouse from the

box and set them next to the desk. "I'll be back in a moment with the monitor. Don't touch anything."

When he returned, he found her lying on her back, legs crossed at the ankle, head and shoulders buried under the desk. She flipped onto her stomach, then crawled backward from under the desk, her long skirt inching dangerously up her shapely calves. "The manual was pretty straightforward," she said, jumping to her feet. "I think I got it all connected."

Even in those dark wool tights her legs were inviting. Made him want to discover—correction, rediscover—what they felt like under his touch, beneath all that sheep's clothing. "You could have hurt yourself, crawling around on the floor like that," he grumbled. He wasn't sure what irritated him more, her stubborn independence or the way his body had sparked to attention.

After connecting the monitor, he sat down at the desk and powered on the machine. "Bingo," he said as the screen came to life. "Once I set your defaults, you'll be ready to rock 'n' roll."

"I can do it," she said, standing next to him. "I've worked with computers before."

"As I recall, you said that office work was never your strong point. Maybe you should take a typing class," he teased.

She leaned over the desk, a whiff of her perfume scrambling his senses. No, not perfume. It was her hair, he realized. And then he remembered. The first time he'd encountered this fragrance was three months ago. Back at his apartment she'd told him to remove the pins from her hair, and as each curl escaped from the upsweep, an exotic scent of peach and champagne had drifted his way.

Who would have thought that hair could smell so...tasty?

She was so close he could feel her breath on his neck. How could he concentrate? If she were any closer, she would be in his lap.

"You spelled my name wrong," she said, peering into the screen. She pushed his hands aside—sending a powerful shock all the way to his toes—and began sweeping her fingers across the keyboard. "Maybe *you* should take a typing class," she said, seemingly unaffected by what he could only describe as an electrical blitz.

Amazing. How could she not have felt it? Either she was made of stone or her shoes were made of rubber.

She turned her head to look at him. "It's asking me to enter the specifications of my printer. I don't suppose you know where I can get a used one, real cheap."

"No, but I know where you can get a new one, free of charge."

She straightened up faster than a puppet on a string. "What did you do, Carter? No, don't tell me. Just promise you'll forget I even mentioned the word *printer*."

"Okay, I won't tell you. But you know that thing I'm not supposed to mention? It's sitting in the back seat of my car."

She knew he was staring at her. She could feel his gaze as she sat next to him in the waiting room, filling out the medical form. He was staring in the same way he'd stared at her in the kitchen last week, over his glass of carrot juice.

Enough of that, she'd decided early this morning. She'd purposely worn a long gray skirt and an oversize sweater, but despite her dowdy appearance—*shlumpy,* Gertie would say—Carter's interest inexplicably kept growing.

Granted, she was just as guilty. Take, for instance, the shock that had zapped her when her hand had brushed against his over the keyboard. It reminded her of how she'd felt after she had fallen in the snow and his fingers had grazed against her injured thigh.

Electricity, pure and simple.

It made no sense. She was pregnant, for heaven's sake. Pregnant women weren't supposed to feel this way.

Were they?

Must be hormones. All those elevated levels. Which also made no sense. She hadn't been pregnant three months ago when all her troubles began. Nope, no raging hormones back then. Just a vulnerable woman, a great-looking guy and one too many glasses of champagne. Obviously a lethal combination, or she wouldn't be here now, waiting to see the obstetrician.

But what was Carter's excuse, outside of being an incurable horndog? For years she'd never been more to him than David's little sister, and three months ago, after they'd made their colossal mistake, he'd reiterated his position with that crude remark, "I hope you don't think this means anything."

Obviously, his sudden renewed interest was all about her being pregnant. Must be a male thing, she thought. A power trip. Primeval. Territorial.

She sneaked a look at him out of the corner of her eye. Still staring. She bowed her head, feigning great interest in the form on her lap. The word *sex* jumped out at her from the page. Well, duh, she thought. How else could she have landed in this situation? She realized that the question was referring to gender, which struck her as odd. What kind of medical concern could a man have that would warrant his going to an obstetrician?

"American Express," Carter said, looking over her shoulder.

"Excuse me?"

"You see where it asks how you intend to pay? You left that field blank."

"I haven't figured that part out yet," she admitted.

"We already agreed that I would take care of the expenses. How many times do I have to remind you that this is my child, too?"

"And how many times do I have to tell you not to use that tone with me?" She sighed. "All right, what's the name of your insurance company? As long as we're covered, I might as well take advantage of it."

"There's no insurance. I can only add you to my policy after we're married."

Ah. So this is why he'd proposed. Cheapskate.

"But even if we got married tomorrow, you wouldn't be covered," he said as though privy to her thoughts. "This definitely qualifies as a preexisting condition."

Oops. Okay, so she'd come to the wrong conclusion, but what exactly did he mean by *after we're married?* Was he talking hypothetically, or did he think she'd changed her mind? The bottom line was, no matter how territorial he was acting, Carter Prescott was not a stay-at-home kind of guy.

She filled out the rest of the form and handed it to the receptionist, who slipped it through a window behind the desk. After picking up a magazine, she sat back down and leafed through the pages.

"What's *he* doing here?"

The sudden edge to Carter's voice startled her. She looked up and saw David and Hannah at the coatrack, hanging up their jackets. "It's time you two children kissed and made up," Hannah said as she and Becky exchanged a conspiratorial look.

"Better keep that maniac away from me," Carter grumbled as David approached. "I'm not responsible for what'll happen to him if he comes near me."

"Speaking of responsibility," David said, "I see you're finally owning up. I'm glad to see you here, Carter. Sorry about your eye. I heard you had one hell of a shiner."

To Becky's surprise Carter burst into a grin. "I wouldn't call that little scratch a shiner. You need to work on that right hook, bud. Or maybe I should call you wuss."

The plan had worked, Becky thought with satisfaction. Hannah had changed her appointment so that they'd all run into each other. But even though Becky was glad the two friends had made up, something felt wrong. Why had her brother caved in so quickly? What happened to his Rocky-like stance on defending her honor?

"I never expected to see you here," he said to Carter. "I didn't even know that Becky was coming. Usually, if I want to find out something about my sister, all I have to do is ask Hannah, since Becky—" he cast her an accusatory look "—never tells me anything. So does this mean what I think it means? When's the date?" he asked, his grin matching Carter's.

Wonderful, Becky thought. David assumed they were getting married. No wonder he was so quick to make amends.

When Carter opened his mouth to reply, she shot him a warning glance. The doctor's office was no place for the scene that would take place once David realized his mistake. All she needed was a brawl right here in the waiting room.

Carter winked at her and said evasively, "Don't worry, David. Becky's kept a few relevant details from me, as well."

"*Mazel tov,* Becky," Hannah said. "Talk about a surprise! I can't believe you didn't tell me!"

"Mrs. Roth? We're ready for you." They all looked up. Manila folder in hand, a nurse stood in the doorway at the back of the waiting room.

"That's me," Hannah said brightly. "This must be a first. No waiting before seeing a doctor. Here I thought I'd have to take the whole day off from work."

"Follow me, Rebecca. I need to take your vitals before you see Doctor Boyd."

Hannah frowned. "I knew it was too good to be true. I think you mean my sister-in-law." She turned to Becky. "Make it fast, girl. I'm about to burst."

After two quarts of water, Becky knew exactly what Hannah meant. Yesterday the receptionist had called to give them their instructions. A full bladder pushes up the uterus, making it easier to scan, she'd explained.

The nurse walked over to the reception desk and glanced at the appointment book. She looked up at Becky. "You wrote 'Rebecca Roth' on the medical form, but the appointment is for Rebecca Steinberg."

Becky stood up. "Both names are mine, but I no longer go by Steinberg."

The nurse made a note in the file. "Good for you! So many women keep their maiden names after they're married. It must be so confusing to their children, don't you think? Come with me, Mrs. Roth. You, too, Mr. Roth." She smiled at Carter. "How wonderful it must be for your mother. Imagine, two sons having babies at the same time!"

Becky was about to correct her, when Carter whispered, "Wonderful? Right now my mother is probably out buying a gas range so she can stick her head in it."

The nurse entered the foyer outside the examining

rooms, Becky and Carter lagging behind her. "You told your mother?" Becky asked incredulously. "Why?"

"Because she's going to be a grandmother. She has a right to know."

Becky hadn't considered this. Carter seemed to accept that he wasn't going to be in his baby's life, but would his mother feel the same way? "What else did you tell her?"

"That you wanted her help in picking out a china pattern."

She felt her patience slipping away. "Be serious, Carter. I can't understand why you're making jokes."

He grinned. "Come on, Becky. Lighten up. Having a baby should be a joyous thing."

Resentment replaced impatience. Who was he to tell her what having a baby should be? He wasn't the one whose stomach felt like it had overdosed on junk food. He wasn't the one who would soon resemble a bathtub. He wasn't the one who'd be raising the baby, assuming complete responsibility for another human being.

They caught up with the nurse, who was removing the blood pressure monitor from a shelf on the wall. "First I'll take your pressure, and then I'll weigh you. After that you can wait in the ultrasound room for the doctor. You'll find a clean gown hanging over the chair. You can go with her, Mr. Roth. I'm sure Rebecca will want you with her."

"I certainly will not," Becky retorted. "He can wait out here until the doctor is done. His name is Prescott, by the way."

"Prescott," the nurse repeated as she rolled up Becky's sleeve. "It's a fine name. If it's a boy, you should consider naming him after his father." She tied the strap of the monitor around Becky's arm and pumped the valve.

"No, you don't understand. Prescott is his last name, not his first name."

For a moment the nurse looked confused, but then her face brightened. "Oh, I see. Mr. Roth is the man in the waiting room. Since Mr. Prescott isn't his brother, you must be Mr. Roth's sister. Which means Roth is your maiden name," she added, her voiced laced with accusation. Once again her forehead knotted. "Then who is Steinberg?"

"Her husband," Carter said with a straight face.

"Ex-husband," Becky quickly qualified. "My mother must have made the appointment under his name." She whispered to Carter, "Will you please behave?"

"Your mother made the appointment? Never mind, it's none of my business." The nurse studied the reading on the monitor, then jotted down her findings. "Take off your shoes and hop on the scale." As she was adjusting the settings, she added, "Some wives are a little embarrassed about being examined with their husbands around, but I assure you, there's nothing embarrassing about having a scan. Are you sure you don't want your husband with you?"

"He's not my husband."

The nurse looked at her and shook her head. "Like I said, none of my business." She made a few more notes, then disappeared down the hallway.

Becky rolled her eyes. "Can you believe that woman? Who does she think she is?"

Carter gave her an impish smile. "From the way she was acting, I thought she was part of your family."

Grimacing, Becky said, "Please, Carter, no more jokes. I need a full bladder for the ultrasound."

"Normally I don't schedule an ultrasound until I've confirmed the pregnancy. But from what you've told me, there's no doubt in my mind.'' The doctor chuckled. ''Besides no expectant mother should have to undergo an examination on a full bladder. Why don't I get your friend in here so he can see the baby, too?''

Your *friend*. Becky appreciated the tactful reference. In her mid-thirties, Dr. Patricia Boyd was as warm and sensitive as she was efficient. She was not what Becky had expected, given Hannah's preference for ancient doctors. After chatting with her for only a few moments, Becky knew that Hannah had made a wise choice.

''All right,'' Becky agreed, though not without reservation. ''He can come in.'' She wasn't convinced this was a good idea. On the one hand, she didn't want Carter to become more involved than he already was. On the other hand, he wanted to be sure the baby was okay. If it took an ultrasound to persuade him, so be it. Maybe he'd finally back off.

Dr. Boyd covered Becky's lower half with a sheet and lifted her gown above her abdomen. She smoothed a cool gel across the slight bulge, then stuck her head out the door and called Carter.

After the introductions were made, Becky took a deep breath and tried to relax. In seconds the image of the baby appeared on the screen.

''Looks good,'' the doctor said, running the hand piece slowly across Becky's belly. ''There's the heart. Can you see it beating?''

Becky felt as though she'd been knocked breathless. Nothing could have prepared her for this moment. She'd known she was going to be a mother, but for the first time she *felt* like a mother. Her baby had a heart. Her baby had a shape. Her baby was real.

She was going to be a mother.

"There's so much movement," Carter said excitedly. "Is that the baby kicking? How can that be? He's not even four months!"

Dr. Boyd laughed. "He's got feet and toes and hands and thumbs—he's practically all formed. He's just tiny."

"You said *he*. Are you saying it's a boy?"

"I refer to all unborn babies as *he*. Would you prefer I say *she*?"

"Can you tell the sex?" Carter asked, leaning in closer to get a better view.

"It's too early to be certain, but I can take an educated guess. Are you sure you want to know?"

"Yes," he answered.

"No," Becky said.

Carter turned to look at her. "That's not what you said the other day."

"I changed my mind. I want to be surprised."

"Becky, I don't think I can survive any more surprises." He looked back at the screen. "It's a boy," he said with more pride than conviction. "Dr. Boyd, you must have seen, uh, something, or you wouldn't have offered to make an educated guess. If you hadn't seen anything, it could be either sex. Am I right?"

The doctor switched off the machine. "Sorry, you won't trip me up that way. If you want to know the sex, it won't come from me until Becky gives the green light." She pressed a button and a videocassette popped out of a drawer. "This is for you. Makes for great show-and-tell. Carter, why don't you wait outside while I finish examining Becky? After that, I'd like to talk to both of you in my office."

After a quick trip to the bathroom, Becky met the doctor in the adjoining room. "Well, that's it," Dr. Boyd said minutes later, after completing the examination. "You can get dressed now.'' She snapped off her gloves. ''Everything looks fine. Your pregnancy is progressing right on schedule, and the baby is developing beautifully.''

Becky waited for her to leave before she swung her legs off the table. In spite of the doctor's words, something in her tone had set off a warning bell.

Mother's intuition, Becky thought. Only, now the thought didn't cheer her.

She dressed quickly and left the room. Carter was already in Dr. Boyd's office, waiting for her. She sat down beside him.

''Let me start by saying the baby is fine,'' Dr. Boyd said. ''Good size, good weight. Everything in its right place. Becky, you'll be delivering in the last week in May, just as you calculated. That said, do either of you have any questions?''

''I have one,'' Carter said, a deadpan look on his face. ''How long can Becky and I have sex?''

''Until you get tired,'' Dr. Boyd answered without batting an eyelash.

Becky shot him a murderous look. ''You'll have to excuse my friend,'' she apologized to the doctor. ''He's obviously deranged. I only hope it's not hereditary.''

Carter gave them a half smile. ''Sorry. Deranged is what I do when I get anxious, and right now anxious pretty much sums up the way I feel. I've never been a dad before.''

Dr. Boyd's smile was gentle. ''Your reaction is perfectly normal, Carter. Joking is a healthy way to relieve tension. And I'm not easily shocked. You'd be surprised at what people ask me.'' Her expression suddenly sobered. ''I'm afraid, though, we have something serious to discuss.''

Becky's stomach clenched tight. "I knew something was wrong."

"It's that crazy diet," Carter insisted. "She doesn't eat anything but vegetables. Dr. Boyd, tell her she has to eat real food. She won't listen to me."

"I eat more than vegetables," Becky protested. "Not that there's anything wrong with being a vegan." The inquiring look on the doctor's face prompted Becky to continue. "A vegan doesn't eat any animal products. I'm a lacto-ovo vegetarian, which means I eat dairy and eggs. Plenty of calcium and protein there."

Dr. Boyd nodded. "Being a vegetarian doesn't mean the baby won't be healthy. Just make sure you get plenty of that calcium and protein you mentioned, including the essential vitamins and minerals. In any case, I'm going to prescribe prenatal supplements. At the moment, however, what concerns me is your blood pressure." She looked down at the chart, then back up at Becky. "It's a little high. Nothing to be alarmed about, but I want to keep an eye on it. You mentioned that hypertension runs in your family."

"Yes, my mother," Becky said. "But it's not serious. She's not even on medication. She's just a little excitable." That was putting it mildly. Gertie was wired tighter than a bowstring. "But what does this have to do with me?"

"Unfortunately, your family history, along with this being your first pregnancy, puts you at a slightly higher risk for preeclampsia."

Becky felt her face grow pale. "Pregnancy-induced hypertension," she said quietly. "Also known as toxemia. I should have made the connection. My ex-husband was a doctor."

"Well, I'm not," Carter said, visibly upset. "Will someone please explain?"

"Preeclampsia reduces the flow of blood to the placenta," Dr. Boyd explained. "It ranges from mild to severe, but it can be managed. There's no evidence of it now, but it usually doesn't manifest until the mother is further along in the pregnancy." She smiled reassuringly. "I'm sure that nothing like this will happen, but it can't hurt to be careful."

"What can I do to prevent it?" Becky asked anxiously.

"There's no known way, but if we catch the condition early, we can keep it under control. You'll need to be seen every week. We'll need to monitor your blood pressure and check for protein in your urine. In the meantime, eat right and get plenty of rest. And try not to worry—I don't want you stressed. Remember, we're just being cautious."

In spite of the doctor's words, Becky was terrified. Her child was too small to come into the world, but to Becky the baby was already a whole person with wants and desires, personality and character. When Becky had first seen the images on the ultrasound screen, she had felt a closeness that, up to that moment, she could not have defined. It was a bond she had never felt with any other human being. This she couldn't risk losing.

A hand reached out for hers. She turned and looked into Carter's eyes. All previous humor had been erased from his expression. He was as scared as she was.

Chapter Six

"This changes everything."

Becky and Carter sat at a table near the floor-to-ceiling fireplace at the Café St. Gabriel. The trendy restaurant, with its wood ceiling beams and colorful tablecloths, was cozy with a French country motif. In the far corner a tall blue spruce gleamed with crystal ornaments, a delicate angel looking down from the top. Candles flickered at every table, adding to the holiday atmosphere.

"How so?" Becky asked. The question was redundant. She knew exactly what he meant. He'd been clucking like a mother hen ever since they'd left the doctor's office, and she was sure he was about to hand out more of the same motherly attention.

"I intend to go with you to all your appointments." He gestured to the small plate in front of her. "Is that all you're going to eat?" On his own plate was a filet of fresh king salmon baked en croute and served with béarnaise sauce. "Now this is what I call food," he said, taking an enormous bite.

"I'm not very hungry," she said, picking at her salad. "This and the orange juice are plenty. I don't know why I let you talk me into coming here in the first place. I could have whipped up something for us at Starr's."

"I know that what the doctor said upset you, but you have to think about the baby. You have to eat, and even the B and B's star chef deserves time off. And I insist on taking you to all your doctor appointments."

The meeting with the doctor hadn't curbed *his* appetite, she noticed as he delved into the salmon. She immediately chided herself for being unfair. In the doctor's office he'd been just as concerned as she.

She picked up her glass and studied him over the rim. He'd changed over the years. The tall, lanky boy she remembered from her youth had grown into an impressive-looking man. Of course, she'd arrived at this conclusion before today, up close and personal that night at his apartment. But it wasn't his appearance she was thinking of now. He'd always been friendly and funny—that side of him hadn't changed. It was what had attracted her years ago, in spite of his bullheadedness. He was still bullheaded; that hadn't changed, either. So what was it? She remembered him having a temper, especially after his father died. Like he was mad at the world. That *had* changed, she realized, recalling how quickly he had forgiven David. But there was something else, something that evaded her...

In any case he was considerate, she had to give him that. Like this morning at the B and B, giving her the computer. Or this afternoon, taking her out for lunch. But she didn't want him hovering over her, and he was bordering on crossing that line. Taking her to the doctor each week wasn't necessary.

"I can go with Hannah," she said. "I'm sure Starr would take me, too, if I asked her, and in a pinch I can always ask my mother."

"No, I'll take you. If there's a problem, I want to be on top of it. This is my child we're talking about."

"You seem to have forgotten one important detail. How do you propose to get me there? Are you planning to fly your private jet back from Colorado?"

He looked at her with surprise. "You know about the job in Denver?"

"Of course I know. You tell David everything, he tells Hannah, she tells me." She noted the uneasy look on his face and laughed. "Don't look so scared. It's not as if you're hiding some deep, dark secret. Are you?" she teased.

"Be serious, Becky." He put down his fork. "I've been considering rearranging my schedule. I think I'll postpone Denver."

This was the kind of thing she'd been afraid of. She didn't want him rearranging his life on her account. "I think not. You can't start shirking your responsibilities."

"My responsibility is to you and the baby," he said, his mouth set in a stubborn line.

"I'll be fine," she assured him. "Trust me, the world won't collapse while you're gone. If something major comes up, you can always catch the next plane home." She looked down at her lap, reluctant to elaborate on what she meant by *major*.

"I'll fly my private jet," he kidded, but she could tell from his expression that he wasn't in a joking mood. He leaned back and crossed his arms over his chest. "I want you to know that after this trip, I don't intend to go anywhere until after the baby is born.''

"It's okay, Carter. I told you, I'll be fine." She took a sip of her juice. "Tell me about Denver. It's just a small job, right? Nothing like that ten-month megaproject in Phoenix. How long will you be gone this time? A week? Ten days?"

"Five weeks, if everything goes as planned."

"Five weeks!" she echoed. "Hannah didn't mention...I had no idea..."

He cocked his head. "What's the matter, princess? Lonely already?"

"Only in your imagination," she returned, feeling the color rise in her cheeks. She didn't want to be feeling this, didn't want to feel one way or another about him, but there it was. She knew she would miss him. It was as if they'd be breaking some sort of connection.

The image of her baby flashed through her mind as clearly as it had been displayed on the ultrasound screen. Carter had been as awed as she. Later, in the doctor's office, his concern had matched hers and she'd been grateful for his reassuring touch.

Grateful? No, it was more than that. For a moment in the doctor's office, the bond she felt with her baby had extended to the father.

"That settles it," she said with a decisiveness she didn't feel. "Five weeks means five visits to the doctor. You can't possibly take me to all my appointments."

A look of resignation crossed his face, but it was quickly replaced with wonder. "It was amazing, wasn't it? That was our son we saw today. His hands, his feet, even his toes!" Carter reached across the table and covered her hands with his. "Becky, I want you to marry me. It's the right thing to do."

No matter what feelings for Carter she believed she was fostering, her views on matrimony hadn't changed one iota. She'd learned that what a man said and what he wanted were two different things, and that a man's view of marriage was different from hers. She pulled her hands away. "We've already been over this. Marriage is something neither of us wants, and having a baby won't change how we feel."

"Having a baby changes everything. I want us to be a family. I want the whole package, picket fence and all."

She regarded him with speculation. "I'm curious about something. You never wanted kids before. Why now?"

"What makes you think I never wanted kids?"

"You were married for four years. I just assumed—"

"You assumed wrong," he said, his eyes becoming as unreadable as a brick wall. "In fact, Wendy did get pregnant, not long before we split up."

Now, this was news. She had to take a moment before continuing. "What happened?" Her question came out in a whisper.

"What the hell do you think happened? Do you see any kids around?"

She lowered her gaze. The thought of miscarrying terrified her; she couldn't imagine anything more painful than losing a baby. "I'm sorry, Carter. I never knew." And neither had David, she guessed. If he had known, he would have told Hannah, and Hannah would have told her.

This is what had been evading her. This is what had changed in Carter.

This explained why he was so anxious to become a father.

Her heart went out to him. Nevertheless, her views on marriage remained unwavering. Marriage wasn't just about having kids, and it took more than empathy to sustain a relationship.

"It's water under the bridge," he said, shrugging. "But we've strayed from the subject. Give me one solid reason why we shouldn't get married."

She didn't have to think twice. "What about your traveling? What about New Zealand? You'll be gone for two years. What kind of marriage could we have with you on the other side of the world?"

"I told you, once I become a partner, I won't be traveling as much. As far as New Zealand is concerned, come with me, Becky. You and the baby. We'll be a family."

"What would I do in New Zealand? My life is here in the States."

He laughed, but not in a funny way. "What life? Your career? Your husband?"

Just when she was feeling sorry for him, he had to go and mock her. "I already have a family," she said. "I don't need another one. And yes, there's my career," she continued, purposely ignoring his remark about a husband. "I've been thinking about starting a catering business after the baby is born. And you know that cookbook Starr has been after me to write? Last night I assembled all my recipes—I have hundreds of them. Okay, so maybe most of them are nothing more than scribbling, but in my head they're perfectly organized. It won't take me more than a few weeks to get them into the computer."

"I'm glad about the writing, but I wouldn't count on making a living from it. And this catering thing—I thought you said you were planning to move back to New York. The city isn't cheap. It takes money to start a business."

"You sound as though you want me to fail."

"This isn't about failure or success," he argued. "It's

about us being a family. All I want is to take care of you. What's wrong with that?''

''You still don't understand. I don't want anyone taking care of me. I won't go through life hanging on to someone's coattails. This is *my* life. This is *my* baby.''

''He's my child, too,'' he reminded her again.

Always, it seemed, it returned to that. She leaned back and stared at him. ''You keep saying *he*. Why is it so important to you that I have a boy?''

''What about you? You've made it clear you want a girl.''

''No, I said I think it's going to be a girl. There's a difference. I have intuition. You, on the other hand, are obsessed.''

A faint smile tugged at his lips. ''It's natural for a man to want an heir, someone to carry on his name.''

The way he talked, you'd think he really did have his own private jet. What was it about men and their egos? What did he think he was, royalty? An heir, she repeated to herself. How ridiculous was that? Remembering the nurse's confusion, Becky asked impishly, ''What name is that? Prescott Roth?''

And then it hit her. *Carter Prescott, IV.* Here she'd been making fun of him, when all the while his heart was breaking. ''Was it a boy?'' she asked gently.

''Was who a boy?''

''The baby you lost.''

He looked down at his plate. ''I don't know. It was too early to tell.''

So, his wanting a boy had nothing to do with the miscarriage. It was his ego talking, after all. She was about to make a remark, when he looked back up, the expression on his face arresting her. Just because he advocated old-fashioned ideas didn't mean he wasn't in pain. It was obvious that talking about the miscarriage still upset him. "Tell me more about Denver," she said, changing the subject. "When do you leave?"

"Right after New Year's." He motioned to the waiter, then turned back to Becky. "Do you want something else? Like maybe a steak?"

"I didn't realize they served vegetarian steaks," she said, trying to keep the mood light. Right after New Year's, he'd said. She felt a cutting pang, and this annoyed her. As far as Carter was concerned—or any man, for that matter—she didn't want to feel anything. "At least you'll be here for the holidays," she said with forced cheerfulness. "You'll come to Starr's Christmas party, won't you? It's the Sunday before Christmas. Even David and Hannah will be there."

A hint of humor glinted in his eyes. "Christmas? Are you planning to convert?"

"No, of course not. Call it a holiday party, if you want. I'll be covering all the bases. For instance, I'll be serving fried potato pancakes for Hanukkah."

"You mean *latkes*. I know what they are. I practically grew up at your house, remember?" The waiter brought the bill, and Carter handed him his credit card. After the waiter had gone, Carter said, "You're supposed to be taking it easy. Cooking for a few guests is one thing, but where in your job description does it say you have to cater a party?"

"Party, shmarty! Cooking is easy for me, and these functions are part of the job."

"How many people are you expecting?" he asked dubiously.

"Just the guests and a few friends," she answered, purposely evasive.

He nodded. "I'll be there, all right. I plan to help. I

don't want you wearing yourself out. So what time does this gala start?''

He was doing it again, going into protective mode. The way his lips were pursed, he looked like a stern parent. Well, it was one thing to want to be a parent to their child, but it was another thing to act that way toward her.

"It starts at six and goes until we all drop," she said. "We're planning an all-night beer bash, so don't forget to bring a keg."

"In that case, I'll have to hire a bouncer," he quipped back, but she could tell he wasn't amused.

The waiter returned with the credit card. After signing the bill, Carter walked around the table and put his hand on the back of Becky's chair.

"I can get up by myself," she said tersely. "I'm not helpless."

He stood back. "Contrary to what you might think, princess, I'm not trying to run your life. You have enough people around claiming that honor. But just because you refused to marry me doesn't mean I have to stop caring about your welfare. And there's something else you should know." He cupped her elbow as they headed toward the coat check. "Just because you refused doesn't mean I'm going to stop asking. It'll take a lot more than your rudeness to get me to quit."

"I suppose I should say *mazel tov*," Gertie said, "but I don't think the words are appropriate."

"What are you talking about?" Becky asked, the phone resting between her ear and shoulder. She scraped the batter from the sides of the mixing bowl. She was trying out a new recipe for a pineapple upside-down cake. After that, she planned on making a loaf of mandel bread, or, as Carter had once called it, Jewish biscotti. "I'm really busy, Ma. We're expecting a houseful of guests this weekend. Could you—''

"Hannah called me this morning, right after the appointment. It might have been nice to hear the news from you, but no, I had to hear it from her. Who am I? Only your mother, that's who. A stranger is all I am."

Ah. Right. When Carter and Becky had left the doctor's office, Hannah and David were already in the ultrasound room, waiting for their scan. Too upset to think of anything but the welfare of her baby, Becky had completely forgotten about David's assumption.

David's erroneous assumption, she thought now, groaning inwardly.

"Ma, don't have a cow. I'm not getting married." She sifted a cup of flour into the batter. "But tell me something, what exactly did you mean by *appropriate?*"

"I'm not one to mix in, but I don't think it's appropriate to marry out of your faith."

"Are you telling me you'd rather me be a single parent than marry a non-Jew?"

"Actually, I was thinking you could tell Jordan it's his baby."

Was her mother nuts? "Ma, Jordan and I haven't had sex in almost a year."

"Don't use that language with me, Rebecca. All I ask for is a little respect, and look how you talk!"

"Is this why you called? To aggravate me?"

"Aggravate *you? Oy!* Do you realize what you've put me through? David said you were getting married! No mother should in one lifetime have such aggravation." Gertie let out a loud, laborious breath. "I have an idea. Invite Jordan for dinner. You'll put on a little makeup, you'll put on some music... So the baby will be born early."

Oy is right, Becky thought. She stared at the bowl. She'd tossed in the oil she'd set aside for the mandel bread. "I have to go," she said, cursing silently.

"Fine, be that way. But call your husband."

What did her mother think? That as soon as Jordan heard Becky's voice, he'd beg her for a reconciliation? Mumbling to herself, she hung up the phone and poured the batter down the disposal. Only a miracle could have saved this cake.

And only a miracle could have saved my marriage, she thought. The memory of a young man, full of dreams and promises, came back to her in a flash. She remembered the way Jordan had talked about medicine, the kind of doctor he would become, how he intended to save the world. She remembered how they had planned their future, where they would live, how many children they would have. She remembered how the corners of his lips would curl in a shy smile, and brushed away a tear.

Becky had been brought up not to question, and she had been certain of three things: she would get married, she would have a family and she would live happily ever after. Jordan had fit perfectly into the plan. He'd been sweet, he was of the same faith and, as an added bonus, he was going to be a doctor. A mother's dream come true.

Becky had bought into the fairy tale, hook, line and sinker.

Carter's face rose before her, replacing Jordan's. She pictured his eyes when he'd first looked up at the ultrasound screen, how they had danced with excitement and pride, and then later, how they had misted with worry when Dr. Boyd had voiced her concerns. At the restaurant when he'd proposed, he'd looked so endearing, so earnest, she'd found herself heading to a place she couldn't go. He was decent and kind and caring, and she regretted the way she had acted, but she had no intention of going where he wanted.

Marriage was a place that was built on trust.

When Becky first learned she was pregnant, she'd told Carter she didn't want him involved, but now that there were complications, she knew that nothing could keep him away. She wouldn't try to stop him. He was looking out for his child—what kind of man would he be if he didn't?

But marrying him was out of the question. She wouldn't allow herself to be dependent on anyone ever again.

Liar, she chastised herself. Oh, it was true she wanted independence, but it wasn't the main reason she'd refused him. Once upon a time she'd believed in promises. Once upon a time she'd believed in forever. But for her the fairy tale had ceased to exist.

She rinsed out the bowl and put it in the dishwasher. So much for pineapple upside-down cake. The last thing she felt like doing was starting over.

With the holidays just around the corner, Carter was worried that Becky was working too hard. Over the next several days he got into the habit of dropping by in the evenings. To lend a hand, he told himself. After helping her set up the dining room for the morning buffet, they'd sit at the kitchen table, sampling some of her recipes and chatting.

Somewhere along the way he got to thinking, I could get used to this.

Somewhere along the way he realized she didn't need monitoring *or* his help. She was doing fine without him.

Until tonight. At least fifty people had shown up for Starr's annual holiday party, and just thinking of the work it must have involved made Carter feel tired. "This is what you call a small gathering?" he asked, his gaze taking in the crowded living room.

"It's quite a turnout," Becky said, obviously choosing to ignore his reproach. "Thanks for coming by early, by the way. You were a great help. If you ever get tired of being an architect, you could probably find work as a sous-chef."

He frowned. "You must have been on your feet all last night after I left. You heard what the doctor said. You need to take it easy."

"Oh, pooh. Dr. Boyd tells that to all her patients. I think it's part of the Hippocratic Oath. Here, have some futari," she said, shoving a platter under his nose. "We're doing all the holidays, even though officially Kwanzaa doesn't start until the day after Christmas."

He was talking about the welfare of their baby and she was pushing food. He sighed. He'd let it go for now, but as soon as the party was over, they were going to have words.

He eyed the yellow mixture with suspicion. "What's futari?" he asked, spooning out a mere morsel. "And what's Kwanzaa?"

"Kwanzaa is an African-American celebration of the oneness and goodness of life. What you're about to taste is a pan-fried mixture of squash, yams and coconut milk." She waited for him to taste it. "Good, isn't it? I added my own secret ingredient."

"Not bad." He shoveled a healthy portion onto his plate.

Not bad was an understatement. She might be a royal pain, but she sure could cook. If the rapidly disappearing food was any indication, it was clear that everyone here thought so, too.

He glanced around the room. She'd told him—ignoring his cautionary words not to tire herself out—that she was going to decorate the tree by herself, but he had no idea she'd intended to make the ornaments. Cutout shapes of hearts, circles and stars, all hand painted with forest animals, hung from the branches of a tall Douglas fir.

There seemed to be no end to her creativity. He was surprised she hadn't insisted on growing the tree itself. A thought occurred to him. "I thought Starr was supposed to be so environmentally conscious. That's a real fir tree."

"For your information, real Christmas trees are more environmentally friendly than artificial ones. They're biodegradable, not like those plastic or metal imitations, and the tree farms give off oxygen, which helps to prevent global warming."

"Okay, okay, I didn't ask for a lecture." But he was smiling. He liked it when she got all worked up. Her passion was contagious. It made him feel alive.

"Oh, there's Maddie!" she suddenly exclaimed. "She's a friend from New York. Here, pass these around while I say hello, will you?" She handed a platter of knishes to Carter.

As he watched her walk away, a pensive mood came over him. Becky was not the person he remembered from his youth. He thought he had known her, but as each day passed, she revealed a side he'd never seen. It was as if she was becoming another person.

Dressed alike in matching Harley-Davidson T-shirts, a man and woman seemed engrossed by what she was saying. Suddenly the three of them started laughing. A child, not more than two years old, tugged at Becky's skirt, and, still laughing, Becky scooped her up and swung her around.

For a reason he couldn't define, Carter's heart did flip-flops.

From across the room he heard Hannah laughing. David slipped his arm around her waist, and she turned her head to his. He bent down to kiss her. It was a light, quick kiss, no more than a gesture.

Flip-flops gave way to loneliness.

Hannah looked up and waved Carter over. "Hi, stranger," she said, hugging him warmly. "Where have you been hiding? I know Colorado's coming up, but I hope you haven't been working too hard. 'Tis the season, remember?" Her gaze traveled from Carter to David's angry expression, then back to Carter. "Oh, no," she said, a look of understanding crossing her face. "Not again. What is it with you two?"

He directed his answer at David. "You haven't returned my calls. What gives, Roth?"

"What gives?" David repeated, spitting out the words. "Don't play innocent with me, Pres. You know damn well what gives. I might be good enough to be your friend, but it's obvious you don't consider my sister good enough to marry."

So this was what it was all about. When David had learned that Becky wasn't getting married, he must have assumed it was all Carter's doing. "You've got that all wrong," Carter said quietly. "I'm not good enough for *her*."

As if a force were directing him, he turned his head and looked across the room. Becky looked up at the same moment, her eyes meeting his. She transferred the child to the woman's arms, then started across the room.

She arrived at his side, smiling brightly. "Your friend is quite a chef," she said to David. "He came by early to give me a hand. You know those blintzes you raved about? He made them. I would have been lost without him.''

''I don't think so,'' Carter said amicably. ''By the time I got here, you had everything under control. But I appreciate the acknowledgment.''

''Under control!'' David blurted. ''Are you blind? Look around you, Pres. Look at this place. Look at these loonies. That man over there is wearing more makeup than Cleopatra! These are the people she associates with? I can't believe you're willing to let her bring up your baby in this kind of environment.''

''Becky can choose whatever environment she likes,'' Carter said, his patience quickly draining. ''She's a grown woman, perfectly capable of managing her life. Did you know she's thinking of starting a catering business? Did you even know she's writing a cookbook?''

Becky's mouth flew open, and Carter almost laughed. His coming to her defense had obviously surprised her. Hell, he'd even surprised himself.

David snorted. ''Come on, Becky in business? She can't even take care of herself, never mind run a business. Besides, are you saying you're going to allow her to work after she has the baby?''

Hannah stared at him as if seeing him for the first time. ''What are you talking about? You know I'm not planning to quit teaching. After my maternity leave, I'm going back to work. And just what do you mean by *allow?*''

Carter had no intention of getting mixed up in an argument between a husband and wife, but he couldn't just stand by and listen to David deride Becky. ''In case you don't know, your sister's a hell of a chef. And for your information, these so-called loonies she associates with are the most interesting people I've talked to in a long while. See that woman over there? The one with the purple hair? She's a best-selling author. Writes science fiction. That man with the nose ring? He's a helicopter engineer. I think it's about time you stopped making assumptions, Roth.''

''And I think it's about time I left.'' David stormed off, leaving an irate friend, an astounded sister and an exasperated wife standing in his wake.

''Sometimes he can be so infuriating,'' Hannah said. ''Will you excuse me? I think I'm about to have my first marital spat, and I don't want it to start without me.''

''She might seem shy and unassuming,'' Becky said after Hannah left, ''but God help the person who crosses her, even David. Do you believe that man?''

''Some *chutzpa*,'' Carter mumbled.

Becky laughed, then looked up at him with shining eyes.

''What?'' he asked, confused by her reaction. ''Why are you looking at me like that?''

Standing on tiptoe, she planted a kiss on his cheek.

He felt a surge of heat rush through him. Her face had *my hero* written all over it, and what flesh-and-blood male could resist such unmasked admiration? To top it off, she looked precious in her Santa Claus hat, the way the pompom kept falling over her forehead. ''So what's a nice Jewish girl like you doing in a hat like that?'' he asked gruffly, mixed emotions raging through him. He didn't know what was stronger, his anger at David or the ache he felt for Becky. At that moment Carter wished *he* were Santa, so he could pull her onto his lap.

He took her arm and led her down the hallway, into the study. ''Mistletoe,'' he whispered hoarsely, motioning to the rafter in the ceiling. He kicked the door closed. With an urgency he couldn't suppress he pulled her to him and wrapped her in his arms, his lips finding hers, his hands in her hair, then down her back, grasping and clutching, everywhere at once. He'd kissed her before—and a lot more—but it was nothing like this. She let out a low moan and pressed against him with a need that seemed to match his own. He nearly came unglued. The way she smelled, the way she tasted, the way her body fit so well with his, released feelings he'd kept restrained for months.

Three months, he thought. Three months spent alone in a hotel room, wondering why he couldn't sleep at night, why he couldn't get her out of his mind.

Now he remembered.

"Marry me," he said for what seemed like the hundredth time.

She froze. Just like that, the light in her eyes went cold, and she pulled away from his reach. "We'd better get back to the party."

She'd refused him before, but this time something was different. He saw it in her eyes just after she'd pulled away, and it was still there now.

Fear, pure and simple, unleashed by his kiss.

He recalled the night the baby was conceived, how she'd run off after they'd made love. It seemed she was always fleeing from someone: Jordan, her mother, him…. "Poor princess," he murmured, softly stroking her cheek with his fingers. "How long can you keep running?"

"I'm not the one who's running," she said in a tight voice. "I'm not the one who can't stay rooted."

In her mixed-up, defensive way, was she saying she would miss him while he was in Colorado? He felt a stitch in his heart. "It's my job," he said gently. "You know that. Besides, I'll only be gone for a few weeks."

She smoothed her blouse as though she could wipe herself clean of his touch. When she looked back up, the fear in her eyes had turned to anger. "It's funny how a man can get away with anything when it comes to his job," she retorted. "It's okay for his career to come first, but the minute a woman calls home to say she has to work late, he starts complaining about her not doing the laundry. How many times do I have to tell you? I want my own life."

So. It wasn't about his traveling. It was that independence thing. He let out a slow breath. "How many times, indeed. You keep singing the same song over and over. It's as if you're trying to convince yourself. Why can't you see that I don't want to take over your life? I just want to be there for you. I just want us to be a family."

"You don't want a family," she replied hotly. "You want a Kodak picture. You have this fantasy about having the perfect life, a dutiful little wife, a son to carry on your name, maybe later a daughter to pamper. Well, I have news for you. Perfect doesn't exist, and you can't build a family from a one-night stand. Go home, Carter. This kiss shouldn't have happened. Nothing between us should ever have happened."

He realized that all the talking in the world wouldn't get her to relent, and with bleak resignation he said, "I'll be out of your hair soon enough. I'm leaving for Denver as soon as I can get a flight out."

An uncomfortable silence fell. "I thought you said you were leaving after New Year's," she said finally, averting her eyes.

"Yeah, well, I changed my mind. This is a good time to take some time off, maybe get in a little skiing. I'm going to be swamped with work soon enough."

"What about the holidays? This is a time for family." She smiled wryly. "Even families like ours."

And what family was that? His father had died years

ago, and his mother was away on a cruise. As for Becky, he didn't want to stick around and be reminded of what he couldn't have.

"I guess I'm not in the holiday spirit." Cupping her chin with his hand, he tilted up her head and said, "For what it's worth, princess, I want you to know I admire you. After Jordan left, instead of wallowing in self-pity, you picked yourself up and decided to make a life for yourself. I have no doubt you're going to be a great chef and that your book will be a success. Take care of yourself, Becky." He left the study and headed down the hallway, feeling her gaze on his back. He pulled out his jacket from the closet, then turned around. "Remember, that's my son you're carrying. Charge anything you need to my American Express."

He didn't look back again.

Chapter Seven

Becky was showing Starr how to create a spreadsheet on the computer, when a small shock caused them both to jump. "What on earth was that?" Starr asked.

"Static electricity." Remembering the shock Carter had given her when they'd set up the computer, Becky burst out laughing. All this time she'd believed that the charge, which had nearly knocked her socks off, had been caused by their mutual attraction.

Static electricity aside, she couldn't deny that the attraction existed. It had been there since they were teenagers—at least on her part. She thought back to the night of the party, three weeks ago. She must have been out of her mind, letting him kiss her. Out of her mind for kissing him back. She'd already made one huge mistake on the night of David's wedding; she couldn't afford to make another. Feelings like these only led to heartache.

"I feel as if I've been zapped by lightning," Starr said.

Becky removed her wool cardigan and tossed it onto the couch near the desk. "Maybe this will help. But we should probably get something to put over the carpet. Sorry for laughing, by the way. I was thinking about something that happened a while ago."

Starr let out a chortle. "I'll bet it has something to do with Carter."

"It most certainly does not," Becky out-and-out lied.

"Fine. Be that way," Starr said, feigning offense. "But you know what they say about she who doth protest too much."

Becky struck a lecturing pose. "Focus," she ordered. "If you don't get back to work, I'll have to make you stand in the corner." For the past hour she'd been trying to teach Starr the fundamentals of accounting, and for the past hour she'd been getting nowhere.

Frowning, Starr turned back to the spreadsheet on the monitor. "This is no way to spend a Sunday afternoon," she grumbled. "Anyway, can't you see it's hopeless? I just don't have a head for this. Maybe I should go back to using the old system."

"What old system? Throwing receipts into a drawer and hoping the numbers come out right? I'm surprised the IRS hasn't come after you with a ten-foot calculator. It's easy, Starr. Just remember, liabilities plus capital equals assets."

"If it's so easy, you do it. Where did you learn all this stuff, anyway?"

Good question, Becky thought. Over the past few years she'd spent more time getting fired from office jobs than she'd spent working. She shrugged. "I guess I picked up more than I realized."

"Since you seem to have a knack for all this computer

hocus-pocus, I hereby appoint you Official Accounting Queen.''

''That's fine with me, but you still have to know what's going on. What are you going to do when I leave?''

A look of horror crossed Starr's face. ''Don't even mention that! I know we talked about it, and I know that someday you'll want to go off on your own, but I can't imagine this place without you. You've brought me more luck than a four-leaf clover. Do you realize that since you've been here the business has more than doubled?'' She slapped herself on the forehead. ''Of course you realize this. The information is right there on the screen. I guess you know, too, what this means. We're now in a position to open the kitchen to the public on Saturdays.''

''Slave driver,'' Becky said, but inwardly she was pleased. She knew that the inn's recent success was mostly due to her cooking, and the knowledge was a bolster to her self-esteem. For once in her life she felt valuable. Like a *mensh,* Bubbe would say.

''Don't say I didn't warn you,'' Starr joked. ''But I have good news—you're about to be liberated. I'm planning to hire an assistant for you. Actually, you're going to hire an assistant for you. I might be the chief cook and bottle washer, but we both know who has the talent in the kitchen. You know better than I do what kind of help you'll need.''

An assistant! Becky had always worked for someone else; she couldn't imagine anyone working for her. A memory from her childhood surfaced, causing her to smile. Her mother used to complain that she had too much to do, what with raising a family, keeping house and occasionally helping Aaron at the carpet store he'd owned since Becky was a baby. Tired of listening to Gertie's complaints, Aaron had hired a housekeeper to come by once a week, but the day before each scheduled arrival Gertie cleaned the house from top to bottom, claiming, "No visitor should have to see such a mess." Later, when Aaron asked why Gertie had fired her, she replied, "The woman doesn't do anything!"

"I think it's wonderful you're expanding, but I don't need help," Becky said with reservation.

"Fiddlesticks. I can afford it now. And you're getting a raise." Starr gave Becky a mock-stern look. "Of course, you'll have to earn these new benefits."

Becky laughed. "You mean you want me to keep doing the bookkeeping. All right, but I'm warning you, you're going to learn this stuff if it kills you. You need to be on top of what's happening, especially now that the business is growing." She closed the accounting program and logged on to the Internet. "But now it's time for recess. Here's something you might enjoy—computer horoscopes. Let's look up what's in store for the baby—she's due the last week in May. That would make her a Gemini like me."

Starr shook her head. "It won't work. To get an accurate reading, we have to know the exact time of her birth. Turn this contraption off. Let's do tea leaves instead."

Becky followed Starr into the kitchen and sat down at the table. She hadn't been living at the B and B that long, but she was amazed at how much she felt at home. She would miss this place when she was gone, the relaxing atmosphere, the hours she and Starr spent talking and laughing at this very table. She would even miss the dolls that were scattered throughout the house.

But she was getting ahead of herself. Starting her own business was only a dream. Her only dictum was that she be on her feet and out of Middlewood before Carter returned from New Zealand—which meant she had a little more than two years to save up enough capital to make her dream a reality.

"All set," Starr said moments later, placing the pot of tea onto the table. She sat down next to Becky and poured them each a cup. "He called again this morning," she said as though continuing a previous conversation. "Are you sure you don't want to talk to him? I'm running out of excuses. You take so many baths, he must think you're a clean-freak."

Playing with the handle of her teacup, Becky asked, "What is there to say? I made my position clear. I don't want to get married. He knows how I feel about remaining independent."

"Keep saying it and maybe you'll believe it."

Becky looked up, startled. "What's that supposed to mean?"

"I'm saying your refusing to speak to Carter has more to do with your fear of getting hurt than it has to do with your independence."

Becky felt her anger rising. "I happen to know my own feelings, thank you very much. Sure, I'm afraid of getting hurt—in my situation, who wouldn't be? Have you forgotten that my husband abandoned me? But even a psychologist would agree that I'm not just commitmentphobic. I need to strike out on my own. All my life people have been telling me what makes me happy, and it's about time I found out for myself." Realizing she was overreacting, she halted. Starr was just being a friend. "Sorry. I didn't mean to snap at you. It's just that these days it makes me crazy when people tell me what to do."

Starr made a dismissive gesture. "Snap away, if it makes you feel better. What are friends for?" Her tone grew quiet. "I'm not telling you what to do, Becky. Only you know what makes you happy. All I'm saying, at the risk of getting my head chewed off, is that you should examine all your options.''

''First you act like a therapist, and now you sound like a stockbroker. But okay, I'll play along. What are you getting at?''

''You were in pieces after your marriage ended, and now you're rebuilding yourself. Right now you don't have all the answers. You're still searching. Which is why you shouldn't discount Carter altogether. What if he's the one?''

Her anger completely dissolved, Becky looked at Starr with amusement. ''So the mystical mage is also a hopeless romantic. Don't tell me you believe that one true love exists for every person! Didn't anyone ever tell you there are no princes on white horses? But you're right about one thing. I'm still searching, but not for a prince. I'm looking for myself, and I don't intend to make any more mistakes.''

''Was your marriage really a mistake?'' Starr asked softly. ''It seems to me that you like the person you're becoming. Did you ever consider that if you hadn't married Jordan, you wouldn't be who you are today?''

It wasn't her marriage Becky had been referring to when she'd mentioned her mistakes, although, heaven knows, it had been a disaster. No, she was thinking of the night of David's wedding, and was about to say so when a jerking movement in her abdomen caused her to flinch.

''What?'' Starr asked, visibly alarmed. ''Are you all right?''

''She kicked! I know it's a little early, but I felt her! She kicked!''

''It's not too early. She might be a wee soul, but she's still a somebody. Some people believe that the spirit enters the body at birth, but I believe it happens at the moment of conception.'' She looked at Becky, her witchy green eyes shining with conviction. ''I also believe there are no wrong turns in life, that everything happens for a reason.''

The baby kicked again, and Becky knew she would never again think of that night as a mistake. It was the night her daughter had been conceived, the night her child, as Starr had pointed out, had become a somebody.

''Are you finished with your tea?'' Starr asked. ''Let's see what the leaves have to say.''

Becky gave her cup a swirl, then handed it over to Starr. ''Well?''

Squinting, Starr peered into the cup. ''Aha.''

''Aha, what?''

''According to what I see, all the pieces to your happiness are right here before you. It's like a jigsaw puzzle. You just have to put them together.''

The woman was incorrigible. ''You think I should marry Carter,'' Becky said.

''Why would I say a thing like that? Just because he's a great guy who's so smitten with you he can't see straight, just because you feel the same way about him except you're too dense to admit it, doesn't mean you should marry him. No, I'm not saying that at all. I'm only telling you what I see.''

''Maybe this is a bad batch of leaves,'' Becky scoffed. ''Or maybe you need glasses. What else do you think you see?''

''Uh-oh.''

''Uh-oh? What is *uh-oh?*''

''You're right—this must be a bad batch. These leaves are saying that the baby will be born in April.'' Starr put down the cup and nodded thoughtfully. ''That would make her an Aries. A born leader, headstrong and courageous. Quick-tempered, too. All your characteristics, I might add.''

''My characteristics? I'm a Gemini, remember? Scatterbrained? Indecisive?''

''Well, then Aries must be your ascendant.''

''Starr, will you please speak in English?''

''Your ascendant is the zodiac sign that was rising on the eastern horizon the moment you were born. It distinguishes your temperament, even your physical appearance. It's the impression perceived by those around you.''

Not once had Becky ever thought of herself as a leader, let alone courageous. ''You must be kidding. Everyone thinks I'm such a wimp. Even my brother calls me helpless. It's exactly that impression I'm trying to change.''

''Not everyone thinks like your brother. And don't forget, you have two sides. It's the twins in you, a trait of the Gemini.''

Becky stood up and carried the cups to the sink. ''It's a good thing you don't do this for a living. My daughter will be born in the last week in May, which makes her a Gemini. The ultrasound confirmed it. Let's hope her ascendant will be a more assertive sign, like Taurus. In this day and age a woman needs to take the bull by the horns.''

Carter sat next to the fireplace, staring out the picture window. The panoramic view before him was unobstructed and resplendent, with mountain peaks disappearing into cloudy drifts. Along the trails snow fell softly, decorating the terrain with myriad sparkles.

He leaned back on the couch and surveyed the room. The old Victorian structure had a welcoming après-ski ambiance. He liked this chalet; in fact, he liked everything about Breckenridge. An old mining town turned ski resort, it was dotted with boutiques, pubs and restaurants. More significantly, with access to thousands of acres of Rocky Mountain skiing, it was less than two hours from Denver.

But he had another reason for choosing Breckenridge over the many other ski locations he could have gone to this weekend. The first time he'd come here, he'd been sixteen, on a high school ski trip with his class. He'd broken his leg coming down an expert hill and hadn't returned since. It was about time he conquered his fear of this mountain, he'd told himself back at the hotel in Denver. Now, after all these years, the fear was behind him.

He was tired, but it was the kind of fatigue that made a man feel as if he'd lived the day to its fullest. He'd had a good workout this weekend, maneuvering the hills with the skill of a professional. Maybe *attacking* was a better word than *maneuvering,* he thought, remembering the way he'd stabbed his poles into the moguls.

It had felt good, pushing himself that way. Allowed him to let off steam. He'd been on the job three weeks now, but it wasn't the work that had him on edge. No matter where he was or what he was doing, his thoughts always returned to the night of the party. Becky had made her feelings clear, and it was time he faced facts. Her interest in him began and ended with the baby.

A gust of cold January air blew in as the door opened and a family of five entered, their ski boots clomping on the hardwood floors. In the corner, several people were gathered around the piano, singing show tunes. Seated on another couch across from him, a woman looked over in his direction. He remembered her from the chair lift. Ski bunny, he'd thought, noting her tight, silver ski pants and short matching jacket.

She sashayed over and sat down beside him. "You're

a real cowboy, you know that?'' she said, smiling brightly.

Amused, he cocked his head. ''Yeah, how's that?''

''You ski like a rodeo star riding a bull. I'd say you're a man with a problem.''

''And you aim to cure me.''

She smoothed her long blond hair with a manicured hand. ''I didn't see a ring.''

''You must have X-ray vision. I was wearing gloves on the hill.''

''You're not wearing gloves now.''

No ring on her finger, either, he noticed, the telltale white line indicating that he might not be the only one with a problem. ''Separated or divorced?'' he asked. He almost added ''or just messing around,'' but stopped himself. What she did was her own business; who was he to judge?

She let out a small derisive laugh. ''Separated. I guess it's written all over me. Abandoned woman seeks revenge in ski chalet.'' She moved in closer, and Carter could smell the fragrance of her perfume. ''What's good for the gander is good for the goose,'' she said, looking at him coyly. ''What about you? What's your sad story? And don't tell me you don't have one. Everyone has a tragic tale. Care to share?''

Suddenly tiredness overwhelmed him, and it had nothing to do with his vigorous workout on the slopes. He had no desire to know this stranger, no desire to talk to her at all.

A face in a crowd, he recalled David once saying. He remembered the conversation in which David had confided his one and only indiscretion. Nothing had happened, but the fact remained that David had considered cheating on Hannah.

It was ironic, Carter thought. Here he was thinking like a married man, except that he was single and the woman he'd set his sights on kept turning him down. He almost laughed. Here he was sitting next to an open invitation, her face less than six inches from his, and he couldn't even bring himself to make small talk.

He stood up. "Maybe some other time. I'm heading back to Denver tonight. I have an early meeting in the morning."

He knew he sounded banal, but what he'd said was true. Besides, the forecast was calling for heavy snow later that evening. Even though his rental was a four-wheel drive, the last thing he felt like doing, after a weekend of snow, was battling a storm. That might be the truth, he acknowledged to himself, but he knew damn well it wasn't why he was declining the woman's offer.

He could almost hear David's taunting words, "Lose your edge, buddy?"

Carter had lost it, all right, on the night he'd taken Becky back to his apartment.

"Okay, cowboy, I can take a hint." The woman stood and nodded in the direction of the lounge. "But if you change your mind, you know where to find me."

Back in his room, his thoughts returned to David. Sometimes his friend could be so lame. What was his problem? David knew that Carter wanted to marry Becky; how could he not know? The Roth family grapevine was faster than a high-speed computer network. Becky would have told Hannah, and Hannah would have told David. What did David expect him to do? Knock Becky over the head with a club and drag her to his cave?

Carter had known David too long to let their friendship slip away, but David was stubborn, even more stubborn than his sister. Carter knew he'd have to make the first move.

He set his laptop on the desk and plugged it in. He knew he could always call him, but e-mail was much easier. More concise. You didn't waste time getting to the gist.

He thought for a moment, then began typing.

Hey, wuss. Super conditions here at Breckenridge. Remember the old days when you had a life? I drove by the baby hill and thought of you.

Carter knew that David liked to spend an hour or two on Sundays puttering on the computer. If David wasn't online yet, he'd get to his messages shortly. In any case, Carter was sure he would take the bait.

After a quick shower Carter packed his suitcase, then checked for messages. Sure enough, there was a reply.

Surprised you didn't break your neck this time, old boy. BTW, little sis explained the confusion. Ditsy as ever, that girl. Gotta hand it to her, though, she showed good taste by refusing to marry a klutz like you. ;-)

Carter grinned, then read on.

Looks like you've created a cyber monster. These days she's surfing the Net. Here's her e-mail address. Thought you might be interested.

Interested? That was putting it mildly. Every night since he'd been gone, he'd lain awake in a sweat, thinking about her. It was Phoenix all over again. Only now she was with him all day, as well, everywhere he went. Whether he was at the job site, working alone at his hotel or crashing down a mountain, her face rose before him, driving him out of his mind.

Dammit, he wanted her. Wanted her more than he'd ever wanted anyone, but she kept pushing him away, using her newfound independence as an excuse.

Except something didn't ring true, only he couldn't figure out what it was. He recalled how she'd practically ravished him in the elevator of his building. Yet three weeks ago she'd acted like a frightened rabbit. He couldn't forget the fear in her eyes after he'd kissed her under the mistletoe. Why had she been so afraid?

He thought about the woman in the bar. She'd obviously been hurt, but that hadn't stopped her from coming on to him. Even though she'd hinted that her motive was revenge, he suspected that what she really wanted was a little TLC, someone to offer a temporary fix. He doubted she was looking for something long-term. Long-term would entail emotional risk.

At David's wedding Becky had been vulnerable and depressed. The furthest thing from her mind—from either of their minds—had been a relationship. But now, she was acting as though she was afraid of getting hurt.

There was no reason for this.

Unless…she *felt* something for him.

Women, he decided, were too complicated.

Men, on the other hand, were much simpler. And they faced their fears. Take, for example, his decision to come back to Breckenridge. For years he had refused to ski here; why return to a place that had nearly done him in? But he knew he had to mount the horse that threw him, so to speak, if he were to ever get over his fear.

Of course, it had taken almost two decades to accomplish this.

In two decades their son would be away at college.

No way, Carter thought. No way would he wait that long. He had to convince Becky that they should be married. Had to convince her that she could trust him. Not an easy feat, considering he was nineteen hundred miles away. Not only that, he hadn't been in contact with her since he'd left for Colorado. He'd tried phoning, but like the last time he'd been away, she wouldn't take his calls.

But now things were different.

She *felt* something for him.

When she was a child, whenever she'd hurt herself, he'd make her laugh to get her mind off her pain. Well, she wasn't a child anymore, and winning her trust would take a lot more work, but he had to start somewhere.

She was still hurting. The first thing he had to do was get her to smile.

And it was hard to hang up on e-mail.

After the breakfast dishes were cleared away, Becky headed straight to the study. She hadn't turned on the computer since yesterday when she'd tried to give Starr the lesson in accounting. She had a pile of receipts to sort through and enter, and after that, she planned on working on her book. She'd already sent off a proposal to a friend she'd gone to college with, an editor at Calyx Editions in Manhattan. Now all Becky had to do, besides entering the final recipes, was wait for a response.

"You have a visitor," Starr said, popping her head into the study. "She's waiting in the living room."

Becky groaned. Just what she needed. It wasn't enough that her mother was making her crazy over the phone; now she had to do it in person. Here it was only Monday morning, and already Becky's week was going downhill.

"Bubbe!" Relief swept through her. Her grandmother was seated on the sofa next to the mantel, wearing what she liked to call her good coat. A no-nonsense beige wool garment she'd owned forever, it had held up remarkably over the years as well as she.

"You were expecting maybe Madonna?"

Becky laughed, then scolded, "How did you get here?"

"I used my feet. How else should I get here? Call a chauffeur?"

"You must be frozen. Come into the kitchen. I'll fix us some tea."

"I didn't come for tea. I came to see you."

Suddenly Becky was alarmed. "What is it, Bubbe? What's the matter?"

"Why should something be the matter? Is it a sin for a bubbe to want to see her grandchild?"

Becky sat down beside her. "I'm sorry, Bubbe. I know I should go home more often. But Ma makes me crazy, and my doctor said I should avoid stress." And if avoiding stress meant avoiding Gertie, it would be a sacrifice Becky would just have to make.

She noted the look on her grandmother's face and quickly added, "Don't worry, Bubbe. Nothing's the matter. I had an ultrasound and everything is fine."

"What means this ultrasound? Hannah, too, had one. In my day the woman didn't even go to the hospital. You're not sick, God forbid."

"The ultrasound is a great tool. It allows the doctor to keep up with the progress of the baby. It can even tell us if it's a boy or a girl."

"*Nu?* Should I start knitting blue booties or pink ones?"

"I didn't ask. I want to be surprised." Becky leaned in closer. "Bubbe, if I tell you something, you won't think it's wrong? You won't think I'm tempting fate?"

"What is it, *bubelah?*"

"Is it wrong for me to want a girl more than a boy? Don't misunderstand, I'll be happy no matter what it is, as long as it's one or the other…I mean…" Becky stopped, embarrassed to be admitting she had a preference.

Bubbe laughed. "You can want what you want, but as soon as you see your baby, it won't matter. You'll forget what you wanted and want what you have. Tell me, what about the father? What does he think he wants?"

"Carter wants a boy. Someone to carry on the family name."

Bubbe nodded knowingly. "When your mother was carrying David, your father prayed every night for a boy. He wanted someone to take over the business."

It's a good thing I wasn't the firstborn, Becky thought, or I might have developed a complex. It was one thing for a parent to secretly harbor a preference, but it was another thing to pray for it.

She remembered the bible story of Jacob and his older twin, Esau. When their father Isaac had grown old, Jacob tricked him into giving him the birthright inheritance normally reserved for the firstborn. The story would have more meaning today, Becky mused, if Jacob had been a girl.

"How come Daddy didn't want me to go into the business? David's a pharmacist. He never even wanted to sell carpets."

"Let me tell you a little something. When David was a *boychik,* he wanted to be just like your father. If your father had been a butcher, David would have wanted chickens. If he had been a tailor, David would have wanted a needle and thread. Every morning he cried your father should take him to work with him. Such a *nudnik,* he was. Little boys want to be like their fathers, and little girls want to be like their mothers. It's the way it works."

There's a notion, Becky thought. Me wanting to be like my mother. "You're missing the point, Bubbe. Daddy never even asked me."

"You're telling me you want to go into business with your father?"

"No, of course not. I'm not interested in carpets."

"So what's the problem?"

One thing about Bubbe, she had a way of putting things into perspective. Becky could just imagine herself in business with her father. He'd probably want to put her baby in all his commercials.

"You're right," Becky answered. "There is no problem. Are you sure you don't want some tea, Bubbe? Take off your coat, at least. Stay for a while."

"No, I just came by to make sure you weren't lying sick somewhere in the house."

"I'm sorry I worried you," Becky apologized again, feeling thoroughly chastised. "I'll come by the house during the week. I'd come for dinner on Friday, but I have to work."

"On *Shabbes* you work? Such a thing, I'm telling you. Never mind, that's not why I'm here. I didn't come to talk about work. I came to remind you that you have a family."

It was no mystery where Gertie had learned the art of guilt. If guilt were a lake, Becky would be drowning in it. "But you know what my mother is like," she protested meekly. "She treats me like a child."

"When you're 105, God willing, you can tell her to mind her own business. In the meantime, you're still her baby. Soon you'll understand for yourself. All a mother wants is for her daughter to be happy. Is that so wrong?"

"No, Bubbe. It's just that she doesn't let me breathe."

Bubbe looked at her sternly. "If you have to be mad at someone, be mad at me. It's my fault she's the way she is. It's how I brought her up. I didn't let her out of my sight for a minute. I was afraid...always afraid..."

Her eyes took on a faraway look. "I lost everyone, everyone but my Chaim. Even my little Judith—your mother's older sister—they took her from my arms. After the war all I wanted was to make a family. Chaim wanted a boy, someone to carry on his name…he also lost everyone…" She paused, and then her face creased in a smile. "After the war we came to America and I had Gertie. Chaim was so happy! She was his little girl, his princess. God didn't see fit to give us another baby, but we were grateful…grateful to be alive and grateful for Gertie. But still we were afraid…always so afraid. Even in America, always looking over our shoulders…" Her voice trailed off, her smile fading.

Becky gave her grandmother's hands a gentle squeeze and waited for her to continue.

"Boy or girl," Bubbe said, her mouth set in a determined line, "it's important the family should continue. I'm going to tell you a secret, so pay attention. Your father prayed for a boy to carry on the business, but in his heart he wanted a girl. He wanted a princess to spoil, just like my Chaim wanted Gertie." She stood up. "Now I'm going to the synagogue. It's not Saturday, but at my age a little extra praying can't hurt. You should come, too. It's important you should honor your heritage."

"I know, Bubbe. I promise I'll go soon." It was a promise Becky intended to keep, if not for herself, then for her grandmother. But she would have to go during the week. She'd be too busy on weekends, catering to the influx of guests.

She took Bubbe's arm and walked with her to the front door. "Wait here a moment, and I'll get Starr. I want her to drive you. It's cold out there."

"It's not Miami, but for a winter in Connecticut it's not so terrible. The sky is clear and the streets aren't icy.

As long as I have my health, I walk. What else can I ask for?''

''But Bubbe—''

''No buts. I can take care of myself. I already had a mother. Another one I don't need.'' She kissed Becky on the cheek and added, her eyes dancing with mischief, ''It's enough I have to live with yours.''

After Bubbe left, Becky returned to the study, intending to play a game of chess against the computer before getting down to work. A flashing icon on the monitor alerted her that she had e-mail. There was one message. It had no subject line, but Becky recognized the sender. Carter's name was part of the address.

She felt a stab of remorse. If a day could be labeled by one specific emotion, today's tag would be guilt. She wasn't just thinking about her family; she knew she'd been too harsh with Carter at the party. She knew, too, that she should have taken his calls these past few weeks, but the truth was, she hadn't wanted to deal with what was happening between them. And something *was* happening, no matter how hard she tried to deny it.

She was a coward, no doubt about it. She'd always been a coward. She'd run from her life to marry Jordan, and when that failed, she'd run back to her parents. She'd made a career of avoiding issues. Like not wanting to deal with her mother. Like refusing to speak to Carter.

Poor princess, how long can you keep running? Her mind still burned with the memory of his words.

She considered hitting the delete button, but then decided against it. What was the harm in reading the message? As far as she was concerned, nothing had changed. In fact, she was determined more than ever to hold her ground. Marriage meant dependence, and that was out of the question. She wanted to live her own life.

She clicked on the message. In spite of herself, a smile found its way to her lips. Evidently he hadn't forgotten that story she'd spun on the night of David's wedding. "The only way I'll ever sleep with you is if we're out on the highway and there's this terrible storm…"

The message said, *It's snowing*.

Chapter Eight

"Hurry up, Starr! I don't want to miss my train!"

"I'll be right there! I'm looking for my purse!"

And they call me scatterbrained, Becky mused. She pushed aside the curtain on the front-door window and looked outside. The day was bright and clear, the sky a brilliant blue. The new year was definitely unfolding favorably. Here it was already February, and not one storm had passed through Connecticut since the holidays. But it wasn't just the weather she was thinking of as she closed the curtain and buttoned up her coat. Last week she'd received a call from the editor she'd contacted at Calyx Editions. After talking on the phone for several minutes, they agreed to have lunch in the city. But the best news was that the editor had asked Becky to bring her completed manuscript.

Actually, that had been the second-best news. Yesterday Hannah had taken her to the doctor for her weekly appointment, and once again Becky had received a glowing report. The pregnancy was progressing perfectly.

Becky didn't consider herself a religious person, but lately she found herself praying for the health of her baby. She'd even kept her promise to Bubbe and gone to the synagogue, and she intended to keep going. She told herself she was doing it for her grandmother, but inside she knew she was doing it for herself. Just being there made her feel connected to the past. It gave her a sense of heritage, which, until her pregnancy, had been something she hadn't given much thought.

"Found it!" Starr called from the hallway, jarring Becky back to the present moment. "Have you seen my gloves?"

I should have called a taxi, Becky thought. At this rate they'd never get out of here.

"Let's go," Starr said, suddenly appearing behind her, purse in hand. She was already in her coat, her zodiac-patterned scarf tucked around her neck. "What are we waiting for?"

Becky pulled open the door—and froze. But it wasn't the chilly February air that caused her reaction. Carter was standing on the doorstep, holding a bouquet of roses.

"You must have ESP," he said, stepping inside. He closed the door behind him. "How did you know I was here?"

She had to remind herself to keep breathing. "I didn't. I just—" She stared at him wordlessly. One of her New Year's resolutions had been to stop thinking of him in a way that made her pulse go haywire. She felt her resolution draining away.

After she'd received his first e-mail weeks ago, she'd replied back with *Hope you remembered to take a shovel.* It wasn't particularly witty or funny, but it was also clearly not flirtatious. She didn't want him to get the wrong idea. Her infatuation, she kept telling herself, was just a silly extension of her teenage crush.

At first she'd considered not answering him, but then she'd changed her mind. What was the harm in keeping up a correspondence? As long as she kept it light, she'd be safe. She could hardly ignore him; soon he'd be back in Middlewood, insisting that he accompany her to the doctor. An antagonistic situation would only create tension, and hadn't Dr. Boyd told her to avoid stress?

Thank heaven for e-mail. It allowed her to remain distant. Allowed her to retain a semblance of control. Yeah, right. What control was that? He'd only been gone seven weeks—two weeks longer than he'd originally intended—but she felt as if he'd been gone for years. Speechlessly she studied him. Had he always been so tall? Were his shoulders always so broad? But his eyes—she could never forget those eyes. Hazy-gray, they bathed her with suggestion, hinting at the fire that lay beneath the smoke.

"Better put these flowers in water," he said, looking at her with those dangerous eyes. Was he looking at her the same way she was looking at him?

"Here, let me," Starr said, when no one spoke. "These roses could wilt from old age before one of you makes a move." She took the bouquet from Carter and disappeared into the kitchen.

"Thank you for the flowers," Becky said with forced composure. "But what are you doing here? According to your e-mail, you weren't supposed to be coming back for another two days."

"The job was done—so what was the use in sticking around? You'll be pleased to know that two hundred gifted children will no longer be forced to sing and dance and play their musical instruments in an old church basement. If I do say so myself, their new school is going to give Juilliard a run for its money.'' Then, as though noticing her coat for the first time, he asked, ''Going somewhere?''

''I have a lunch date in New York. An old friend of mine is an editor at Calyx Editions, and she wants to see my book.''

''You finished it already?'' he asked, not masking his surprise.

''It didn't take long at all. I told you, it was all written out on paper. All I had to do was enter the recipes into the computer. But I'll tell you all about it when I get back. Right now I have to go. Starr is taking me to the train.''

''The train! You can't be serious. You can't take a train in your condition. I can't believe you'd even consider doing something so dangerous. And how do you propose to get from the station to the meeting?''

He talked as if she were planning to hop a freighter, not ride a comfortable commuter into the city. ''I thought I'd hail a cab. Or is that too dangerous, too?''

''I'm going to drive you to the city. I insist.''

''Carter, don't be ridiculous. I'm not an invalid, for heaven's sake. I'm pregnant.''

''Don't argue with me, Becky. My mind's made up. I'll take you wherever you want to go. Besides, this gives me an opportunity to drop in on an old friend and colleague, Rob Parker. He left the firm a few months ago to go out on his own, and I'd like to see his new office. When you're done, you can call me on my cell and I'll come get you.''

''Sounds like a plan,'' Starr said, returning to the front door. She'd already taken off her coat and hung it in the closet.

''Traitor,'' Becky muttered. Just what she needed, to

be confined in a car, alone with Carter for more than an hour each way. Confined in a car, her body inches from his. Whether or not she liked it, she'd missed him, but she had no intention of going down that particular road, no matter how fast her pulse was racing.

Starr laughed. "No, not a traitor. An eavesdropper. You'll thank me one day, I promise."

The first thing Carter noticed as he pulled over and double-parked outside the restaurant was Becky's smiling face. It warmed him to see her so happy, and for a moment he was back in the past. He pictured her on roller skates, playing hopscotch in the driveway, skipping rope with her friends. He'd been an only child, and she'd managed to kindle his big-brother instinct. She'd been sweet and funny, exactly the way little sisters were supposed to be.

She was still sweet and funny, when she wasn't lashing out at him.

She'd also been undemanding and accepting, he remembered. Whatever her parents or David told her to do, she'd done without question.

That certainly had changed. It was as if she had awakened one morning and suddenly become a different person.

She noticed him and waved. Even pulled back in a knot, her hair couldn't be kept constrained. Dark tendrils had escaped onto her forehead, giving her the appearance of someone carefree, someone at ease with the person she'd become.

The little girl he remembered had grown up. She was still as bubbly and enthusiastic as she'd been as a child, but it wasn't his big-brother instinct she was kindling now, he thought as he watched her weave her way across the crowded sidewalk.

He waited for a break in the traffic, then got out of the car and walked around to the passenger side. "From the look on your face I'd say that the meeting was a success," he said, opening the door.

"It was wonderful!" she gushed as she climbed into the car. "Sandra Meyers is just as I remembered, full of life and enthusiasm."

"Funny," Carter said softly, "I was thinking the same about you."

Becky laughed, her cheeks flushed with joy. "She said she loved the idea of my book. I decided to call it *The Lover's Guide to Vegetarian Cooking,* did I tell you? Can you believe it? I'm going to be published!" Her forehead crinkled. "Well, probably. Maybe. But she loved the idea, Carter. She loved it!"

"I knew you could do it," he said as he closed the door. Once back in the driver's seat, he started the car and pulled away from the restaurant, listening as she chatted excitedly about her day.

"What's the matter?" she asked abruptly. "You're not talking."

He chuckled. "You won't let me get in a word edgewise. Seriously, princess, I'm happy for you. Nothing's the matter."

"No, something is wrong. I can tell."

He sighed. Was he this transparent to everyone? Or did Becky know him better than he'd like to admit? "It's just that it's already after four. I didn't think you'd be so late."

Silence filled the car. It was so thick he could almost see it.

"I'm sorry if I inconvenienced you," she said finally, her voice as cold as ice water, "but I told you I would be a while. I knew I should have taken the train. Tell me something, why does a woman always have to bend to a man's schedule? It's always the same old story.''

At times, being around Becky was like waiting for a bomb to explode. This was fast becoming one of those times. ''This has nothing to do with convenience,'' he said with forced patience. ''There's a storm brewing, and I don't want to get caught in it.''

''What storm? The forecast is calling for clear skies throughout the rest of the week.''

''That storm.'' He pointed through the windshield. ''Look at those clouds.''

By the time they had merged onto the I-95, the snow had begun to fall in thick, heavy clumps, and traffic had slowed to a crawl.

''Damn,'' he said. ''At this rate we won't get back till midnight.''

''Sorry for ruining your plans,'' she said, her tone dripping with sarcasm.

Being stuck on a highway was stressful enough; he didn't need attitude, as well. He glanced at her in the passenger seat. She was sitting rigidly, her hands clenched tightly in her lap. She was even tenser than he was. Remembering Dr. Boyd's warning about stress, he was instantly filled with concern. He had to get Becky to relax.

He recalled the first e-mail he'd sent from Breckenridge, the one that had moved her to bury the hatchet. Why not? he thought. Wasn't laughter the best medicine? ''Becky?''

''What?''

''It's snowing.''

''The joke's getting old. Just concentrate on your driving, okay?''

''Let's see if I remember this correctly. You said we'd

be coming home from a business trip, right? Seeing how I came from the office of an old associate and how you met with your prospective editor, I'd say this trip definitely qualifies as business.''

''Will you please keep your eyes on the road?''

''Why? We're not going anywhere.'' It was true. Traffic had come to a halt.

She slumped back in her seat and stared straight ahead.

He raised his eyes heavenward. It was turning out to be a long day. A very, very long day.

The cars ahead began to inch forward, but the wind had picked up and now the snow was swirling in billows. Even with the wipers on max, Carter could barely see through the windshield. Shoulders hunched over, he leaned forward and peered through the glass.

An hour later they'd progressed less than a mile. He could see the next exit up ahead. ''Maybe the back roads will be better,'' he grumbled, pulling off the highway. She didn't answer. She was fiddling with something at her feet.

After a few minutes of plowing along the whitened road, something darted out of the rapidly descending darkness, its eyes like headlights glowing through the blowing snow. Instinctively Carter swerved to the right, and the car went into a skid. It slid along the shoulder for what seemed like miles—unending, terrifying miles—and then, with a jolt and a thud, came to a stop, smack in the middle of a snowdrift.

And then there was quiet. Complete and utter quiet.

Carter turned toward Becky. In the dim light from the dashboard he could barely make out her profile. She was sitting perfectly motionless. ''Are you all right?'' he whispered, his voice shattering the eerie silence.

"I'm okay," she answered in a tremulous voice. "What about you?"

She was safe. She and the baby were all right. "I'm fine," he said, though still feeling shaken. "Hold on. I'm going to get us out of here."

He stepped on the gas, but the only response he got was the hissing of tires. He shifted into reverse. The wheels dug deeper into the snow. He tried rocking the car backward and forward. Nothing moved.

"Wonderful," she said. "Now what are we supposed to do?"

He clenched the steering wheel. She acted as if he'd called ahead and ordered the storm just to tick her off. "I'm thinking," he answered.

It wasn't as if they were stranded in Siberia. As far as he knew, this exit was still part of the Western world, even if it did resemble the frozen steppes. He felt a smile tug at his lips. "The *ruchas*," he said.

"Excuse me?"

"The middle of nowhere. You said we'd be out in a snowstorm, coming back from a business trip, when we get stranded in the middle of nowhere."

"I can't believe this. Here we are stuck in a blizzard, and you're making jokes? We could turn to ice out here and not thaw out till spring!" She folded her arms across her chest. "I was perfectly willing to take the train, but *nooo*. You can't take a train in your condition, you said. It's too dangerous, you said. And this isn't dangerous?"

"Will you relax? I have it covered. Once again, technology saves the day." He took out his cell phone from his coat pocket and pressed the speed-dial button for roadside assistance.

After several rings a recorded message came on the line. He listened for a few moments, punched in his phone number, then hung up. "Seems everyone in the Northeast needs a tow. It'll be at least twenty-four hours before someone can get here. I left my number so they can call us."

"Great. The way I see it, either we stay in the car with the heat on and die of carbon monoxide poisoning, or we turn off the engine and freeze to death."

Carter knew Becky had studied Greek mythology in college. He wondered if she knew that the Greek word for uterus was *hyster,* as in hysterical. Somehow he didn't think this was a good time to mention it. "I think I'll choose door number three. Wait here. I'm going to scout around."

"You're going to leave me here alone? What if I get mugged?"

"I have no choice. We have to find shelter. Besides, who's going to mug you in this weather? Frosty the Snowman?" He immediately felt guilty for snapping at her. She wasn't hysterical; she was worried. People handled stress differently. When he got nervous, he made wisecracks. When she got nervous, she ranted.

"But it's so dark out there—no streetlights or anything! The power must be out. How can you get anywhere if you can't see where you're going?"

He reached into the glove compartment for a flashlight. "Keep the car running and open the window just a crack. I'll be back before you know it. And don't worry," he added, forcing himself to sound reassuring. "It'll be all right. Something's bound to be open—a gas station, a convenience store, a McDonald's...." He gave her hand a gentle squeeze.

"Carter?"

"Yeah?"

"Be careful," she said softly.

Less than twenty minutes later he was back at the car, his long black coat frosted with snow. He knocked on the window and she rolled it down. "There's a motel just down the road," he shouted over the howling wind. "We can wait there until the tow truck comes."

"I thought you said it wouldn't get here until tomorrow. I'm not going to a motel with you, so you can just forget it."

He let out a frosty breath. "At the moment our options are limited," he said, reminding himself to be patient.

"I can't go. I have a problem."

Oh, she had a problem, all right, and it was driving him insane. "Becky, if you don't get out of the car, I'm going to have to physically remove you."

"You don't understand. I can't go anywhere. My feet were hurting, so I took off my boots."

He gritted his teeth. "So put them back on."

"I can't. They don't fit anymore. My feet are too swollen."

He opened the door and handed her the flashlight. He removed his scarf and wrapped her feet in the woolen fabric, then scooped her up in his arms and lifted her out of the car. "That should keep your feet warm and toasty. Now, shine the light on the ground ahead and we'll be fine."

"What are you doing? Put me down! You can't carry me in this snow! It's slippery out here!"

"Do I have a choice? My God, what did you have for lunch today? Rocks? You're as heavy as a piano."

"Nice," she said tersely. "In case you've forgotten, I'm in my sixth month."

The statement nearly stopped him in his tracks. He hadn't seen her without her coat, and, until this moment, in his mind he'd pictured her just as he'd left her back in

December. The whole time he'd been away, he'd thought of her as just a little bit pregnant.

They were so close to becoming parents.

He trod through the snow slowly and carefully, making sure she remained secure in his arms. One slip, he knew, and they'd fall.

He didn't want to think of the consequences.

He had to lighten the mood. "Let me get this straight. It's snowing, we're coming from a business trip and we get stranded in a storm. What was that other condition? I think it had something to do with a farmhouse."

"Give it up, Carter. The joke is over. It's no longer funny."

No matter how hard he tried not to pant, puffs of steam appeared in the air in front of him. "Funny? My fingers and toes are frozen, my arms are numb from carrying you and if I don't get a hernia it'll be a miracle. If you think I think this is funny, you're a mighty strange woman."

"Then why are you laughing?"

"Who me?" he returned innocently.

Looming in the dark, the motel appeared in the gleam of the flashlight. On a swinging wood sign in the front yard, above the Vacancy sign, was the name of the motel.

In bold block letters were the words The Red Barn.

"We'd like a room, please," Carter said to the man behind the counter.

"Two rooms," Becky chimed in.

A short, balding man looked up from behind the desk. "Do you have a reservation?"

"You're kidding," Carter said. "Aren't you?"

"No, sir. We get mighty busy during these storms. I'll have to check to see what's available." The man held up the lantern and leaned over a ledger. "You're in luck," he said, looking back up. "I've got one cabin left with a woodstove. I don't think you want a room inside the lodge. Gonna get mighty cold tonight with the power out."

From what Becky could make out in the light of the lantern—and from what she'd seen on TV—this motel looked more like the kind of place that had overhead mirrors than the kind with woodstoves. Hanging on the wall was a poster-girl calendar, with Miss February smiling down at them, wearing three strategically placed Valentine's Day hearts.

"We'll take it," Carter said.

"Carter—"

"Becky, I have no intention of sleeping in a refrigerator. If you think—"

"The cabin's got an extra bed," the man interrupted. "It's a pullout, but it's comfortable. 'Least that's what the husbands tell me."

Becky's cheeks grew hot. She couldn't believe they were having this conversation with a complete stranger. To make matters worse, her stomach started growling, adding to her embarrassment. "Excuse me, but is there a restaurant in the vicinity?"

"You just had lunch," Carter said. "Don't tell me you're hungry again."

"That was hours ago. I'm famished."

"Nothing within walking distance, ma'am," the man answered. He looked down at her stockinged feet. "Doesn't look like you're wanting to go hiking. But the cabin's got a kitchenette, and the range is gas-powered, if you got a notion to do some cooking."

"Perfect," Becky said. "We have an oven but no food."

He gave her a toothy smile. "Wish I had some pork

chops or bacon, but I'm not running a grocery store. Tell you what. I'll get the missus to bring you some bread and cheese. She baked fresh just this morning. Might even have an unopened bottle of juice sitting in the fridge. The cabin's outside to the left.'' He handed the key to Carter. ''You go on ahead. The missus will be by shortly with the food, fresh towels, too. You might not be getting a hot meal, but 'least you got hot water. All the water tanks are heated by gas.''

Once again Carter lifted Becky into his arms. He carried her back outside, trudging through the drifting snow. ''You'll have to get the door,'' he said when they arrived at the cabin. ''Right now my hands are full. Can you get the key from my pocket?''

Twisting her body into his, she reached down and pulled out the key. Even in the cold of winter, even through their coats, she could feel the heat of his chest pressing against her. Adding to that, mingling with the fresh mint of winter, his musky aftershave created a heady elixir. *Get a grip,* she ordered herself. *You're just tired.* She reached down again to unlock the door.

He put her down only after they'd entered the cabin. ''Wait here,'' he said, leaving her at the door. Moments later, light from an oil lamp flickered throughout the room, casting long shadows across the walls and ceiling.

The cabin was not what Becky had expected. Unlike the reception area, the decor was warm and welcoming. In the glow she could make out rustic furnishings and wildlife artwork. To the left of the king-size bed was a cast-iron woodstove, and in front of the stove lay a thick faux-fur rug.

Across the room, next to the kitchenette, was a sofa covered with cushions. This, Becky thought, had better be the hideaway bed.

They weren't inside the cabin more than a minute before someone knocked at the door. Just as the man had promised, his wife had come with food and towels.

A stack of bundles in her arms concealed her face. "Thought you might need these, as well," she said. "Take the plastic bag before my arms fall off. I brought you bathrobes, too."

"Thank you," Becky said. "That was very thoughtful."

"No need to thank me. We sell these robes in the gift store. I added them to your bill. The food, too."

After the woman had gone, Carter burst out laughing. "This place sure is an enigma. If I had to rate it, I don't know whether I'd give it five stars or any at all." He plopped down on the sofa and pulled off his boots. "Why don't you freshen up while I get the stove going? This way, it'll be nice and warm when you come out."

The bathroom, too, surprised Becky. It was completely modern with a large whirlpool bath, which wasn't working because of the power failure. Not that she would have used it. She'd read that it could be dangerous to pregnant women or anyone with high blood pressure. No matter. As long as she could take a shower. She was still shivering.

She pulled off her sweater and removed her skirt, catching a glimpse of her reflection in the full-length mirror. She still couldn't believe the changes her body had undergone. She remembered the calendar in the reception area. Not exactly centerfold of the month, she thought, studying her round belly. Why had she been so insistent on separate sleeping arrangements? It wasn't as if Carter would be getting any ideas.

After her shower she found him kneeling by the stove,

kindling the fire. "Hi," she said shyly, pulling her robe closer to her body. "Nice fire."

He turned around and smiled. "Hi, yourself. This place sure got warm fast, didn't it? If you have any wet clothes, they'll be dry in no time."

She draped her skirt over the chair by the stove, then folded her remaining clothes and placed them in a drawer. "Shower's hot, too," she said. She felt awkward, standing there in her bathrobe, trying to make conversation.

"The phone's dead, so if you need to make a call, use my cell." He handed her his cell phone and stood up. "My turn now. I'll be out in no time. But go ahead and eat. Our charming hostess even brought peanut butter and jelly."

"I'll wait for you," she said. "You waited for me."

After calling Starr to let her know she wouldn't be back until tomorrow, she curled up in front of the stove. Listening to the crackle of the flames, she felt herself drifting. She was in that somnolent place between wakefulness and sleep, when a loud pop came from the stove, jolting her fully alert.

"Have a nice nap?" Carter asked, stirring the fire with an iron poker.

"I wasn't asleep," she answered drowsily. "How long have you been here? You must be starving. I know I am."

"You should have started without me," he reproached. He handed her a chipped plate. "Look what I found in the kitchenette. Not exactly fine china, but at least it's clean."

"I told you I'd wait for you. Besides, what fun is a picnic if you have to eat alone?"

She attacked the food like a ravenous bear. Nothing she'd ever prepared, nothing she'd ever eaten anywhere, compared to this feast. She was so hungry she would have believed him if he'd told her that the cheese, peanut butter and bread was an exotic vegetarian stew.

"That was some meal," Carter said after they had finished eating. When Becky reached for the dishes, he said, "Relax. I'll take care of it."

She lay back on the rug, basking in the heat from the stove. "And now, for dessert," she said when he returned. "A nice long nap right in front of the fire. I might even stay right here on the rug, all night long."

He sprawled out next to her, propping himself on his elbow. "You must be exhausted," he said, his voice coming to her as if from far away.

She closed her eyes. "Mmm," she answered lazily. "It's been a long day."

"I know you're tired, but are you sure that's all? Are you sure you're all right? I'm worried about you, Becky. I have a feeling that today was only the tip of the iceberg, that you've been overdoing it at work."

"I'm fine," she assured him. She turned onto her side, tucking her hands under her head. "You should be pleased to know I now have an assistant."

"I'm glad," he said, reaching over to brush away a curl that had fallen onto her forehead. "So the B and B is doing well."

"Are you kidding? At first I was against hiring someone, but I had to give in. During the holidays we were serving three full meals a day, and it got to be a little much. Now, even though we're back to being a basic bed and breakfast, I still need help. We have a full house every weekend, and we've added a fixed menu for the public on Saturdays. Not only that, I've been doing a lot more office work since the business increased." She noticed Carter's expression and laughed. "I know what you're thinking. I always believed I was terrible at anything that involved a calculator, but it turns out I was wrong. It seems I have a knack for numbers. Anyway, hiring an assistant was a good move. She's very organized and she's a natural in the kitchen. Also, she lives just down the block from the B and B. We've never been busier, and this way Starr doesn't lose a room.''

"So who's the miracle worker?"

"You remember Christina from the diner where I used to work, don't you? Merlin fired her. He goes through staff faster than I go through tofu.''

"You mean Chrissy? The one with the…uh, long po-nytail?''

"I should have known you'd remember her. No one ever forgets Christina. Everyone who came into the diner was crazy about her.'' Every man, she thought but didn't say.

"Do I detect a note of jealousy?'' he asked, his eyes shining with amusement.

Becky rolled onto her back and stared up at the ceiling. "Now why should I be jealous? She's got long, silky blond hair, legs up to her armpits, a minuscule waistline and huge…dimples. Next to her I'm a beauty queen, haven't you noticed? A beauty queen who's as big as a house.''

"A piano,'' he said jokingly. "I believe I compared your weight to that of a piano.''

Without warning a tear rolled down her cheek. Morti-fied, she wiped it away. Why now did she have to have one of her hormonal attacks? If she wasn't laughing these days, she was crying.

"Aw, princess, I'm sorry. I was only teasing. If there's an award for being the most insensitive clod on the planet, hand it over. I deserve it.'' He grazed the side of her face with his fingers. "Becky, look at me.''

"No," she said, refusing to turn her head.

"Do you have any idea how beautiful you are? It's true what they say about pregnant women. You're positively glowing."

"That's not a glow. That's sweat. Even when I'm cold, I sweat. Do you know why pregnant women are always perspiring? It's because they have to lug around all this extra weight, and don't go telling me that this bulge is attractive. Not only do I look as though I swallowed a basketball, I've got the butt to match. If you think I'm beautiful, I'd say you need glasses."

"Then I guess I should make an appointment with an optometrist. Me and every other expectant father." He chuckled. "And about Chrissy, trust me, she doesn't have anything you don't have."

Becky smiled through her tears. "But the problem is, lately I have twice as much of it everywhere. Sure, I finally have cleavage, but no one ever told me how much my chest would hurt. While I'm complaining, you might as well get the whole picture. The morning sickness might be gone, but I'm always hungry. Not to mention I always have to pee. And let me ask you this, when did a pregnant woman suddenly become public property? It seems that everywhere I go, someone wants to touch my belly. You'd think they'd never seen a pregnant woman before. You'd think—oh!"

"Becky?" Carter asked, pulling himself to a sitting position. "What is it?"

"The baby. She's kicking. That's another thing. Sometimes she keeps me awake all night. I swear, I think she's in training for the Olympics. I know they start them young, but this is crazy. Here, feel for yourself."

"Are you sure you want me to?" he kidded gently. "I

wouldn't want you to feel as though you're public property."

She reached for his hand and placed it just below her belly button, on top of her robe. "Actually, I lied. I love it when she moves. It's so incredible, I can't begin to describe it. There's this whole other person inside, getting ready to emerge into the world."

Something poked out from under her robe, making a visible lump. "What's that?" he asked, his face filled with wonder.

She laughed. "I think it's her foot. She must be practicing her gymnastics routine."

Becky wasn't sure what prompted her to do what she did next. Maybe it was the look on his face, or maybe it was the way his hand felt on her body, even over the fleece of her robe. All she was certain of was that she wanted him to keep touching her.

Kneeling beside her was the concerned, caring man who had carried her to safety through the blinding snow, and she regretted having doubted him, even for a minute. She should have known everything would turn out all right. She should have known he'd never let anything happen to her or the baby.

But it wasn't gratitude that led her to guide his hand to the sash of her robe. As much as she had tried, she couldn't deny what she felt. Couldn't deny what was happening between them.

He loosened the sash, then slid his hand inside her robe and moved it slowly across her belly. She closed her eyes as he caressed her, his hands making lazy, wide circles.

"So beautiful," he murmured. "So incredibly beautiful."

She felt his hands leave her belly and make their way

up to her breasts. "Tell me if I'm hurting you," he said tenderly. "I'd never want to hurt you."

Feeling his gaze burning through her, she opened her eyes. "No, it feels wonderful."

His eyes never leaving hers, he opened her robe, continuing to caress her as though afraid she would break.

It was making her crazy. Crazy with desire she'd kept locked up for months. Outside the cabin the wind was whistling, inside the fire crackling. She moaned softly. His soft, tantalizing fingers were like feathers against her skin, maddeningly languid, driving her slowly, steadily, to the edge of paradise.

She sat up and reached for him. Deliberately matching his slowness, she untied his robe and moved it off his shoulders. Mesmerized, she watched as it glided downward, his chest and arms gleaming in the light from the stove. He smiled at her, then slid her robe down her arms, bathing her with his gaze. He cupped her face with his hands, and in his eyes she saw the confirmation she'd been desperately seeking. In his eyes she was beautiful.

Facing her, he eased her onto his lap and she curled her legs around him. He wrapped her snugly in his arms, clasping her body tightly to his. "Just for the record," he said playfully, "I'd like to know one thing. Who's seducing who?"

"Just for the record," she answered, her lips barely touching his, "I came on to you in the elevator, the night of the wedding. But if you ever remind me of it, I swear I'll deny it."

His mouth brushed against hers. "Now that we're owning up, I have something to tell you, too. Being with you was all I thought about that entire evening. In fact, the whole wedding was just a ploy to get you back to my apartment."

She laughed. "And here I thought the wedding had something to do with David and Hannah being in love."

Suddenly he pulled back, his eyes probing hers with intensity. "Becky, are you sure this time?" he asked softly. "Are you sure this is what you want?"

The memory of the car skidding out of control flashed through her mind. She could have lost the baby. They could have all been killed. Yet here they were, safely nestled in an obscure motel, somewhere off the I-95. It was true what they say, she thought. Life was as precarious as a throw of the dice. Only a fool would put her chips on tomorrow.

She thought about Jordan, how he had walked out. She thought about Carter going to New Zealand. For her the last line of the story was always the same. Plain and simple, nothing was forever.

No, she wasn't sure, but at the moment she didn't care. If the present moment was all she could count on, to hell with tomorrow.

"Tell me if you want me to stop," he said, his voice barely a whisper. "Tell me anything you want, and I'll do it."

Part of her wanted to play the odds. Part of her wanted to tell him, "Tell me you'll never leave," but she held back the words. She might be a lot of things she never was before—a vegetarian chef, a bookkeeper, a writer, an expectant mother—but she was no gambler.

In response, she pulled his head to hers.

Chapter Nine

Becky realized she was an avid fan of snowstorms. She liked the feeling of being safely cocooned inside a warm room, listening to a fire crackling in a stove while outside the wind howled and drifts of snow swirled.

So much had changed in just one night, she mused as she lay snug and cozy, curled up under the blankets. She found herself conceding that maybe, just maybe, she could make a place in her child's life for Carter. She wasn't sure what kind of place, or how large, but she and Carter were mature adults, weren't they? Mature adults compromised, didn't they? What if she started her catering business in Middlewood? The only reason she'd been considering moving to New York was so she wouldn't risk running into him. She didn't want a fly-by-night dad in her child's life. But what if he decided to curb his traveling, as he'd said when he'd first proposed in her kitchen? Wasn't it all about compromise?

Well, no. There was more to a relationship than that.

Wait a minute. A relationship? As in the two of them?

Well, why not? Maybe she couldn't depend on tomorrow, but she could stretch out today a little while longer, couldn't she? A lot longer if he did in fact compromise and didn't go off to New Zealand. No question about it, she could easily become accustomed to her new Live For Today attitude.

She remembered how she'd felt lying in his arms, all night long, first in front of the fire and then after they'd moved to the king-size bed. Dreamily, her eyes still closed, she rolled onto her side and reached across the mattress.

He wasn't there.

Her eyes shot open, and a searing pain sliced through her head. Sunlight streamed in through the blinds, making her wince. She forced herself to a sitting position, but a wave of dizziness sent her back to her pillow.

She realized that the heat she felt wasn't coming from the stove; at some time last night the power must have been restored. Or was the heat coming from her body? The glow she'd felt upon awakening had suddenly become a sweat bath. And it wasn't the wind she heard in the distance; outside the cabin the plows were clearing away the snow. Wrong again, she thought. The noise she heard was the buzzing in her ears.

She lay back and draped her arm over her eyes, willing the pain to go away. She must have fallen back to sleep, because the next thing she remembered was Carter standing in the doorway. The only thing she was fully conscious of was the throbbing in her head.

"Hey, sleepyhead," he said, kicking off his snow-covered boots. "It's a beautiful morning out there—one of those days that makes you glad just to be alive. There's not a cloud in sight, and most of the roads have been cleared. I brought in your boots, but if you still can't get them on, at least I won't have to carry you cross-country. The tow truck's already been here, and I've moved the car out front.'' He hung up his coat and sat down on the bed. ''Of course, we don't have to leave right away. I could be persuaded to stick around for an hour…or two.'' He smiled at her. ''You know, we should consider coming back here sometime. It's the kind of place that makes you want to sit in a rocker on the porch, sipping a glass of wine while you watch the sunset. It would be just the two of us—'' he gently patted the bulge in her tummy ''—and of course, Junior.''

''The baby…'' she said in a weak voice.

He smoothed the hair from her forehead, then quickly pulled his hand away. ''You're so warm,'' he said, his voice suddenly taking on a worried tone. ''Do you feel okay?''

''It hurts…so much…''

''My God,'' he whispered, ''what have I done?''

''Not your fault…'' She wanted to say more, to reassure him that what had happened last night had nothing to do with what was happening now, but she couldn't speak…couldn't move…

Feeling like a rag doll, she was vaguely aware of him talking on the phone, then helping her get dressed. ''My legs,'' she moaned when he reached for her boots.

''I'm taking you to emergency. We'll be in Danbury in less than an hour.'' He picked up her boots. ''Don't move. I'm taking these to the car. I'll be back in a minute.''

''The bill,'' she said when he'd returned.

''No time. Besides, they have my credit card number at the front desk.'' As he'd done the night before, he wrapped her feet in his scarf and lifted her in his arms.

She squeezed her eyes shut and pressed her face against his chest as he carried her out to the car. "I called the hospital," he said, settling her into the passenger seat. "Dr. Boyd is there, making rounds. She's going to meet us in the ER."

The light was so bright through the windshield, she had to keep her eyes closed. "Breakfast," she murmured.

"We'll get you something to eat as soon as the doctor says it's okay."

"No, the guests...I have to make breakfast..." What was the matter with him? Why couldn't he understand that she had a job to do? She felt the tears trickle down her cheeks. "Why does it hurt so much? You're a doctor, Jordan. Make it better. Promise me you'll make it better." Why didn't he answer? Why didn't he ever answer? Then she remembered. Jordan was going away. Jordan didn't want her.

She didn't open her eyes until the car had pulled into a parking lot and come to a full stop. She saw an ambulance parked in front of an entranceway, heard sirens approaching in the distance.

"Becky?" The voice was Carter's. The door on her side of the car was open, and he was leaning in. "I'm going to lift you again. Are you ready?"

The bristles on his face grazed her cheek as he hoisted her into his arms. Why hadn't he shaved? she wondered through her haze. And then it all came back—the meeting in New York, the storm, the cabin...

The baby. Dear God, she could lose the baby.

"It'll be all right, won't it?" she asked, fighting back panic.

"Nothing is going to happen," he said as he hurried down the emergency corridor. "I won't let it."

* * *

After an interminable three hours, he was finally allowed to see her. She'd been moved to a private room and was lying on her side, her back to the door. He walked around the bed to face her and felt his heart drop. She was as pale as the sheets on the bed.

He forced himself to sound jovial. "Hey, princess. Hell of a way to get out of work."

"I'd offer you a cup of tea, but they said I should keep completely still. Lying like this on my side will help get the blood flowing to the placenta."

He swallowed hard. "Becky, I'm so sorry…I…"

"I know," she said softly when he faltered. "They made you leave. I told them I wanted you to stay with me in the emergency room, but they wouldn't listen."

"No, I'm not talking about that." It was his fault she was lying here, and he'd be damned if he allowed her to think she was in any way to blame. "Last night—"

"Will you wipe that sheepish look off your face? I know what you're thinking and you're wrong. Last night had nothing to do with what's happening now. I know you'd like to think the entire world is your responsibility, but believe it or not, some things are beyond your control."

He didn't respond. He looked down at the floor, unwilling to meet her eyes.

"I wish you could see yourself. You look ridiculous, Carter. Sorry, but you just don't wear guilt well. You have to be Jewish to pull it off with any credibility."

"But if I hadn't—"

"Enough already. Come closer, you idiot."

Tentatively he approached the bed. She looked so frail, he was afraid she might bruise if he so much as touched her. "You're the one lying in a hospital bed, and here you are comforting me,'' he said, not trusting his voice to remain steady.

''You're the one who drove like a maniac to get me here in record time, and now my blood pressure is back to normal. My fever is broken and I feel so much better.'' She reached for his hand. ''One of the nurses said that because of the storm all the trains had stopped running. What would have happened to me if you hadn't been there? Thank you, Carter. Thank you for being there and for knowing what to do.''

She was something else. This whole catastrophe was his fault, and she was thanking him. He felt his throat tighten. ''I have no doubt you would have been okay. You're a lot more resourceful than you give yourself credit for.''

''Are you kidding? Last night I was one big panic attack. I was sure we were going to turn into human Popsicles, but you kept assuring me that everything would turn out all right. And it did.'' She patted the spot next to her on the bed. ''Come here. I have something to say to you.'' She waited for him to sit down before she continued. ''I've been doing a lot of thinking, and I realize I might have been too stringent in my decision to exclude you from our baby's future. You keep proving over and over that you're caring and responsible, and up to now I've been too pigheaded to admit it.''

He cleared his throat. ''I've also been doing a lot of thinking about the future—yours and mine, not just the baby's.'' He held out his hand when she started to protest. ''No, hear me out. I know you're not ready to accept my proposal, but rest assured, one of these days you're going to change your mind. I'm a patient man and I can wait. In the meantime, I want you to know you can depend on me. From now on I intend to be there for you, every step of the way.''

''I don't understand. What are you saying?''

''I'm saying we got lucky. Your blood pressure is back to normal and your condition has stabilized. It's as if we've been given a second chance. I've been thinking about the New Zealand job. I'm considering not going. If everything works out, I intend to stay right here with you and the baby.''

There was a long pause. ''Right. If everything works out. That's big of you, Carter. If I don't lose the baby, I'll keep your words in mind.''

Shoot. There she goes again, he thought. Purposely twisting his words to make him the bad guy. ''Come on, Becky, don't be like that. You know I want us to be a family more than anything. After last night—''

''I hope you don't think it means anything,'' she said dryly.

''Pardon?''

''Don't you remember? Those were the words you used at your apartment. Now I'm throwing them back at you. Leave me alone, Carter. I'm tired and I want to get some sleep. Sorry if I've damaged your ego, but right now the baby is my only concern.''

He stared at her, dumbfounded. For the life of him he couldn't figure out what he'd said to set her off. He wanted to get to the heart of the matter, but he held back, remembering the doctor's warning about stress. ''You're right,'' he said reluctantly. ''You need your rest. I'm going home to change, but I'm coming right back.'' He leaned over to brush his lips against hers, but she turned her head away.

And he thought *he* had commitment issues. He'd told

her he wanted to be there for her, and she'd turned off faster than a firefly trapped in a jar.

Disheartened, he left the room, trying to force his hurt feelings aside. All that mattered was Becky. Becky and the baby. He thought about how close he'd come to losing them. Not once but twice, yesterday and today.

He shuddered, trying not to dwell on the what-ifs. Didn't these things happen in threes? Hell, he was beginning to sound like Starr.

"Carter!"

Speak of the devil. He turned around to see her running down the corridor. She approached him and immediately began bombarding him with questions.

He led her to the row of chairs against the wall. "I can't tell you any more than what I told you on the phone. Except that she's fine now. She's sleeping." He looked away. "She could have lost the baby, Starr. She could have—"

"Don't even say it. Everything will turn out all right, you hear?"

In spite of the situation he forced a small smile. "Been reading those tea leaves?"

"Laugh if you want, but you'll see I was right. I have every intention of saying, 'I told you so.'"

"I certainly hope so," he said gravely. "Thanks for bringing her things, by the way. She'll want her own toiletries."

"Have you called her mother?"

"No one was home and I didn't want to leave a message. I'll call again later."

The sound of footsteps caused him to look up. Dr. Boyd approached him, and he rose to his feet. "How is she?" he asked, dispensing with preliminary chitchat. "She says she feels better, but she looks so tired."

Dr. Boyd gave him a reassuring smile. "She's doing fine. Nevertheless, I want to keep her in the hospital for a few days, just to keep an eye on her. If she remains stable, I'll release her. But she's going to need complete bed rest, maybe for the duration of the pregnancy. Is there someone who can take care of her?"

"I can," both Carter and Starr answered simultaneously.

"Don't be silly," Starr said. "You have a job."

"And you don't? Becky told me that the B and B is busier than ever. Look, right now my schedule is pretty flexible. I want to bring her back to my place."

"But you still go to meetings," Starr protested. "She can't be left alone."

Carter turned to the doctor. "What about a nurse?"

"Becky's blood pressure needs to be checked daily, but you can rent a monitor from the hospital pharmacy. Outside of that and weekly office visits, she doesn't require any special medical treatment. Remember, the key words are 'bed rest' and 'no stress.' Her preeclampsia is mild and can be managed at home, providing she has someone to look after her. If hiring a nurse is her only alternative, I'll arrange it. But what about her mother? Becky mentioned that she lives nearby. Maybe Becky could move back home for a while. Of course, this is something you'll need to discuss with her."

"Does she have to lie in bed the whole time?" Starr asked. "Can she get up to go to the bathroom? Can she sit up to read?"

"She can leave her bed to tend to her hygiene, and I still need to see her at the office for her weekly blood tests, but that's it. And yes, she can sit up."

Dr. Boyd talked a while longer, detailing the management of Becky's condition. "If she follows these instructions,'' she concluded, ''she'll greatly increase her chances of carrying to term.''

After Dr. Boyd left to continue on her rounds, Carter gave Starr a wry smile. ''Becky's mother? I don't think so. The woman is a walking stress machine.''

Starr's face grew somber. ''Seriously, Carter, the B and B is the best place for Becky. If I have to go out, Christina can stay with her. Becky will never be alone.''

''She'll feel like a freeloader. After all, she's your employee.''

''She's my friend.''

''All this is academic. In the end, the decision is hers. Not that she has much choice. There's no way she'll go to her mother's, and she can't stay at David's. Hannah teaches during the day.'' He sighed. ''She'll agree to stay at the B and B, but she's not going to like it. You know how she hates feeling dependent.''

''As you said, it's all academic. She has no choice.''

Carter stood up. ''Are you planning to stay here a while? I'm going home to shower and change. I'll be back as soon as I can, but she might wake up while I'm gone.''

On the drive home he debated stopping at his mother's. He hadn't called her since he'd been back from Denver, and he knew she'd be eager to see him. He decided against it. He didn't want to be away from Becky any longer than he had to. Besides, dealing with his mother was difficult at the best of times, never mind when he was feeling so low.

Back at his apartment he threw his keys down on the credenza, then checked his answering machine for messages. He'd been collecting his voice mail daily since he'd left for Denver, but the flashing light indicated that new messages had been left since yesterday.

The first was from David. *Where are you? My mother*

phoned and she's frantic. Last night she called the B and B, but Starr told her that Becky wasn't there. What's this about you and Becky getting stranded in the storm? Call me.

Carter frowned. When was Gertie not frantic? He knew he had to call her, and he dreaded what was coming. After what he had to say, she would probably call out the National Guard. First he impregnates her daughter, then he kidnaps her, then he nearly gets her killed, and then he lands her in the hospital. In spite of what Becky had said, nothing could convince him that her condition wasn't his fault.

The second message was from his mother. *Where are you? I heard you were back. Wendy told me that you and your ex-colleague had lunch in New York. It seems that Wendy and his wife keep in touch. And speaking of Wendy, why have you been ignoring her calls? I've also been hearing some pretty nasty rumors about you and that Roth girl. I hope you aren't considering doing something stupid. Call me.*

Something stupid? Sorry, too late. He'd already filled his quota.

Becky sat propped up in bed, reading a magazine. She glanced at the clock on the wall. Almost one. She was being released first thing in the morning, and Starr would be here shortly to bring her a change of clothing. She knew why Starr couldn't come by tomorrow, and it filled her with guilt. These days her employer was spending her mornings in the kitchen with Christina.

And while they were on the subject of guilt…Becky knew that Carter had rearranged his schedule so he could spend more time at the hospital. Right now he was at a meeting, but she'd had a hard time convincing him to go.

She also knew that even if Starr could come by tomorrow, Carter would still insist on driving Becky home.

Being around Starr and Carter was like having mismatched parents. They were always at odds with each other, yet both were so concerned. Carter had wanted Becky to stay at his apartment after her release, intending to hire someone to take care of her when he had to go out, but Starr wouldn't hear of it. Why should Becky stay with a stranger when she had a friend who was willing to help?

Both choices filled Becky with dismay. She didn't want to be dependent on Carter, and how could she continue to live at the B and B without working?

But what was the alternative? Stay at her mother's as Dr. Boyd had suggested?

"What do you mean you have to stay in bed the whole time?" Gertie had asked earlier that day when she'd come by to visit. "That's exactly how you got into this mess in the first place. Come home. I'll make chicken soup, gefilte fish, a little chopped liver...I'll have you back on your feet in no time."

"Ma, you're missing the point. I have to stay *off* my feet. Besides, have you forgotten I'm lacto-ovo?"

"It doesn't matter what you are, you still have to eat. And when you're better, we'll go shopping. Just because you're having a baby doesn't mean you should dress like a *shlump*."

Becky had felt like climbing the walls. Her talk with Bubbe had helped her understand why Gertie was the way she was, but just because Becky now saw her mother in a different light didn't mean she could live with her.

She put down the magazine and stared out the window, her thoughts returning to Carter. Over the past few days he'd remained by her side almost constantly. If they had allowed him to move in a cot, she was sure he'd have set up camp right next to her bed.

Good Lord, she hoped he wasn't planning on moving into the B and B! She could just see him with Starr, their heads bent over a deck of Tarot cards as they tried to map out the future. In spite of herself she smiled. "Poor, helpless Becky," she could hear Carter saying. "Whatever will become of her?"

She tried to imagine what it would be like living with him—when she *wasn't* so helpless. Since the night they'd spent at The Red Barn, he'd proposed to her daily. But a relationship was one thing, marriage another. She had her reasons for not accepting his proposal, and just because she'd let down her guard that night at the motel didn't mean those reasons had disappeared.

The first reason, she recapped, was Carter himself. No matter how her feelings for him had grown—and she couldn't deny that they had—what he was offering was illusory. There was no such thing as a happy ending, no such thing as forever. Just because he was singing one tune today didn't mean he'd be singing the same one tomorrow.

She recalled what he'd said to her the first day in the hospital. "If everything works out, I'm not going to New Zealand." No matter how she turned the words around in her head, the meaning was always the same. His being there for her was conditional. If she lost the baby, he was history.

She hadn't told him why his words had angered her. She'd realized that in a crazy way he made sense. Everything in life was conditional. Everything was subject to change.

The second reason—

A loud knock broke into her thoughts. "Come in," she said. "It's open."

—was standing in the doorway.

The second reason was about trust. She stared wordlessly, her heart pounding in her ears.

"This must be a first," Jordan said, crossing the room. "You're speechless."

Lean and muscular, he was just as she remembered. He wore his dark curly hair cropped short, and his eyes, as blue and cold as a clear winter sky, were sharp and assessing. She forced herself to remain calm. "What are you doing here?"

"You could at least pretend to be happy to see me," he said, sitting down in the chair by the bed. "So what have you been up to this past year?" His gaze swept over her body. "Never mind, no need to answer. I can see you've been busy."

"What do you want, Jordan?"

"Now don't go off on a rampage. I only came by to bring you some news."

"You're getting married," she said flatly. The last news he'd delivered was that he was running off with the redhead. Wouldn't marriage be the next step?

He gave her a look that meant she'd hit the nail on the head. What did she care, anyway? And why would he think she'd be interested? He had some nerve, coming here like this. She studied him coolly. "How did you know I was here?"

"I ran into your mother in the lobby. Last month I applied for a surgical residency here at Danbury Hospital, and today I had my interview."

I should have known my mother was behind this, Becky thought. "Remind me to thank her," she said, not bothering to hide her sarcasm.

"Just so you know, she didn't want me bothering you. She made it sound as if you were on your deathbed. But then she told me you were being released tomorrow, and I figured, how sick could you be? So here I am. Aren't you going to wish me luck? If I get accepted into the program, we'll be neighbors. I'll be moving to your neck of the woods."

"I'm sure you and your new wife will be very happy," Becky said coldly. So much for her remaining in Middlewood. How could she live in the same vicinity as her ex and his redhead? "What was her name again? Bambi?"

"Barbie. But I'm not seeing her anymore. You were right about one thing, though. I'm getting married. You're going to laugh when I tell you this. She's an old friend of yours, Carol Weinstein."

Weinstein...the name sounded familiar. Then she remembered. They'd been in the same class in grade school. Friends? Hardly. Carol's father was some kind of big-shot movie producer, and Carol had made it clear that she and Becky were in different leagues.

Apparently, Carol had broadened her social sphere. Either that or Jordan had charmed himself into hers. Either way, Becky knew that where the money was, Jordan's nose followed. "I gather Carol doesn't want to leave Middlewood."

He shrugged. "Why shouldn't we live there? It's a great little town, and it's close to Danbury. It's not as if this hospital is a mom-and-pop shop. They have a great residency program."

"I'm sure. Thank you, Jordan, for coming by and sharing all this with me. It's been a pleasure seeing you again, but could you just leave?"

"Come on, Rebecca, give me a break. I came here to make amends. I was planning on calling you, but when your mother mentioned you were here, I figured there was no time like the present. Telling you about my marriage isn't the reason I came. I came to tell you I intend to pay back every cent of what I owe your father. I want to move forward. You know, get on with life. Who knows? Maybe in time you and I can even be friends.''

Friends? When pigs flew they could be friends.

He laughed. "Speechless again. Twice in one day, must be a record. So how do you want to go about this? Should I mail the checks to you or directly to your father?''

Never in a million years had she expected him to repay that loan. If he meant what he said, she would have one less financial burden. She eyed him suspiciously. "You must want something pretty badly. Level with me. What's going on?''

His gaze met hers, and, for the first time in as long as she'd known him, in his eyes she saw regret. "I know you despise me,'' he said quietly, "and I don't blame you. What I did was despicable. I could spend the rest of my life apologizing, and it wouldn't be enough. But let me ask you something, and I want you to answer truthfully. Did you ever love me?''

The question took her off guard, and she had to take a moment to compose herself. "I married you, didn't I?'' she said, unsure of where this conversation was headed.

His expression was wistful. "We were so young, what did we know? We knew nothing of life, nothing of the world outside. We had similar backgrounds and we did what was expected of us, no questions asked. Our parents had our whole future sewn up before our second date.'' He chuckled. "Your mother wasn't thrilled that my father was just a butcher in the kosher deli. Then I told her I was going to be a doctor, and she started planning the wedding.''

"But I was happy," Becky said in a meek voice. She hated the way she was feeling, hated the way she knew she sounded. Whiny. Pathetic. But she couldn't help herself. She'd lost a part of herself the night he walked out.

"Were you? Be honest, Becky. You were unhappy the whole time we were married." When she didn't answer, he stood up. "Well, I've said my piece. Let me know what you decide. Should I send the checks to you or your father?"

"My father," she said without hesitation. She wanted nothing more to do with Jordan. In a way, though, she was glad he had come here rather than call her. His visit had given her a sense of closure. There was one thing, though, one small thing she had to know before she could finally shut that door. "Why now, Jordan? What made you decide to pay back the loan?"

He flashed her that shy smile, the one in which only the corners of his lips curled up, the one that used to make her heart turn over. "It's my fiancée. She insists. She wants to make an honest man of me."

Becky fought to keep herself from laughing. Honest? Apparently, he still had his own interpretation of what the word meant. Borrow from Peter to pay back Paul, she thought, as she watched him leave. In this case, however, he didn't have to borrow the money. He was marrying it.

She picked up her magazine but found she couldn't concentrate. She kept replaying Jordan's visit in her mind. Maybe he had his own definition of honesty, but one thing he'd said was true. The whole time they'd been married, she'd never been happy.

But he'd been wrong when he'd suggested she hadn't loved him. The proof was in her pain. Pain she'd felt when he'd walked out on her, a year ago this March.

She put down the magazine. Something was different.

It was too quiet in the room. All she could hear was the ticking of the clock on the wall.

She looked around. Everything was exactly as it had been before Jordan's visit. Nevertheless, she had the feeling something was missing. Something had changed.

It was the pain, she realized. It was no longer there.

Chapter Ten

The numbers on the computer screen all added up. There, Becky thought with satisfaction. If I ever decide to give up cooking, I can always become an accountant.

But giving up cooking was precisely what she'd done. Dr. Boyd had given her the go-ahead on resuming some of her activities, but had told her to stay off her feet as much as possible. Nothing strenuous, she'd warned. And no cooking. At least I no longer have to remain in bed all day, Becky thought gratefully.

Carter had brought up the computer from the study so she could do the books, and had set it up under the window. Converted into a sitting area, the alcove now accommodated a small sofa, a credenza, a TV and a VCR, all confiscated from the living room downstairs.

Over the past several weeks a routine had set in, with Carter pampering her shamelessly. He claimed he didn't have much going on at work right now, but Becky knew he'd had to juggle his schedule. Starr and Christina, too, doted on her, making sure she didn't exert herself.

Knowing that her pregnancy was high risk, Becky considered each new day without complications a blessing. But even though her condition was stable, she always felt tired and her back ached constantly. No surprise there, given her size. A piano, Carter had called her. She felt more like a hotel. Her symptoms were normal, Dr. Boyd had assured her, but Becky found it difficult to remain cheerful. It wouldn't be so bad if she could get out of the house for something other than her weekly appointments, but being stuck inside day after day only worsened her mood.

"Becky?" Starr stood outside Becky's open door. "Can you come to the dining room? I want to show you something. I'll help you down the stairs."

Becky looked at her with curiosity. This must be important. Starr knew that Becky had to spend as much time off her feet as possible, which meant no stairs unless absolutely necessary. In fact, Starr could have been a drill sergeant, the way she made sure that Becky followed Dr. Boyd's orders.

"Surprise!" came a chorus of voices as she and Starr entered the dining room. Sitting at the long central table were Becky's parents, David and Hannah, Bubbe, Christina—and Carter. Starr was grinning like a cat with milk on its whiskers.

"What's going on?" Becky asked.

"Ask your boyfriend," Christina said, smiling widely.

Carter stood up and guided Becky to the seat next to his. "Welcome to the annual Starr DeVries Easter/Passover celebration."

"The annual Starr DeVries Easter/Passover *vegetarian* celebration," Starr added.

"Only in America." This from Bubbe.

"Annual?" Becky asked. "Exactly when did this tradition begin?"

"Just now," Starr said, "but we've been preparing all afternoon. Besides the traditional matzo ball soup—made with vegetable broth, of course—there's matzo lasagna, matzo pizza and matzo farfel pie. I never realized you could do so much with matzo!" She motioned to the table. "I even got out my special china. Your mother said that special dishes and silverware are all part of the seder meal."

The table was formally set with a white lace cloth and linen napkins, candles glowing at each end. Becky shook her head. "I had no idea. I didn't hear a thing."

"Your mother and grandmother have been here for hours. They did most of the cooking. This was all Carter's doing, by the way. He arranged everything. He even decided to make it a surprise. He said you could probably use some fun, being cooped up so much."

Carter shrugged dismissively. "I was afraid that if you went home for Passover, you'd probably overdo it. So I brought the holiday to you."

Becky smiled at him, her heart filled with gratitude. In spite of her constant complaining about her family, he knew what they meant to her. She looked around the table, and a knot rose in her throat. These people were her family and her friends. Everyone here had helped make this happen. "I...don't know what to say."

"Enough with the talk," Bubbe said. "*Nu*, when do we start? I'm getting hungry. Reading the Haggadah should only take an hour, but if we don't start already, we won't get to eat until Purim."

After the ritual blessing over the wine, Aaron began reciting from the Passover prayer book. "Since Christina is the youngest, she should ask the four questions," he said, looking up from the book. "Becky's been doing it for a long time now, but in a few years that's going to change permanently."

David smiled at Hannah with pride, then looked back at Becky. "What do you say we start a pool on who's going to deliver first?"

Hannah shot him a look of reproof. "What do you think this is, a horse race? I have to say, though, if I were a betting person, I'd put my money on my coming in first. This baby doesn't stay still for a minute."

Becky laughed. She recalled comparing her own baby to an Olympic gymnast. Lately, however, she felt as if she were carrying an entire soccer team.

"Uh, excuse me," Christina interjected, her brow creased with anxiety, "but what four questions are you talking about? What do I have to do?"

"These are questions that were designed to encourage participation in the seder," Becky explained. "They're usually recited by the youngest person at the table." Christina seemed reluctant to speak in front of the group, so Becky added, "I think, however, we can dispense with the normal routine. This isn't exactly a normal Passover." Smiling, she gestured around the room. Scattered everywhere were pastel-colored Easter decorations. She picked up the prayer book and read aloud, "Why is this day different from all others?"

"In Hebrew," Bubbe said. "You didn't go to Hebrew school for nothing."

Becky gently reminded her grandmother that she didn't know how to read Hebrew. It was David who had attended Jewish school, not Becky. A thought occurred to her and she looked up at her father. "Daddy, how come I didn't have a bat mitzvah?" It wasn't the first time the question had crossed her mind, but it was the first time she'd been inclined to mention it.

"A bat mitzvah? Since when—"

"You know we're not religious," Gertie interrupted.

"Ma, what are you talking about? What about David? You sent him to Hebrew school, and he had a bar mitzvah."

"That's different. He's a boy."

Becky rolled her eyes. "What century are you living in? I'm surprised you and Daddy didn't provide a dowry for me when you put me on the marriage block."

Gertie pointed her finger at Becky. "All the time with issues. Just once, why can't we sit down to a meal without you making a big *megilla?* Young people today think they have all the answers. You think it's easy raising a family? Just wait till you have your baby."

I'm the one making a big *megilla?* Becky was about to reply, when she remembered what her grandmother had told her. Gertie was the way she was because of her upbringing. And, Becky surmised, Bubbe was the way she was because of her own mother, and so on, and so on...

She looked at her grandmother's happy face. Then again, she thought, there was something to be said for tradition. Bubbe always said it made you feel connected to something larger than yourself. Becky felt the baby stir, and once again she found herself marveling at the miracle of life.

She began to read aloud phonetically: *"Mah nishtanah ha-lahylah ha-zeh..."*

After the recounting of the story of Exodus, the meal was served. When everyone had eaten, they ended the ceremony with prayers, then sat at the table for another hour, talking and laughing. When both Becky and Hannah yawned, Gertie announced it was time to clean up, and everyone except the two expectant mothers helped clear the table. After the dishes had been put away, the last of the leftovers packed in foil, the family embarked upon a lengthy goodbye, which was accompanied with hugs and kisses, ending with Becky promising to call her mother first thing in the morning.

Carter helped Becky up the stairs. "Tired, princess?" he asked when she plopped down on the sofa and closed her eyes. He sat down beside her and eased her into his arms.

"Just a little." She leaned her head against his shoulder. "I still can't believe you arranged the whole thing. Imagine, Carter Prescott, III, arranging a Passover seder! What would your mother say?"

"She'd probably tell me to take a pill," he joked.

"Oh, you." Becky swatted him playfully. "Talking about your mother, why didn't she come?"

He paused. "She didn't come because I didn't ask her."

"Why not? It was a family meal, and she's going to be the baby's grandmother. Soon we'll all be related. Through blood, that is," she added quickly. These days Carter was still proposing and she was still refusing. Except for the little tiff she'd had with her mother, the evening had been wonderful. She didn't want to spoil it with talk of marriage.

Apparently, her blunder had gone past him, because he let out a sarcastic laugh and said, "My mother wouldn't have come if I'd sent her an engraved invitation."

Knowing that his relationship with his mother was strained, she proceeded with caution. "Parents can be a pain, but remember, your mother is the only mother you'll ever have. Tonight convinced me that you feel the same way I do about family, so don't try to deny it. You wouldn't have done what you did if you felt otherwise.''

He began caressing her belly through the fabric of her skirt. "I'm not denying it. I feel very strongly about my family.''

She felt a wave of heat flow through her. It wasn't what she'd meant by *family,* but she had no objection. She was surprised he'd made the gesture in the first place, not that she was complaining. Since she'd been home from the hospital, he'd been treating her like a china doll, acting as if he were afraid she would break if he so much as breathed on her.

Just because they couldn't make love didn't mean they couldn't be a little physical, did it? All she had to do was raise her head slightly, tilt it a little to the right, move her lips close to his...

She thought back to when she had cornered him in the elevator in his building, the night it had all begun. Tonight, however, was different. She didn't make a move. Without champagne to bolster her, she was a coward, plain and simple.

This is crazy, she chastised herself. Here she was in her eighth month of pregnancy, obsessing about sex. I thought it wasn't supposed to work that way, she mused, amazed at how easily her body could betray her. Either she was so tired she couldn't see straight or she was having fantasies. Trust her hormones to have a mind of their own.

"Speaking about family," he said, his voice tinged with amusement, "since when are you the dutiful daughter?''

Acting like a dutiful daughter wasn't foremost on her mind, but it was obvious he couldn't take a hint. "Since I realized my mother can't help the way she is," she answered. "I might not always agree with her—okay, I *never* agree with her—but I know she means well and I respect her opinion.''

''Come on, you can't be in the same room with her for two minutes before you start arguing. What was that business about Hebrew school? I never even knew you cared about all that. Then later, after the meal, she kept bringing up the baby shower you're having on Sunday. Why is she so against it?''

''My mother believes that accepting gifts before the birth will attract evil spirits. It's an old Jewish superstition. I don't put any stock in it, but I understand why she thinks that way. She can be just as traditional as Bubbe. As for Hebrew school, I never really cared about all that until recently. Having a baby makes you look at things differently, I suppose. I just want our daughter to have the same opportunities a boy would have. Did you know that the bat mitzvah ceremony is a recent development? It was always considered unnecessary, since women didn't have the same rights as men.''

''I'm confused. Are you talking about women's rights or religion?''

''I guess both. On one hand, it irks me that religion can be so male-dominated. Yet on the other hand, I think it's important for our daughter to grow up knowing her heritage. How else can she learn the importance of family?''

''You're saying you want her to have a bat mitzvah,'' Carter stated. ''Or a bar mitzvah, if it's a boy.''

''You sound surprised.'' Something in his tone bothered her. She looked up at him, trying to read his face. ''What is it? What are you thinking?''

''What I think,'' he said, stretching leisurely, ''is that we've both had enough family for one night—in person and in conversation. It's been a long day, and you need your rest.''

It was back to the china-doll syndrome. "I'm fine, Carter. Will you relax?"

He kissed her on the forehead and stood up. "I'll be by tomorrow with more movies."

Disappointment filled her. All through dinner she'd been refilling his wineglass, dropping hints, hoping to loosen him up. How was she supposed to practice her Let's Live For Today lifestyle if he refused to cooperate?

Let's live for today, my foot, she thought. She could make light of her feelings all she wanted, but nothing could dispute the fact that she was falling for him, heart and soul. Sure, sometimes his constant doting got to be a little annoying, but she knew he was that way because he cared. He brought her flowers daily, along with a constant stream of books and movies, and he never seemed to mind her mood swings, taking them all in stride.

More importantly, over these past weeks they'd talked for hours on end about everything under the sun. *Almost* everything, she reminded herself. His marriage was still off-limits. But Becky understood this. After all, she had no desire to talk about Jordan. In fact, as far as she was concerned, the entire subject of marriage was taboo.

Carter arrived back at his apartment after eleven. He'd just hung up his coat when the buzzer rang. By his standards it wasn't late—he was used to burning the midnight oil—but this was Middlewood, a sleepy little town that retired early. Even on weekends, restaurants pulled in their awnings somewhere around ten.

The voice over the intercom caused him to swear under his breath. Wendy had been leaving him messages for months. He knew he should have returned her calls; it would have been the polite thing to do to. But when it came to his ex-wife, he didn't exactly feel like being polite.

He buzzed her into the building. Moments later she was knocking on his door. Muttering to himself, he pulled it open. "So, what brings you to Middlewood? Slumming it?"

"I see you haven't lost your sarcasm. Aren't you going to ask me in?"

"Suit yourself." He turned his back and headed into the living room.

She pulled off her gloves and put them in her pocket. "Aren't you going to take my coat?"

"No." He didn't want to give her the impression that she'd be staying. "You have five minutes," he said coldly.

She opened her coat, revealing a low-cut sweater and short tight skirt, then sat down on the couch. "I suppose you're wondering why I came."

Here she was, alone with him in his apartment, at eleven o'clock in the evening. He let his eyes roam over her. Tall and willowy with sleek blond hair, she'd always been able to turn a man's head with just a flick of the eyes, a hint of a smile. She wanted something, and she intended to use all the ammunition she had.

He sat in the wing chair across from her. "I have no doubt you're going tell me."

"Believe it or not, I came here to tell you I'm sorry. I was wrong for running off the way I did." She lowered her voice. "Wrong for a lot of things."

Wendy wrong? She'd rather be run over by a bus than admit she'd made a mistake. He regarded her warily. "After all this time you've suddenly decided you're sorry? Spill it, Wendy. What do you want?"

"My, my, so hostile. I was hoping you'd be over all

that by now. Which is precisely why I'm here. I don't want us to go on hating each other. I know you think—''

"You have no idea what I think," he snarled. "This might come as a shock, but I don't sit around all day pining for you." He knew he was being rude, but dammit, what made her think she could come waltzing back and expect him to be understanding?

She snatched up her purse and made a gesture to rise. "Never mind. I can see this is going nowhere."

One thing about Wendy, she'd always had a dramatic flair. "Sit down," he said, knowing damn well she wouldn't leave without first presenting her case. It was the lawyer in her. "I'm sorry if I'm a little abrupt. It's been a long day and I'm tired. Go ahead. I'm listening."

She sat down again and smoothed her skirt. "I'll get straight to the point. I want to have a baby."

And this concerned him how? "Congratulations," he said dryly. "Don't forget to send me a cigar."

"Please, Carter, I'm being serious. I'm talking about my biological clock."

"For Chrissake, Wendy, you're only in your thirties." He eyed her with a critical squint. "Did you get fired?"

She let out that nasal high-pitched laugh, the one she always made whenever she found something amusing. "Hardly. In fact, the firm offered me a promotion." Her expression sobered. "My priorities, however, have changed. My career doesn't seem to be all that important anymore. There's something to be said about baking bread, attending Little League games—even suburbia. I've decided I want the whole package, picket fence and all."

The whole package. Funny, those were the words he'd said to Becky when he'd proposed to her at the Café St. Gabriel.

Then it hit him, and he felt like a moron. He should have seen it coming. She wanted a reconciliation. "Wendy—"

She put out her hand as if to ward him off. "No, let me talk. I've been doing a lot of thinking about the child we could have had. I was hoping we could try again. A complete change of scenery might be just what we need to start over. I hear New Zealand is beautiful and unspoiled with a wonderfully temperate climate. It would be the perfect place to start a family. Carter Prescott, IV— doesn't it have a nice ring?"

For a moment he thought he saw something in her eyes, something he'd never seen in them before. Sadness? Regret? He quickly dismissed the notion. He doubted if she'd ever had an honest emotion in her life. "You can't be serious," he said flatly.

"Why not? I always knew we would get back together. I just didn't know when. We understand each other, Carter. We travel in the same circles. Our parents grew up together, for heaven's sake. Our mothers belong to all the same clubs."

Was she delusional? Did she think these past years apart were just an extended vacation? "Why now?" he asked, curious in spite of his shock.

She leaned back and crossed her legs. "Until now I had no reason to hurry. I always believed we had plenty of time. You had your career and I had mine. But I made sure I kept in touch with you—kept the embers burning, so to speak. I knew you'd come around sooner or later." She smiled sweetly. "But now circumstances have forced the issue. You're going away for two years."

It didn't add up. She'd waited this long to start a family, so what was another two years? No matter how hard he tried, he couldn't imagine her living in New Zealand, never mind leaving Manhattan. Besides, their marriage had been a dismal failure; why would she even consider going down that road again? He didn't flatter himself by thinking she was still in love with him. She wanted marriage so that she could start a family; surely a woman with her looks and savvy could find someone else to fit the bill. "Forget it Wendy. Find someone else to wind your biological clock."

She shook her head as if tired of explaining the obvious. "Do you think it's easy finding someone with all the right attributes? Call me an elitist, I don't care. But you and I, we're cut from the same cloth. Oh, I considered other men, all of them successful, but just thinking of the words *nouveau riche* was enough to make me ill. Old money, however, has a certain feel, a certain smell. It's authentic, it's pure and it's in our genes. I want our children to have all the advantages. Call it good breeding, if you want. Of course, I realize there's more to marriage than having children." She cast him a suggestive look. "If I recall correctly, you used to leave our bed whistling."

She was delusional, all right. Now she was inventing things. "Whatever we had has been gone for a long time," he said, reminding himself to be tactful.

She smiled smugly. "You don't really believe that. I saw the way you were looking at me when I first sat down. Admit it, that part hasn't changed. But don't you see? Everything else has. I'm different now. *You're* different. We were so young when we got married—what did we know? This time we'll try harder. We'll make it work."

Becky had an expression, "Forgive but don't forget." He knew that what Wendy had done would haunt him forever. Maybe in time he could forgive her, but as long as he kept breathing, he knew he could never forget.

Maybe she did feel regret. He wasn't sure. One thing he did know was that she was stuck in some kind of social warp and believed he belonged there with her. He almost felt sorry for her. In fact, he did feel sorry for her. Anything else he might have felt had died a long time ago.

"It's not going to happen," he said quietly.

"But I told you, I don't mind living abroad. And I wouldn't mind your working on-site after we returned."

"In any event, I won't be going to New Zealand. In fact, I plan on cutting down on all my traveling."

Where had that come from? When had thinking about changing his lifestyle actually become a plan? Wendy claimed to have changed her priorities; apparently, so had he. For some peculiar reason it had taken his ex-wife to make him see clearly. With gut-wrenching certainty, he realized he wanted to stay here with Becky, no matter what lay ahead for them.

"What about the partnership?" Wendy asked. "Your mother said—"

"My mother says a lot of things."

Her mouth twisted into a sneer. "I see. It's that Roth girl, the one you got pregnant. So you *are* considering marrying her. Support the child if you feel you have to, but don't do this, Carter. She's not one of us. Don't ruin both our lives because of one stupid mistake."

Ah. Now it made sense. It was Becky's pregnancy that had prompted Wendy to come here today. He didn't have to question how she'd found out. She was in cahoots with his mother, wasn't she?

My biological clock, she'd said. That was a load of manure. Until recently she'd believed she had all the time in the world. Until she'd learned of Becky's pregnancy, she'd never had any intention of chasing him down.

"Yes," he said.

"Yes, what?"

"Yes, it's 'that Roth girl.' Yes, I'm going to marry her—if she'll have me."

"You haven't changed at all," Wendy retorted. "You keep making one mistake after another. Let me tell you something, as far as mistakes are concerned, you're about to make a doubleheader—first by turning me down and second by marrying that girl. I told Eleanor you'd never go for it."

"And you were right. Congratulations. Being right was always your biggest passion." Suddenly tired of the whole conversation, he stood up, expecting her to do the same.

She didn't disappoint him. "Go ahead, marry her," she spat as she stormed toward the door. "But at least be honest with yourself. The only reason you're drawn to her is because you think she needs you. She makes you feel important. Admit it, our marriage ended because I wouldn't be your clinging vine. How long do you think it'll be before she gets tired of living just to stroke your ego?"

She pulled on her gloves. "And I'll tell you something else. If you give up working on-site, you'll start to rot. How long will it take before you get tired of being tied down? I know you, Carter. You've got itchy feet. How long will it be before you leave your little tramp to go back on the road?"

When Carter walked through Becky's door on Sunday morning, he was carrying a large box wrapped in shiny gold foil and tied with a bright-blue bow.

"You have to stop giving me things," Becky scolded, but secretly she was delighted. Being around Carter was like being a kid at Hanukkah. He was always bringing her presents, like a handcrafted thimble, or a book on the migratory habits of birds. "Little nothings," he called them. The gifts weren't expensive or even things she needed; he brought them to keep her spirits up, and he always succeeded.

This box, however, was too large to be one of his little nothings. "It's tall, but it's too skinny to be a new computer," she said, eyeing it suspiciously. "Unless it's a laptop. Please tell me you didn't, Carter."

"I didn't," he said, setting it onto the floor. "Not yet, anyway." He sat down next to her on the sofa. "This is a gift for your baby shower. Go ahead, open it."

"If it's for my shower, I should probably wait." She wasn't planning to wait, but he was so cute when he became impatient that she couldn't resist teasing him. "Why don't you join us?"

He gave her a horrified look. "I have no intention of sticking around and listening to a bunch of females man bash. Isn't that what you do at these hen parties?"

"No, we play Pin the Tail on the Man. Starr made voodoo dolls of everyone's significant others. Are you sure you don't want to stay?"

"As tempting as the offer sounds, David and I have other plans. While you ladies are ripping us men to shreds, we'll be tending to our wounds at Max's Bar and Grill."

Becky looked at him dubiously. "A bar? For lunch?"

"Voodoo is pretty powerful stuff—we'll need all the fortification we can get. But we'll be having dinner there, not lunch. After the shower you'll probably want to rest, and since Hannah is having dinner with her cousins, David and I figured we'd make a whole day of it. I'm picking him up in about an hour. We're planning to grab a quick bite at the taco shop, then it's off to the car show, then Max's. I'm guessing I should be back here around eight."

He motioned to the box. "Are you going to open it or should I?"

He was worse than a kid in a toy store, except that he was the one giving the toys, not receiving them. Which was something she loved about him. He was generous to a fault.

Leaning over, she ripped opened the top. She reached inside and pulled out a—

"A parrot?" she asked, perplexed. "You bought me a toy parrot?" What kind of baby gift was a parrot?

"This isn't just any parrot. This is a kakapo."

Well, *that* explained everything. "It's...unusual."

"It's the world's only flightless parrot—get it?"

No, she didn't. And why did it have to be so big? The thing had to be at least two feet long. But not wanting to hurt Carter's feelings, she said, "I'm sure our daughter will love it." She reminded herself that it was the thought that counted, not the gift.

Just what had he been thinking?

"The kakapo comes from New Zealand," he said, his face beaming. "Except for a couple of bat species, there were no mammals on the islands for millions of years. Since it had no natural predators, it evolved without the ability to fly. It's an endangered species, very rare and very unique."

"Like you." It was true. Carter was definitely unique. Most fathers-to-be went out and bought teddy bears; he went out in search of parrots. "So why is this the perfect gift?" she asked, her curiosity piqued.

"Don't you see? It's flightless. And so am I. I thought I'd bring a little of New Zealand here, since I won't be going over there."

Remembering that first day in the hospital, she felt her

heart constrict. "Yes, I know. If everything works out.
You said—"

He raised a finger to her lips. "Everything *will* work
out," he assured her. "But I want you to know that I'll
be there for you, regardless. I'm tired of living on the
road. The reasons I chose that lifestyle no longer exist.
Now I have a reason for staying put, and I'm not just
talking about the baby. I'm talking about you."

Was he saying he was willing to give up New Zealand
unconditionally? "Can you do that?" she asked, her heart
thumping wildly. "Can you just bow out of the job? Who
would take your place? And what about your promotion?"

"My becoming a full partner doesn't hang solely on
my going overseas. And yes, I can bow out. Mark Brad-
shaw has been making noises about wanting to go over
there. He and Phil Thompson make a good team." He
smiled at her coyly. "Look under the beak."

"Excuse me?"

"The kakapo, Becky. Look under its bill."

She looked back at the parrot. It really was kind of
pretty with its moss-green feathers. Tentatively she lifted
its beak. Tucked in a small pocket was a sleek platinum
band embracing what had to be two carats of square-cut
glittering diamond. Speechless, she looked up at Carter.

"Here, let me," he said, his voice filled with tender-
ness. He picked up the ring and slid it onto her finger. "I
picked it out right after you were released from the hospital. But you kept turning me down. Now there's no reason. You said you wouldn't settle for a part-time husband,
and I've decided to stay put."

He was right. She had no reason to refuse him—no
reason except pure, unadulterated fear. Fear of what tomorrow might bring. "Actually, I said fatherhood wasn't

a part-time job.'' She bit down on her lip. ''I...I don't know if I can accept this.''

He looked at her with confusion, then slapped himself on the forehead. ''I can't believe how stupid I am—I should have realized you'd want to choose your own engagement ring. But don't worry, the jeweler has a return policy.'' He chuckled. ''A little pessimistic of him, wouldn't you say? But we'll be exchanging the ring, not returning it. We'll just be doing everything backward. We'll get married as soon as possible, and after the baby is born, we'll go ring shopping together. How does that sound?''

She felt a squeezing in her heart. ''No, the ring is exquisite. I'm glad you picked it out. It's a symbol of your promise.''

She moved her hand, watching the light as it flashed from the stone. Making promises was the easy part, she thought. It was keeping them that was difficult.

''Then what's the problem?'' he asked. ''I know it probably doesn't fit just right, but we can get it resized.'' He took her hand in his. ''Talk to me, Becky. Are you trying to tell me you're still not ready?''

Her gaze met his. Devotion shone in his eyes with as much brilliance and fire as the diamond on her finger. He was giving up New Zealand of his own accord, not out of a sense of duty. He was giving it up to be with her.

The ring fit perfectly. For once her hands weren't swollen. Starr would probably tell her it was a sign. She was always saying that signs were everywhere to help you find your way. You just had to open your eyes and trust your instincts.

Trust. Now there was a word for you. And what about love? These past few months she'd come to know Carter better than she'd known anyone else, and somewhere along the way she'd made a place for him in her heart. But did she love him? She wasn't sure. Did he love her? Another blank. All she knew was that he seemed to want to spend every minute with her, and she felt at loose ends when he wasn't there.

Signs? Becky didn't need any more signs. All the proof she needed was right there beside her, holding her hand, waiting for her to reply.

She let out a breath. Okay, so she wasn't a gambler, but sometimes you had to take a chance. "Yes," she said in a shaky voice. "I mean no. Yes *and* no." Then, with a confidence that surprised her, she smiled and said, "No, I'm not saying that I'm not ready, and yes, I'll marry you." Without waiting for him to respond, without champagne to boost her courage, she threw her arms around him.

Damn abstinence, she thought. Well, they might not be able to celebrate in the manner she'd like, but she couldn't let this moment go by without some kind of seal.

He didn't disappoint her. At first his kiss was slow and tender, his lips as soft and caressing as a midsummer breeze. Then, with an urgency that left her breathless and wanting, he crushed his mouth to her lips. His warm breath mingled with hers, his tongue probing, searching, searing. She leaned backward, half sitting, half reclining, clinging tightly to his neck, slowly pulling him down.

He released her and sat up. "Becky, we can't..." Agitatedly he ran his figures through his hair.

She relaxed against the sofa cushions and smiled innocently. "Cold showers help."

"I have to tell you, it's not easy. Ever since your brother's wedding...let's just say I can't wait to start practicing for the next baby."

She laughed. "Slow down, lover-boy. One baby at a time."

He snuggled her back into his arms. "The operative word is *practicing*. But let's not wait too long for the real thing. It would be nice to have our kids close to each other in age. A girl for you, a boy for me."

"Too expensive," she said lightly. "Do you know how much it costs to have a bar mitzvah these days?" She curled into him, resting her head on his chest. "Two kids coming of age at the same time—you'd have to take out a second mortgage."

I could get used to this, she thought contentedly. The easy bantering, the dreaming, the planning... She had a momentary flashback to another life, but it vanished as quickly as it had arisen. This time around would be different. This time around was for keeps.

"I'm just kidding," she said. "I want to have a houseful of kids. We can always rob a bank." When he didn't say anything, she turned her head and looked up at him. His face was a mask of stone. "Carter? What's the matter?"

When he finally spoke, it was with hesitation. "I want you to know that I had a good time the other night. I appreciate that Starr threw in some Easter decorations for my benefit."

"But..."

He sighed. "But you have to admit, it was basically all about Passover."

"I know," she agreed. "Next year will be different. Our daughter will be a toddler. We'll put Easter baskets everywhere, and she can hunt for eggs."

"That's not what I'm getting at. I think it's wonderful that you intend to go on honoring your heritage. I also think it's important that our children be aware of their roots. But don't you think having two religions could get to be a little much? You even said so yourself. 'Talk about confusing a child,' I believe were your exact words.''

She stared at him as though seeing him for the first time. "I thought we understood each other. I thought it was agreed that we'd be following both faiths. Are you saying you want me to convert?''

"No, of course not. All I'm saying is that the baby should be raised with just one religion.''

"And that religion would be yours," she said, comprehension setting in. "Did you know that according to Jewish law the child always takes the religion of the mother? That's because we're always sure who she is, but you can never be too sure about the father.''

"Becky, this is serious. Children should take the religion of the father. It makes sense. After all, the father hands down his name. Why shouldn't he hand down his faith?''

The other night after the seder, he'd asked her whether she'd been talking about women's rights or religion. One thing she knew, religion was not what he was talking about now. It was all about his ego, all about his having a son to carry on after him. It was the same, she decided, for all creeds and cultures. The male of the species had a doctrine of its own.

She twisted the ring off her finger. "I can't wear this.''

He stared back at her incredulously. "What are you saying?''

She should have known it was too good to be true. She should have known the floor would open up right under her. "I'm saying I can't marry you. A marriage should be a partnership, a blending of ways. You seem to forget—''

The phone rang, startling her. After a moment she turned to Carter and said, "That was Starr calling from downstairs. My mother and grandmother are here in the kitchen, setting up. The rest of the party will be arriving shortly.''

"Looks like we'll have to continue this discussion later,'' he said. His eyes were remote, his face devoid of color. "Think about what I said, princess. You'll see that I'm right. In the meantime, hold on to the ring.''

Fuming, she watched him leave, angry with him for being so pigheaded. But more than that, she was angry with herself for ever having believed in him.

Chapter Eleven

Becky sat on the couch in the study, her feet propped up on the ottoman. The baby shower had lifted her spirits, as once again she'd come to realize the importance of family and friends. But now that the party was over, she felt disheartened. She couldn't see how she and Carter would ever get over this latest hurdle, and all the family and friends in the world couldn't fill the aching gap in her heart.

She picked up a colorful mobile from the stack of gifts. A present from Starr, the musical carousel supported magical wizards and hobbits from the movie trilogy, *The Lord of the Rings*. Nursery toys sure have changed over the years, she thought. She put down the mobile and looked around, her gaze roaming from gift to gift. So much stuff! She'd been to baby showers before, but only now did she fully realize how much paraphernalia was required to care for a baby. I guess you never really think about it, she mused, until it's your turn.

When Starr had first offered to host a luncheon for Becky's baby shower, Becky had refused. Starr had already switched roles from employer to caregiver. Not only that, she and Christina had taken over all of Becky's kitchen duties. How much could one person do?

But Starr wouldn't take no for an answer, and had even suggested that Becky and Hannah have their baby showers together. It made sense, she insisted. Their delivery dates were so close, and the guest list for each mother-to-be was practically identical. Despite her reservations about receiving gifts before the birth, Gertie had offered to help, and in the end Becky had relented.

After the last guest had left, Starr had moved all the gifts to the study. A heaviness settled inside Becky's chest. She wondered where she'd be setting up the nursery.

All the progress she and Carter had made had sifted away like sand in an hourglass. She wasn't what anyone would call a hard-nosed feminist, but the nerve of him! Why should their child's religion be determined based on gender? Specifically, *his* gender.

Not wanting to fall asleep in the drafty study, she forced herself off the couch and went slowly upstairs to her room. Her back ached, and she was more tired than usual. She couldn't understand why she was feeling this way. No one had allowed her to lift a finger. She hadn't budged from the wing chair in the living room during the entire party; her mother had even insisted on opening the gifts.

She looked around the alcove. She would have to go back to her original plan and turn the nook into a nursery. After she was on her feet financially, she and the baby would live in New York.

Her eyes wandered over to the toy parrot by the credenza, and a tangle of emotions assailed her. Carter had never actually said he loved her, but she felt it in every cell of her body. If his constant caring for her these past weeks hadn't convinced her, his willingness to give up New Zealand had definitely tipped the scales.

She knew he'd been looking forward to the trip abroad. He was being narrow-minded about this religion thing, but no matter how hard she tried to convince herself that her feelings for him were shattered, she couldn't erase from her mind the sacrifice he was willing to make.

But was love enough? She walked over to her dresser, opened the top drawer and took out the ring. A symbol of his promise, she'd said. What promise was that? There had to be more to a marriage than love. She'd loved Jordan, and look what had happened. What about respect and equality? Wasn't marriage supposed to be a partnership?

What Jordan had done was despicable, but she couldn't absolve herself of her share of the blame. With no dreams of her own, she'd allowed herself to live in his shadow. What man wanted to be married to a nonperson? If she'd learned anything from that whole fiasco, it was that she could never afford to let herself disappear again. How could she not bring her religion into her child's life? Her religion was part of her. If she started chipping away at who she was, how long would it be before nothing was left?

Blinking back a tear, she put the ring back into the drawer.

Too tired to undress, she lay down on her bed and closed her eyes. In a state of half sleep she dreamed of New Zealand. Then, like a scene in a movie, the dream suddenly shifted. Large green parrots transformed into strange-looking mythical creatures, and New Zealand became an exotic Middle Earth landscape. She saw herself running across a land lush with giant ferns and ancient beech trees, glaciers and volcanoes looming in the background. She didn't know what she was running from or where she was going. All she knew was that if she stopped, she would vanish into the depths of the strange terrain.

"Another beer," Carter said, motioning to the waiter. He picked up the bottle in front of him and polished it off.

"Take it easy," David said from across the table. "Don't you think you should slow down?" He turned to the waiter. "Make that a pot of coffee instead. A large pot."

Carter peered at his friend. "Why should I slow down? I'm not going anywhere."

"You got that right. I took your keys, remember? After we leave here, I'll drive you back to your apartment, and tomorrow morning you can come by my place and get your car. I have a feeling the walk will do you good."

"I'm perfectly fine," Carter grumbled.

"You're already over your limit, pal. What's going on? You and Becky fighting again?"

"No. Yes. Maybe. I gave her the ring."

"Finally," David said, nodding his approval. "And?"

"She accepted."

"So what's the problem?" His face clouded over. "Don't tell me you're having second thoughts. Because if you are—"

"Hey, take it easy yourself. I'm not in the mood for another black eye."

David raised one hand in a mock oath. "No violence, I swear. Now level with me. What's bugging you?"

"I put the ring on her finger, but then she took it off. She's your sister, all right. Stubborn as a mule."

"You're talking in riddles. Are you getting married or not?"

Carter hesitated. Even though he and David had been friends for years, he wasn't sure he should be talking about his premarital problems with the brother of the bride. But it wasn't just the family connection that made him uncomfortable; it was the whole religion issue. In the past their separate faiths had never posed a problem, but now that Carter intended to marry into the family, all that could be history. "I'm not sure you're the person I should be talking to," he said after a long a pause.

"Come on, what are friends for? Look, Becky might be my sister, but I'm the first to admit she's a pain in the neck."

The waiter returned with the pot of coffee, and Carter poured himself a cup. He knew he was stalling. He was afraid he'd say the wrong thing, something that might offend his best friend. He couldn't just come out with, "By the way, old boy, nothing personal, but I don't think my son—your nephew—should have a bar mitzvah." He honestly didn't know how David would react, and Max's Bar and Grill wasn't the place for a brawl.

He took a sip of his coffee, studying his friend over the top of the cup. He chose his words carefully. "She wants us to be a two-religion household."

"And you want to raise the baby as a Christian," David said flatly.

Carter cleared his throat. "Uh, sort of." He waited for David to explode.

But David's response took him by surprise. "Hey, I'm with you," he said, lifting his cup as though making a toast. "Sure, I'd like my nephew or niece to be raised in the Jewish faith, but it's *your* family. You're the head of the household. Which means you get to make the decisions.''

''You make it sound as if I want her to work for me, not marry me,'' Carter said, suddenly feeling unsettled. ''I'd like to think of us as being equals. The only reason I want to raise our child with one religion is so he doesn't grow up confused.''

''Then why not take her religion?'' David challenged. ''I'll tell you why. It's like I said, you're the head of the household. You're the male, bottom line. We live in a patriarchal society. It's the way it's always been, and it's the way it'll always be.''

''Yeah, but does Hannah know this?'' Carter joked uneasily. Something about the conversation was making him uncomfortable, only he wasn't quite sure what it was.

''Laugh if you want, but you know that what I'm saying is true.'' David leaned forward. ''Think of it this way. Marriage is like a ship, and there can only be one captain.'' Suddenly he chuckled.

''What's so funny?''

''You sure have your work cut out for you. My sister could sure use some steering.''

''Now wait just one minute—''

''Come on, you said it yourself. She's as stubborn as a mule. You've got to take charge, show her that you're at the helm. Take Hannah, for instance. She has it in her head that she's going back to work after the baby comes, but there's no way I'm going to allow that. A mother should stay home with the children.''

Carter was getting tired of David's caveman philosophy. ''What are you saying? That I should give Becky orders? I'll tell you one thing, she sure as hell wouldn't take them.''

"And you call me a wuss." David shook his head. "Obviously I'm not getting through to you. Let me put it another way. You're not planning to give up meat, are you?"

"No, of course not. Why would you think that? Get to the point, Roth."

David gave him a twisted smile. "I'm talking about her strange eating habits. You're not planning to let her serve you that vegetarian garbage after you're married, are you?"

"I still don't understand what you're getting at," Carter said, his patience draining away. "If Becky wants to remain a vegetarian, it's fine with me. I'm happy to eat whatever she prepares—she's a great cook. And as far as her *serving* me, I don't expect her to be my personal chef. She wants to make cooking a career, and the last thing she might feel like doing is cooking at home. I intend to help out as much as possible."

David let out a scornful laugh. "Give me a break. You cook?" He gestured to Carter's empty plate. "So was that your last steak? You're really going to give up meat?"

"Sure, I'll cook. Why not? And no, this wasn't my last steak. I'll eat vegetarian food at home, and when we go out—" Carter stopped abruptly.

"What is it? You look like you swallowed a ten-pound bagel."

"I just realized I've been acting like a jerk." That's putting it mildly, Carter thought. He hadn't merely been a jerk; he'd been a total shmuck. Now he knew why the conversation was making him feel so uneasy. He'd begun to recognize himself in David, and he didn't like what he saw.

"I don't get it," David said.

"Oh, you will, all right," Carter answered. "I've gotten

to know Hannah a lot better these past few months. On the surface she might seem shy and quiet, but I suspect that you're going to be in for a shock. You don't really believe she's going to continue putting up with your crap, do you?''

"Hey, watch it. It's a good thing you're not sober. I might have taken that the wrong way."

Carter rolled up his napkin and tossed it onto the table. ''You didn't.''

He felt disgusted with himself. He couldn't believe what he'd said to Becky. When had he become so intolerant? He recalled something Becky had once said about God being in the heart. She'd also told him that she wanted to bring up her child with an open mind. Maybe there was just one truth, she'd said, but there were many paths that led to it.

He thought about last Christmas, and about the holiday they'd just celebrated. On both occasions diverse backgrounds had blended together in harmony and joy. Who was he to say that one path was better than another?

He felt like an idiot. Ever since he found out he was going to be a father, he'd let his ego take over. His stupid, obnoxious ego. All that poppycock about handing down a legacy—it was a wonder she hadn't given him the boot.

She *had* given him the boot, he reminded himself. She'd told him she wouldn't marry him. But she hadn't given him back the ring, he thought with hope. She'd taken it off, but she'd kept it. That said something, didn't it? If she'd been serious about not marrying him, wouldn't she have insisted he take back the ring?

He stood up quickly. ''Let's go,'' he said with urgency. ''You're not driving me to my apartment, you're taking me to Becky's. I need to talk to her.''

He had to see her right away. Had to tell her he'd been a jackass. Had to tell her—

"Aren't you forgetting something?" David asked. "I think they're expecting us to pay the bill. Besides, I think we should stay a while, like we planned. You don't want my sister thinking she's marrying a drunk."

David had a point. Carter was far from three sheets in the wind, but why give Becky an excuse to turn him away? He sat back down. An hour and a half later, after the game on the big-screen TV had ended, he felt completely sober. Nevertheless, David insisted on driving. He was a good friend, even if he did have some strange notions. Like his views on marriage. He'd been wrong when he'd said that Carter had his work cut out for him. Carter wasn't the one with the harrowing task ahead; it was Hannah.

"Becky?" Christina called through the closed door. "I know you said not to wake you, but Starr and I were worried that you might be hungry. Your phone's not working, so I came right up."

Becky groaned. Her phone wasn't out of order; she'd taken the receiver off the hook. She glanced at the clock on her bureau. Good heavens, it was almost eight! She'd slept right through dinner.

She lumbered out of bed and opened the door. "Thanks, but I'm not hungry. I'm still full from lunch."

"If you change your mind, just call me on the kitchen extension. In the meantime, you have a visitor. She says she couldn't make it to the shower, and she has a gift for you. Should I send her up?"

"Who is it?"

The answer left Becky feeling numb. "Eleanor Prescott."

Panic took over. Eleanor Prescott! Becky had asked Starr to invite her to the shower, but Eleanor had declined without offering any explanation. Why was she here now? "Give me a moment," Becky said. "I need to freshen up."

After Christina went back downstairs, Becky closed the door and hurried into the bathroom. Running a comb through her hair, she studied herself in the mirror and winced at her reflection. Her clothes looked as though they'd just been pulled from an overstuffed suitcase.

She was debating whether or not she had time to change, when she heard a loud knocking. Well, that decided it. She straightened her skirt as best as she could, then took a deep breath and opened the door.

Next to the older woman, Becky felt even dowdier than she knew she appeared. Eleanor's silvery blond hair, pulled back into an elegant chignon, accentuated the gleam in her diamond-drop earrings. Worn over expensive-looking kid leather boots, her coat was a full-length black mink. Hadn't she heard of animal rights? She undid the coat, revealing a designer gray tweed suit, the only color in her entire ensemble coming from an azure silk scarf tied loosely around her neck.

"Won't you sit down?" Becky asked nervously. She motioned to the sofa in the alcove.

"Very well," Eleanor replied, "but I can't stay long."

Becky wheeled her desk chair into the alcove and sat down across from her. "I'm sorry you couldn't make it to the shower," she said, at a loss for something better to say.

Eleanor handed Becky a small box. "This is for you. You can open it later. Under the circumstances, I'm sure you can understand why I didn't bring it earlier."

And what circumstances were those? That Becky was

the unmarried mother of her son's child? That Eleanor wouldn't say two words to her if they passed each other in the street? Becky forced herself to remain calm. "Thank you," she said, taking the gift.

When she'd told Carter that she wanted his mother to come to the shower, he'd been against it. But she'd finally convinced him that it was the right thing to do. After all, Eleanor was their child's grandmother. But now, sitting across from this formidable woman, Becky understood Carter's reluctance. Eleanor had a way about her that made a person feel as small as an insect.

Surreptitiously Becky studied the older woman's face. How could two people look so much alike yet be so different? Like Carter Eleanor's eyes were gray, but hers were as cold as ice. Like Carter she had a proud, square chin, but unlike him she appeared austere.

"I suppose you're wondering why I'm here," she said, pulling off her gloves. "I won't beat around the bush. The other night I got a disturbing phone call from my daughter-in-law. You remember Carter's first wife, don't you? Of course you do. Wendy St. Claire comes from one of the best families in New England. Well, she told me that Carter was thinking about marrying again. I remembered him mentioning that he thought he might be the father of your baby, and it occurred to me that he might in fact be considering marriage. Is this true?"

Becky hesitated. She knew that Carter had told his mother about the pregnancy, but he never would have intimated that he might not be the father. Not only that, Eleanor was implying that Carter and Wendy were on speaking terms. That, Becky knew, was highly unlikely. Carter could barely bring himself to speak his ex-wife's name, let alone talk to her.

"Carter and I are in the talking stage," Becky said noncommittally.

"I see. In that case, it's a good thing I came."

Becky regarded her with suspicion. "Just why have you come, Mrs. Prescott?"

"I came here to stop you from making a mistake. If you go through with this, you'll be ruining my son's life."

Eleanor was right; she didn't beat around the bush. Take a deep breath, Becky ordered herself. Relax, stay calm. "Mrs. Prescott, I assure you—"

"Yes, I know. You have only Carter's happiness in mind. If that's true, then tell me, how can you do this to him? Don't you realize that if he gives up the New Zealand project, he'll be saying goodbye to the partnership?"

The woman might be Carter's mother, but how dare she come here and accuse Becky of not thinking about Carter's happiness! "The promotion doesn't depend on the project," Becky answered with forced patience. But as soon as the words were out of her mouth, doubt began to set in. Would Eleanor be saying this if she didn't believe she had good reason?

Eleanor nodded. "That's our Carter for you. Inventing truths to spare the other person. Yes, I can see why he would have told you that. He's always been like that, quick to give up what's important to him for the sake of the other person." She gave Becky a conspiratorial look. "I'm going to tell you a few things, dear, that he probably never told anyone. After what I have to say, I'm sure you'll see why a marriage between the two of you couldn't possibly work."

Inventing truths to spare the other person. Something occurred to Becky. Carter hadn't actually said he'd be getting the promotion.

Tell her to leave, her inner voice directed. Tell her now,

before it's too late. You and Carter can work out your differences. You love him, and he loves you. That's all that should matter.

She drew in her breath. "Please, just say what's on your mind."

"I presume he never told you what happened between him and Wendy."

Becky averted her gaze. "We don't talk about our previous marriages."

"Just as I thought. Secrets. Not a very good way to start a marriage, wouldn't you agree? I'm not surprised he didn't tell you, though. It's not something he's proud of."

Becky knew she shouldn't be listening to this. If Carter wanted her to know, he would tell her himself. But she didn't tell Eleanor to stop. It was as if an invisible force were standing there, making her listen. "Go on," she said in a thick voice.

"After he married Wendy, he turned down an opportunity with a major architectural firm in Los Angeles so that she could practice law in New York. He went to work for Joe Sullivan in Middlewood—the firm was small back then—and she took the job in the city and commuted. But when her law career flourished, he couldn't stand it. His own career wasn't going anywhere, and he resented her." Eleanor let out an ugly snort. "He's just like his father was, couldn't stand a strong woman. Carter couldn't stand that Wendy's career was more successful than his, and he wanted her to quit work to start a family. They argued constantly. When she did get pregnant—an accident, I'm sure—he was thrilled. He was going to be a father. His own wife didn't respect him, and now he would finally shine in someone's eyes."

How could a mother talk about her son this way? Becky

thought. She forced back a caustic reply, and waited for Eleanor to continue.

Eleanor's voice took on a disapproving tone. "When he insisted she stop work immediately, they had another argument. According to Wendy, he stormed out of the house like an angry child and didn't come home all night. The next day she miscarried. It was just one of those things, never meant to be, but he felt sure that the stress he'd put her through had caused it. After that the marriage collapsed. He never did get over his resentment, and the added guilt just tore them apart."

"What does this have to do with me and Carter?" Becky asked, trying to keep her voice steady. But in her heart she knew what Eleanor was going to say, and she dreaded hearing the words.

Eleanor pointed a manicured finger in Becky's face. "If Carter stays in Middlewood, he'll be kissing his future goodbye. The partnership hinges entirely on the job, no matter what he told you. He's wanted it for so long—do you honestly believe he'd be happy without it? Right now he thinks he's doing the right thing by marrying you, imagines himself to be some sort of knight in shining armor, but don't think for a moment that this will last. He resented Wendy for denying him the job in California. How long will it be before he resents *you?*"

Becky's anguish was like a huge knob inside her. She wanted to turn back the clock to that morning and tell Carter she'd marry him, tell him that whatever problems they had, they could work out. But it was too late. It would be one thing if she hadn't found out why his marriage had failed—ignorance was bliss, right? But she *had* found out, and now everything was different. How could she knowingly destroy his happiness?

"I can go with him," she said, her mind whirring.

Could she? Could she sacrifice the next two years of her life?

"You're not being realistic, dear. I know how you people like to stay rooted. You all like to stick together. Are you really willing to traipse around the world with a new baby? Even if you did go with him, what about later?" Eleanor gave her a sickly half smile. "Admit it, dear. You're the clingy type—you wouldn't want to be away from him for any length of time." She rose from the sofa. "I've said what's on my mind. The rest is up to you. I have no doubt that once you've thought over what I've said, you'll come to the right decision. I'm sure you and Carter will reach an arrangement agreeable to both of you, but if what he proposes isn't sufficient, please feel free to contact me. We'll draw up our own terms."

Becky looked at her with disgust. Did Eleanor really believe that Becky could be bought? Not wanting to acknowledge the insult with a comment, Becky bit back her reply.

Misery quickly replaced anger. She knew that most of what Eleanor had said made sense. Here Becky was, fighting to preserve her identity; how could she expect Carter to deny his own? She could no more expect him to turn away from his dreams than she could turn away from hers.

She walked Eleanor to the door, desperately trying to hold back tears. No way would she cry in front of this woman. No way would she give her the satisfaction.

After Eleanor left, Becky unwrapped the gift. Inside a jewelry box was a little silver rattle. Becky picked it up and shook it. Nothing. It was just a showpiece, purely ornamental. She put it in her dresser drawer, next to the ring.

She went back to bed and stared up at the ceiling. She couldn't possibly go with Carter to New Zealand. Her life was here with her family and friends. And what about her catering business? Was she expected to give up on that just because Carter had a thing about successful women?

But more than that, she was terrified of losing herself. Never again could she put herself in that kind of situation. Never again could she sublimate herself for someone else's dreams. She'd become invisible once before. She couldn't risk it happening again.

Was she being selfish? Maybe. Probably. Part of her wanted to shout, To hell with it! To hell with her life here, to hell with her plans. But as much as she desperately wanted to be with Carter, she knew she could never put her life on hold again. She'd done that once before, and look what had happened. She'd become no more than an empty shell. No wonder Jordan had left. Who could respect a nonbeing?

And what about later, after New Zealand? She still felt strongly about her child having a full-time father, but if she made Carter stay grounded, how long would it be before his resentment turned to hatred?

She rolled over and buried her head in her pillow, hoping to muffle her sobs. She knew what she had to do. She had to convince him to go to New Zealand, and then she had to let him go.

Carter paced back and forth in front of the sofa in the alcove. "You're not making any sense. I said I was wrong, and I meant it. This morning you told me that marriage should be a partnership, a blending of ways. I don't understand why you've changed your mind."

"Because I realized you were right. It's what we've been saying all along. Having more than one religion would be too confusing. I'm sorry, Carter. I can't marry you. We need to have common goals, common backgrounds. With so much going against marriage today, what chance do we have if we start out with so many strikes against us?''

Suddenly he stopped in his tracks, his face brightening. "I'll convert."

"Don't be ridiculous. You can't change religions the way you change your clothes. That would make you a hypocrite."

A hypocrite was exactly what she felt like, she thought miserably. But what choice did she have? She knew she couldn't tell him the real reason she was turning down his proposal. He'd never accept her decision. He'd make all kinds of noises about not wanting to go to New Zealand, and she was sure he'd believe what he was saying—but what about tomorrow? What would happen when he realized the price he'd paid for marrying her?

Bubbe always said, "A man can do what he wants, but it's up to the woman to let him know what that is." Well, this was one of those times. Oh, he might believe he wanted to remain in Middlewood, but she knew he would live to regret it. She had to make him go, and there was only one way she could do this. She had to convince him that they couldn't be a family. Once he accepted that, he'd have no reason to stay.

He sat down next to her on the sofa. "I don't understand why you're acting this way. Is it because you're still angry with me? I already told you I was wrong." A glint of humor shone in his eyes. "You can thank your brother for helping me see the error of my ways. Actually, you're not going to believe this, but Wendy also made me realize a thing or two. Ever since she came to see me—"

"Excuse me? Run that by me again."

"I, uh, was going to tell you about that."

She pursed her lips. ''And when was that? When did you see Wendy, and when were you going to tell me?''

''You're missing the point. What I'm trying to get across here is that two people don't have to come from the same background for a marriage to work. Look at what happened in my marriage. Wendy and I were supposed to be so well suited, and we ended up in the divorce courts. Just like you and Jordan.''

''No, the point is that you never told me you saw her. Next you'll be saying you want us all to be friends. You sound just like Jordan—that's exactly what he said, too.'' She frowned with exasperation. ''What is it about men and their ex-wives? You screw us over and then you decide you want to be friends.''

''What are you talking about? And when did you talk to Jordan?''

''I...um...''

''And you accuse me of keeping secrets! When did you see him? Why didn't you tell me?'' He let out a scornful laugh. ''Oh. I see.''

''What?'' she asked, confused. ''What do you see?''

''Ever since your brother dropped me off here, you've been trying to pick a fight. It's as if you can't wait to send me packing to New Zealand. Now I understand. It's Jordan, isn't it? You're getting back together with your ex.''

She stared at him incredulously. ''Have you lost your mind? I'm more than seven months pregnant with another man's child. What would Jordan want with me?''

''He was the one you called out for on the way to the hospital, the morning after the storm. Sure, you were irrational with fever, but you can't deny that it was your ex you wanted, not me. Admit it, he still has a hold on you. That's why you're always talking about going back to New York.''

He thought she wanted Jordan back? He had to be kidding. She looked at his face closely. He *wasn't* kidding. She was about to make a snappy retort, but then stopped herself. She had to admit, she liked that he was jealous. It made her feel secure.

Wait a minute. The idea was to set him free, not rope him in.

Nevertheless, no way would she send him off to New Zealand thinking that she and her ex were conspiring behind his back. "First of all, Jordan is accepting a position at Danbury Hospital. And he's getting married. Did you hear what I said? Married, Carter. Like us. Only we're not. Getting married, I mean."

Carter shook his head. "We're something else, you and I. Arguing about our exes." His voice turned serious. "What's going on, Becky? What are we really fighting about?"

She sighed heavily. So much for her noble attempt to set him free. She could no more lie to him than she could lie to herself. "Your mother was here. She gave me a gift for the baby, and then she told me why you and Wendy split up. She also told me the truth about your promotion." She looked into his eyes. "I can't let you give up New Zealand. You'd lose the partnership. You've worked far too hard to let it slip away."

A muscle flicked at his jaw. "My mother. I should have known. She has a habit of rewriting history, especially when it comes to my marriage. And I already told you that the partnership doesn't depend on my going to New Zealand. I'm not going to be passed over. But that's not the issue. What do I have to do to convince you that you're my future? You and the baby. I want us to be a real family, but you keep inventing excuses to push me away."

"A real family," she repeated. "Don't you see? You have this idea about what a real family should be. But it's just a fantasy. It's not who you are, Carter. You need to be out in the world, working on-site. You can't be stuck at home with a wife and child. You'd only resent me, and then you'd leave, anyway."

"I'm not going anywhere. Not without you."

"Everyone leaves," she said, choking back tears. "Jordan left me, and you left Wendy."

She knew she sounded pitiable, but she couldn't help how she felt. Men walked out; it was as simple as that. If Becky took away Carter's dreams, she'd be stacking the deck against them, even before the game started.

He smiled sadly. "I know you think I ended my marriage, but that's not what happened. Yes, we'd been fighting, and yes, I walked out. She'd told me she didn't want the baby. I told her she was talking crazy, but she wouldn't stop. I was so angry, I left to spend the night at David's apartment. But I came back, Becky. I came back the next morning to reason with her. We had a child coming, and I wanted our marriage to work. I wanted to tell her I'd be willing to move to New York. I'd be the one to commute. I didn't think she should have to exert herself any more than necessary." He put his head in his hands. "I wish to God I hadn't left that night. I wish to God—" He stopped abruptly.

The only sound in the room was the ticking of the clock on the bureau as Becky waited patiently for him to speak. "What happened?" she prodded gently when he didn't continue.

He raised his head, and in his eyes she could see the depth of his sorrow. "I waited for her all day," he said quietly, "but she never came home. I called her office, but they said she hadn't showed up. I called her friends.

No one had heard from her. I was frantic. The following morning she called me from a hotel in New York. She said she'd be coming back on the weekend to pack her things. She said the marriage was over.''

"That was when she had the miscarriage," Becky said, feeling his anguish as acutely as if it were her own.

"You don't understand," he said in a monotone. "She didn't have a miscarriage. She had an abortion."

Becky felt all the color drain from her face, and instinctively her hand went to her abdomen. "Oh, Carter. My God. I—"

And then the pain set in.

"Becky? Are you all right?"

"Hurts," she said. "Oh, God, it hurts so much." Pain as sharp as a razor sliced through her, and she doubled over on the sofa.

"Becky!" he cried out. "What is it? Becky!"

She couldn't answer. One moment her breath was stuck in her throat, and the next moment there was blackness.

Chapter Twelve

"I want to know what names you picked out."

Carter looked up at Gertie from his uncomfortable chair in the maternity waiting room. She stood in front of him, hands on hips as though she meant business. "Wh-what?" he asked, feeling dazed.

The past few hours had gone by in a blur. At the B and B, Becky had regained consciousness almost immediately. Even though she'd claimed she was all right, her swollen hands and face had told him differently, and he'd insisted on taking her to the emergency room. He'd scooped her up in his arms and was halfway out the door before he remembered he didn't have his car. Not only that, Starr and Christina had gone to a movie as soon as he'd arrived, leaving him with no way to get to the hospital. Frantic, he was about to call an ambulance, when his mother called on his cell phone, babbling something about Wendy. He cut her off and told her to come right over. Five minutes later she arrived at the B and B, and Carter took over the wheel, driving to the hospital at breakneck speed.

"You have to name the baby after someone who's dead," Gertie said. "It's a Jewish law."

"It's not a law," David contradicted her. "It's a tradition."

Gertie raised her chin. "Then it's settled. We'll call her Judith, after my older sister, God rest her soul."

"What if it's a boy?" Eleanor asked. "His name should be Carter. Carter Prescott, IV. That's *our* tradition."

"Pooh, pooh," Becky's grandmother said and then pretended to spit, which, Carter knew, was a custom to ward off evil spirits. "He's not dead."

"Chaim," Gertie said. "We'll name him after my father. He *is* dead."

Becky's grandmother shook her head. "I loved my Chaim and may he rest in peace, but you want all the children should laugh at him in the schoolyard? This is America, not the old country. If it's a boy, his Hebrew name can be Chaim, but we'll call him Charlie."

Gertie nodded. "Charles."

"Chuck," David said.

"Don't I have a say in this?" Eleanor interjected. "What's wrong with the name Carter? Both Carter, I, and Carter, II, are dead."

"But not the third," Carter pointed out sarcastically.

"Bite your tongue," Gertie said.

"Pooh, pooh," Becky's grandmother repeated.

Carter couldn't believe the conversation. Why on earth were they discussing his demise? What was wrong with everyone? Here they were arguing about what to name the baby, while Becky was having surgery. He wished he'd left his mother at the B and B, and he wished he hadn't called Gertie. But, of course, he'd had no choice. They were family.

It was tension, he realized. It made people act strangely. Look at his mother. She hadn't stopped crying since they'd arrived at the hospital. It was uncanny what having a baby could do, he thought. It had the power to make a heart from a stone.

He rose from his chair and paced. Wasn't that what expectant fathers did? Pace? Only he wasn't merely expectant. Despite Dr. Boyd's assurance that everything would be all right, he was terrified.

He'd called Dr. Boyd from the B and B, and she'd met them in the ER. After an examination, she'd told them that Becky's blood pressure was alarmingly high and that she needed surgery. The baby would have to be delivered by cesarean section.

Feeling helpless, he sat back down, resting his chin on his fists. The nurses had told him that if Becky were having a normal C-section—if there was such a thing—he could have remained by her side. She would have been given a spinal block, allowing her to remain awake through the entire procedure. But time was of the essence, and she'd had to be put under immediately.

Eleanor took out a hankie and delicately wiped her eyes. "This is all my fault," she said, sniffing. "Becky and I had a talk, and I must have upset her. I should never have interfered."

"Her condition has to nothing to do with you," Carter snapped, "but you're right about one thing. You shouldn't have interfered. I'll tell you something else. If you want to be part of your grandchild's life, you'd better learn to stop meddling, starting now."

"Such a way to talk to your mother," Gertie said, shaking her head. "You think it's easy being a parent? Wait till your child is older. I wish you the same aggravation! So maybe your mother has some mixed-up ideas, maybe she's a little *farfufke,* but is it such a crime to want what's best for your child?''

"You mean what's best for *her,*" Carter mumbled.

"In my day, children did what they were told," Gertie said huffily.

"I admit I've been a little rigid," Eleanor said, blowing daintily into her hankie. "It's just that after Carter's father died, I couldn't…I didn't want to…"

Carter rolled his eyes. This had to be his mother's best performance yet. "Mother, you drove Father away. He died after you'd been separated for three years."

"What's the matter with you?" Gertie admonished him. "How many mothers do you have? You think she's going to be around forever? All right, so she's a little snotty, but we can work on her. After all, we're going to be family."

Becky's words came back to him, and he sighed. "Parents can be a pain," she'd said, "but remember, your mother is the only mother you'll ever have." A pain? That was an understatement. His mother was the reason they'd invented Prozac.

"Machetunim," Becky's grandmother said. "That's what we call our relatives by marriage." She went over to Carter and gave him a hug. "I want you should call me Bubbe." She turned to Eleanor and said, "You, too. Call me Bubbe."

Eleanor stiffened visibly, but then, to Carter's astonishment, she took the older woman's hands and held them.

"Excuse me." All heads turned to see a pretty young nurse standing by the row of chairs. "Carter?" she said to David. "Is that you? What brings you here?"

"You have the wrong person." David nodded in Carter's direction. "You want him."

"No, it's you, all right. Carter Prescott, III. I'd recognize those dimples anywhere." The young woman frowned. "You don't remember me. I'm Marla. Marla Taylor. We met at Snooky's Lounge."

David's face turned bright red. When he made no motion to stand, Marla said, "Don't bother getting up. I wouldn't want you to exert yourself."

Carter recalled the conversation he'd had with David at the racquetball club. David had told him he'd met a woman at a bar, but he'd also insisted that nothing happened. Carter studied the woman's face. She didn't look pleased.

"I should be very angry," she scolded. "You never called."

"Aren't you going to introduce us?" Hannah asked, glaring at her husband.

If looks could break legs, Carter thought, David would be in crutches.

"Who is this woman?" Gertie demanded. "David, what have you been up to?"

"This is none of our business," Aaron said. "Let the kids—"

"What's the matter with you, Aaron? A strange woman threatens to break up your son's happy home, and you tell me it's none of our business? Do something!"

"Marla, this is my wife, Hannah." David said, squirming in his seat, "and this is my family. We're here to see Becky Roth, soon to be Becky Prescott. Maybe. But maybe not. My wife's having a baby, too."

"Well!" Marla exclaimed. "You certainly have been busy. You never even told me you were married." She shot him a poisonous look, then said to Hannah, "Good luck, Mrs. Prescott. I have a feeling you and the other Mrs. Prescott are going to need it.''

Gertie held a hand over her heart. ''Oy. No mother should have to hear this.''

''I can't believe you gave her my name,'' Carter said to David after the woman flounced off. ''What were you thinking?'' But he knew exactly what David had been thinking. For Hannah's sake more than anything, it was a good thing that thinking was all he'd done.

''What was that all about?'' Hannah asked, her voice rising.

''Nothing,'' David muttered. ''She's just someone I met at a bar. Before we were married,'' he added quickly.

''Why didn't you tell me about her? And why did you tell her you were Carter?''

David took Hannah's hands. ''Aw, honey, don't get like that. It didn't mean anything. It was after that argument we had. When you gave me that ultimatum, remember? But nothing happened, I swear. All we did was talk, have a few drinks. Afterward I went straight to your house and told you I wanted to get married. See? It all worked out.''

''That doesn't make any sense! You said nothing happened. You also said it didn't mean anything. Which is it? And if it didn't mean anything, why didn't you ever mention it?'' She yanked her hands free. ''Poor Hannah, so sweet, so understanding,'' she mocked. ''Poor, naive Hannah, she has no idea what goes on behind her back.'' She shook her finger at him. ''I'm sick and tired of you telling me what I can and can't do, while you seem to think you can do exactly as you please! You're a bully, and that's about to change. For one thing, I intend to go back to work after the baby is born, with or without your blessing. Oh, don't worry, I don't think you and your nurse actually played doctor, but I can't believe you never told me about this…this rendezvous!''

David slumped in his chair. ''Now look what you've done,'' he hissed at Carter.

''Me? What did I do?''

''Hannah only started getting these ideas when Becky got pregnant. This is all your fault.''

''You're nuts, you know that?'' Carter looked at him with amusement. ''What are you going to do? Hit me again? She's right, you *are* a bully.''

''*I'm* a bully? I can't believe the way you speak to your own mother! And talk about being nuts! It's a good thing Becky won't marry you. You've made the whole family crazy enough already. Ever since you knocked her up—''

''Why you—'' In an instant Carter was across the narrow aisle, grabbing David by the collar and pulling him to his feet. He clenched his fist and was about to take a swing, when he felt two thin arms encircling him from behind.

''Let him go!'' Gertie ordered her husband. ''Your condition!''

Aaron didn't move. ''David, apologize for that remark or I'll set your friend loose on you. If it were up to me,'' he said to Carter, ''I'd let you sock him. I should have taught him a thing or two a long time ago. But if I had, my wife would never have spoken to me again. Of course, that could be considered a blessing.''

Carter knew that with one swift jerk he could be free of Aaron's hold—free to put out David's lights—but he feigned weakness. In all the years he'd known this family, this was the first time he'd seen evidence that Aaron had a pulse.

Besides, he knew what the real problem was. Stress.

And people handled stress differently, he reminded himself.

"Sorry," David murmured, then sat back down next to his wife. Hannah stared straight ahead, her mouth a thin line.

Aaron released Carter and said to the others, "All this arguing has to stop. I'm about to become a grandfather and this is what I have to listen to?"

"Aaron, sit down," Gertie said.

"And you! For your information, I don't have a medical condition. The only condition I have is you. All I ever hear is how you want to be a grandmother, and now that the time is finally here, you have to make a scene. Always with the scenes! Well, I forbid you to speak until this is over. Do you hear me? I forbid you!"

"Aaron, please. You're making a fool of yourself."

"Quiet!" he shouted, turning purple.

"Oh!" Gertie stared at him, wide-eyed.

"Mr. Roth?" A woman in green scrubs had entered the waiting room.

David and Aaron looked up. "Yes?" they both answered.

She glanced uncertainly at Aaron, then turned to David. "Congratulations, Mr. Roth. You're a father. I'm Sally Reynolds, one of the ob-gyn nurses who assisted in the delivery. Everything went perfectly. Becky is just coming out of surgery now, and I'm happy to report that both mother and baby are doing fine."

"I'm the Mr. Roth you want," Carter said excitedly, scrambling to his feet. "When can I see Becky?"

"She won't be awake for hours, but you can go up to the neonatal unit, if you want. The pediatrician took the baby upstairs about ten minutes ago. I can take you there myself. I'm going up there now."

If he wanted? He took two long strides toward the door, then stopped abruptly. "Wait a minute. What is it? A boy or a girl?"

"A girl," the nurse replied, smiling. "A four-pound, six-ounce healthy baby girl."

A daughter! He thought of Becky, what she was like as a little girl, what she must have been like as a baby, and he was sure his heart would burst through his rib cage.

"Four pounds!" Gertie exclaimed. "That's not a real baby, that's a Beanie Baby!"

The nursed laughed. "She's tiny, but she's perfectly healthy. She's in an incubator in the preemie ward."

"An incubator?" Eleanor asked. "But you said she was fine. How long does she have to remain in the hospital?"

"The incubator is only to make sure her temperature remains constant," the nurse explained. "She'll have to remain in the hospital for at least a few weeks, just as a precaution. No matter how healthy, a preemie can't go home until she weighs five pounds, and of course, until the sucking instinct has kicked in."

This time the clamor in the waiting room was joyous. Amid a chorus of *mazel tovs,* everyone was laughing and crying and talking at once. Gertie and Eleanor were weeping happily into handkerchiefs. David was hugging Hannah—and apologizing profusely. Aaron was vigorously shaking Carter's hand. And Carter just stood there, numb with elation, his entire world having turned upside down. Knowing he was going to be a father was one thing; learning it was now a reality was something else entirely.

A daughter. He had a daughter.

"A girl!" Gertie said, her face glowing. "Come on, Eleanor, let's go see our granddaughter!"

"Only the father is allowed in the preemie nursery," Nurse Reynolds said. "Sorry, hospital rules."

"But we're family!" Eleanor protested. "Rebecca is going to be my daughter-in-law. We're maka...maka-toon..."

"*Machetunim,*" Gertie said. She smiled at the nurse. "And that's our grandchild you're talking about. Judith Roth."

"Catherine Prescott," Eleanor contradicted. "You said that your people like to name your children after dead people. Catherine was my mother's name."

"Judith," Gertie said resolutely. "Her name is Judith."

"I fail to see—"

Carter followed Nurse Reynolds out of the waiting room, leaving the others to their bickering. He should have known the reprieve wouldn't last. He wondered what he was getting into, marrying into this family. *If* Becky married him, he reminded himself. But no matter what the future held for them, this baby was concrete proof that their worlds had merged. The crazy and the uptight, he thought wryly, then laughed out loud. The way he felt now, not even their families could erase the grin that was spread across his face.

Before entering the preemie ward, he was instructed to put on a hospital gown, a cap and mask, and then wash his hands. When he was done, he followed the nurse to a row of incubators. Suddenly an alarm went off, startling him. Another nurse rushed over to one of the incubators and began to shake it gently. "Come on, Allan," she crooned. "Breathe, Allan."

"Sometimes these little ones forget to breathe," Nurse Reynolds said. "I realize it can be a little disconcerting the first time you see this, but it happens all the time. That's another reason why we have to keep the preemies here. They can't be released until at least forty-eight hours have passed without an episode."

The nurse who had shaken the incubator joined them. "I'm Candice Walker, the night nurse in charge. But please call me Candy. I'll be looking after your little girl." She gestured to the third incubator along the wall. "And here she is."

Carter's heart was hammering. My daughter, he repeated to himself. No matter how often he said the word, he still couldn't believe that he was a father. He placed his hands on the incubator, and the baby let out a squeak.

Candy laughed. "Noisy, isn't she? Squeaks louder than any of the others. That's a good sign. Her lungs are maturing nicely. That's always a worry with our preemies. Would you like to hold her?"

"Is that okay? She's so small."

"She's small, but she's strong," Candy said. "And she needs to feel your touch." She motioned to one of the rocking chairs. "Go ahead, sit. I'll bring her to you." A moment later she handed him the baby. "If you need me, just holler. I'll be across the room. I'm afraid your visit will have to be a short one. She can't be out of the incubator for more than a few minutes at a time. But you can watch her for as long as you want. Some parents like to sing to their babies right through the Plexiglas."

Carter was in awe. Carefully he loosened the blanket and stared at his daughter's hands. Her palms seemed no larger than pennies, and her fingers were like matchsticks. But her face—her small, perfect face—was a vision, the most beautiful face he'd ever seen. She looks like Becky, he thought. "Hi, sweetheart," he whispered. "I'm your daddy."

He could have sworn she looked up at him and smiled. The nurses would say it was impossible, but they would be wrong. This was his kid.

He sat in the chair, gently rocking his daughter, and far

too soon Candy came to take the baby and put her back in the incubator. Knowing it would be hours until they'd let him see Becky, he remained in the chair, across from the incubator, unable to tear himself away.

When Becky opened her eyes, Carter's face was the first thing she saw. "Did you see her?" she asked groggily. "Is she okay? They didn't lie to me, did they? She's fine, isn't she?"

"She's wonderful," he said, his voice breaking.

"I can't wait to hold her. When I woke up in the recovery room, they'd already taken her upstairs. Then they gave me a shot and I fell back to sleep." She chewed her lip nervously. "You're not disappointed, are you?"

"Disappointed? What do you mean?"

"I know how much you wanted a boy."

"No, you're wrong. I wanted a girl right from the start, only I didn't realize it. She's perfect, Becky. Just like you." He sat down on the edge of her bed. "I want us to get married. Today. I'll call a justice of the peace and our family can be the witnesses."

She looked away. "I can't," she said, a dark mood settling over her. "Don't you see? The baby doesn't change a thing. What your mother said makes sense. I can't keep you chained. You think this is what you want now, but it's not. You can't give up everything just because you believe I need you. A marriage built on need can't survive."

"It's okay to need someone. It's perfectly fine, especially if it's mutual. Give and take, remember? I have news for you. I need *you*. I'm in love with you, Becky, can't you tell? I'm in love with you and I want us to spend our lives together. You, me and our baby. The perfect family."

Finally he was telling her he loved her, but hearing the words only made her feel miserable. She couldn't do this to him. Couldn't destroy his future. "You have this idea of what the perfect family should be," she said, trying to keep her tears in check. "What happens when you get tired of living a fantasy? What happens when you realize what you gave up?" She clasped her hands together and stared at them. "You say you're in love with me, but I think you're more in love with the idea. I'm a real person, and so is our daughter. We're not part of some fairy tale."

"Don't you think I know that? For the past few hours I've been sitting across from our daughter, staring at her face, her hands, her fingers. She's real, all right. She's only been in our lives for less than a day, and already I can't imagine life without her. I can't imagine life without *you*. I go crazy every time I think about how I could have lost you. I love you, Becky. I've loved you from the first time I saw you, when you first moved to Middlewood. You were only seven, cute as a button. I remember thinking how lucky David was to have a little sister like you."

In spite of her decision she felt herself melting. "I remember that day," she said softly. "We were at the park. David was baby-sitting me while my parents were unpacking. This big kid came over and knocked me down. You were so angry—even back then you wanted to protect me." A tear spilled down her cheek. "You can't make that your entire life, Carter. Besides, I can take care of myself. In case you haven't noticed, I'm a big girl now."

"Oh, I've noticed." He brushed the moisture from her face. "Sure, I want to keep on protecting you, but what's wrong with that? You've convinced yourself that being grown-up means having to fend for yourself. But being your own person doesn't have to mean being alone. We can be there for each other. That's what it's all about.''

"What about New Zealand?" she asked tremulously. "I know how much you wanted to go. And what about later? I can't expect you to change your whole life.''

"I can't stand the thought of being away from you, even for a minute. Nothing could send me away. As for later, truth is, I never wanted this hectic lifestyle to begin with. I had no desire to live in the city, no desire to do much traveling. But after my marriage ended, I threw myself into my work, trying to fill the emptiness. Now circumstances are different. How can you say you're not real to me? You and our daughter are the only real things in my life.'' He took her hands in his. "Marry me,'' he said again, this time with urgency. "Now. Right away. I'll get a judge here within the hour. Or a rabbi. Or a minister. Hell, I'll get them all to come. Just say you'll marry me, once and for all.''

With all her heart she wanted to believe him. Wanted to believe in the fairy tale. But she was tired…so tired…. "I'm sorry,'' she whispered. She felt her eyes closing. Her eyelids heavy with tears, she drifted back to sleep.

Even while she slept, she was aware of him beside her. Once again New Zealand pervaded her dreams, only this time she wasn't alone. She was with Carter, strolling through a colorful meadow that overlooked a shimmering lake. When she awoke, sunlight was streaming in the room through the slats of the blinds. Carter was asleep in a chair by the bed. As if sensing that Becky was looking at him, he opened his eyes. "What does she look like?'' Becky asked. "Tell me every detail.''

"Why don't you judge for yourself?'' Standing in the doorway was Dr. Boyd. "How are you feeling this morning? Are you up to making a trip upstairs?''

"It feels like I've been cut in two. But I don't care. I want to see my baby."

"I'm going to take a quick look at you, and then I'll get a nurse to give you a shot for pain. Then we'll see what we can do about getting you together with your baby." She turned to Carter. "And how is our new father? Have you seen your daughter?"

Becky and Carter talked with the doctor, and then Carter left the room. After a few minutes Dr. Boyd poked her head through the doorway and said, "You can come in now. I'm done with my examination." She turned back to Becky. "Everything is perfect. You won't be mountain climbing for a while, but you're healing just fine."

A nurse arrived, pushing a wheelchair. She gave Becky a pain shot, then maneuvered her into the chair. "I think Daddy can take over now," she said after hooking the IV bag to the hanger.

Carter wheeled Becky down the hallway toward the elevator, and they talked excitedly about the baby all the way to the preemie ward. Once inside he pointed to the row of incubators. "There's our daughter," he said proudly. "She's the third one on the right."

Becky turned her head, and in that instant her world was transformed. She stared at her daughter in awe. The baby let out a squeak, and Becky laughed with joy. "She's beautiful!"

Carter smiled at her. "She looks like you."

A woman approached them and introduced herself as Susan Gold, the day nurse in charge. She instructed Becky to sit in the rocking chair. "Someone's been very anxious to meet you," she said, handing Becky the baby. "I'll leave the three of you alone. It's time you got properly acquainted."

Becky cradled her newborn gently, touching her face,

marveling at her perfection. "You're wrong," she said to Carter after the nurse had gone. "She doesn't look like me. She looks like herself. She's her own person."

"She might be her own person, but we made her, Becky. We're a family now."

A family, Becky repeated to herself as she sat rocking her baby, Carter by her side. This bundle of joy in her arms was, and would always be, a reminder that their lives were intertwined. Yet each person was unique, bringing something wonderful and special to this life. Every living thing had a place in this world.

Never had Becky felt so alive. Never before had she felt so connected. How could she have kept pushing Carter away? How could she have believed that loving him would make her disappear?

She looked up at him, her heart brimming over. "Did we create her or is she on loan to us from God?"

"Either way, she's ours to love and care for."

She caressed her daughter's cheek. "There's an old Jewish saying... 'God can't be everywhere and that's why he made mothers.'"

"Hey, fathers, too," he said, chuckling. "As I recall, you weren't alone in the room when she was conceived." His voice thickened. "And as her parents, we have an obligation to give her all we can."

"Our love and our guidance. How can we go wrong? She'll have the best of both worlds."

"Do you love me, Becky?"

His question had come out of nowhere, but she wasn't surprised. "More than I ever thought possible," she whispered.

"Then marry me." He knelt before her. "In case you don't know, this is a formal proposal. Correction. Almost a formal proposal, since the ring is back at the B and B. But how can you refuse a man on his knees?"

Trying not to laugh at his antics, she glanced around the room. "Carter, get up! Everyone is watching!"

"Who, the babies? I'm not moving until you say yes— and this time mean it. There's no use fighting it. You're stuck with me, princess. Actually, you've been promoted. You're now the queen. That little bundle you're holding can be our princess-in-training."

It was ironic, Becky thought. At first she hadn't let herself love him because she was afraid she would become invisible, and, if she became invisible, he would leave her. Then she'd wanted him to leave because she loved him. But all that was over. Now she was certain of two things. One, she knew that loving him didn't mean she had to lose herself. On the contrary, he had helped her find her way. And two, she would love him forever.

"You realize," she teased, "that in chess, the king is just a figurehead. The queen has all the power."

"Don't I know it," he said, smiling. "You've had a hold on me forever."

Forever. There was that word again. Funny how it no longer scared her now that the reasons she'd had for refusing him were gone. Like pawns in a game of chess, they'd all been removed, one by one.

She took a deep breath, then exhaled. "Yes, I'll marry you. And yes, I mean it."

The baby squeaked again, and Becky and Carter both laughed. "And that," Carter said, "makes it official. Our princess-in-training approves."

Diaper bag over one shoulder, baby in a pouch in front, Becky waited with Carter at the check-in counter at the airport. "I see you'll be flying with us all the way to

Christchurch International,'' the attendant said, examining the tickets. She looked up inquisitively. ''There's no return date. Are you emigrating?''

''Visiting,'' Carter said, handing her the visas. ''For two years.''

The attendant began punching information into a computer, and Becky thought back over the past three months. Dr. Boyd had told her and Carter they'd have to wait six weeks before starting their ''married life,'' as she'd put it. Carter had wanted to get married immediately, but Becky had insisted on waiting. A wedding wasn't a real wedding, she'd claimed, unless a honeymoon followed.

So, six weeks later they were married at the B and B. The ceremony was conducted by both a rabbi and a minister, and after a huge vegetarian feast, Becky and Carter drove off to The Red Barn, with little Sarah nestled safely in her infant seat. The trip was to be a short one, just a weekend getaway. After all, they'd soon be off to New Zealand.

The cabin was just as Becky had remembered: the rustic furnishings, the woodstove, the whirlpool bath. Carter had once said it was the kind of place that made you want to sit in a rocker on the porch, sipping a glass of wine while you watched the sunset. Becky smiled to herself. They'd done a lot more than watch the sunset. Their daughter was one smart cookie; she'd known just when it was time for her to sleep.

And she was sleeping now, completely oblivious to the bustle in the airport. ''Sarah,'' Becky whispered, gently stroking the top of her daughter's head. Sarah. What a beautiful name. The whole family had tried to talk her and Carter out of naming the baby after no one in particular, but Becky hadn't relented. ''She's her own person,'' she'd tried to explain. Truth was, she'd always loved the name. Ever since she was a little girl, she'd known that her firstborn would be a daughter and that she would name her Sarah. And Carter couldn't have been more pleased. In Hebrew the name meant *princess.*

The entire family had come to the airport to see them off. Even though it was the weekend, Starr and Christina had managed to slip away from work to be here, too, leaving the B and B under the watchful eye of Christina's assistant. Becky looked over at the entourage. Her father was holding his new grandson, Charles, and was cooing to him softly. Gertie and Eleanor were crying into handkerchiefs, Bubbe trying to console them. David and Hannah were holding hands, looking at each other adoringly. These people were Becky's family, her lifeline, and she knew she would miss them. Two years was a long time. After New Zealand, though, it was home to Middlewood.

The attendant handed back the paperwork. "You're going to have a wonderful time in New Zealand," she said to Becky, smiling at the baby. "The people are friendly, and the climate is wonderful. Two years! I'm envious. Living there will be like an extended vacation. I'd love to be able to get away from it all, to put my life on hold."

Becky couldn't remember exactly when she'd realized that giving up New Zealand would mean giving up the experience of a lifetime. She'd always wanted to learn to ski, and what place would be more exhilarating than the spectacular Southern Alps? But more significantly, Calyx Editions had decided to publish her book, *A Lover's Guide to Vegetarian Cooking,* and had offered her a contract to write another one. She could hardly wait to start her collection of New Zealand recipes.

Once back in the States, she planned to open a catering business, using all her culinary creations. Maybe she'd even include a line of vegetarian food for children. Children meant birthdays, and didn't birthdays mean parties? But for now, she was looking forward to the excitement that living in a new country would bring, not that her new husband wasn't providing plenty! Ever since Dr. Boyd had given them the go-ahead, Becky and Carter had been making up for lost time—when Sarah was asleep, of course. When she was awake, she was either wailing to be fed or howling to be changed or just filling their lives with the sheer delight of her being.

"But then it's back to the States to roost," Carter said to the attendant.

He wrapped his arm around Becky's shoulders, and a warm glow spread through her. She leaned into him, resting her gaze on their child. She hadn't put her life on hold; the journey was just beginning.

* * * * *

If you enjoyed what you just read,
then we've got an offer you can't resist!

Take 2 bestselling love stories FREE!
Plus get a FREE surprise gift!

//

Clip this page and mail it to Silhouette Reader Service™

IN U.S.A.	IN CANADA
3010 Walden Ave.	P.O. Box 609
P.O. Box 1867	Fort Erie, Ontario
Buffalo, N.Y. 14240-1867	L2A 5X3

YES! Please send me 2 free Silhouette Special Edition® novels and my free surprise gift. After receiving them, if I don't wish to receive anymore, I can return the shipping statement marked cancel. If I don't cancel, I will receive 6 brand-new novels every month, before they're available in stores! In the U.S.A., bill me at the bargain price of $3.99 plus 25¢ shipping and handling per book and applicable sales tax, if any*. In Canada, bill me at the bargain price of $4.74 plus 25¢ shipping and handling per book and applicable taxes**. That's the complete price and a savings of at least 10% off the cover prices—what a great deal! I understand that accepting the 2 free books and gift places me under no obligation ever to buy any books. I can always return a shipment and cancel at any time. Even if I never buy another book from Silhouette, the 2 free books and gift are mine to keep forever.

235 SDN DNUR
335 SDN DNUS

Name	(PLEASE PRINT)	
Address	Apt.#	
City	State/Prov.	Zip/Postal Code

* Terms and prices subject to change without notice. Sales tax applicable in N.Y.
** Canadian residents will be charged applicable provincial taxes and GST.
All orders subject to approval. Offer limited to one per household and not valid to current Silhouette Special Edition® subscribers.
® are registered trademarks of Harlequin Books S.A., used under license.

©1998 Harlequin Enterprises Limited

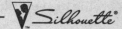

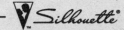

Silhouette®

COMING NEXT MONTH